# Prisoner of Wallabout Bay

## JANE HULSE

FIRESHIP
PRESS

Cover image: Wood Engraving 1906, Meeder, Philip, -1913, engraver. Library of Congress. The Prison Ship "Jersey"

Cover and interior design: Jacqueline Cook

ISBN: 978-1-61179-413-7 (Paperback)
ISBN: 978-1-61179-414-4 (e-book)

10 9 8 7 6 5 4 3 2 1

BISAC Subject Headings:
FIC002000 FICTION / Action & Adventure
FIC014070 FICTION / Historical Colonial America & Revolution
FIC031020 FICTION / Thrillers / Historical

Address all correspondence to:
Fireship Press, LLC
P.O. Box 68412
Tucson, AZ 85737
fireshipinfo@gmail.com

Visit our website at:
www.fireshippress.com

*To the thousands of men who lost their lives on British prison ships during the American Revolution.*

# Chapter One

Surely this is hell.

I can't think, I can't sleep. Not with Mother snoring up a storm on the ragged straw mattress near my feet. Not with the occasional boom of cannon fire in the distance.

Please: Just a moment of privacy and peace in this cramped, leaky attic we now call home. Is that unreasonable?

I tiptoe across the rough floorboards and retrieve my diary from its hiding place behind the chimney. A necessity since Mother feels compelled to know every last thought in my head.

With my quill pen, I write, *November 1, 1776: Samuel's touch sends ripples of pleasure through my body. I ache for more. Am I wicked for such thoughts when I don't even know if I'll marry him?*

The candle flickers out before I finish. Damn! In the dark, I slip under the patchwork quilt beside Mother and little Benjamin and close my eyes. The warmth feels good, but sleep doesn't come. I hear the skittering of mice, interrupted by the earsplitting racket from Mother's gaping mouth.

A year ago, we lived in a stately brick house with a mahogany grandfather clock and rugs in every room. Father, the only person on earth who's ever understood me, was alive then. Unlike Mother and Samuel, he never thought me a fool for wanting to be a writer.

Just as I'm remembering the woodsy smell of Father's pipe, a sharp rap on the front door jolts me. Likely someone needing Mother's services. Again. Why babies always choose to be born in the middle of the night mystifies me.

Despite the pounding, Mother barely twitches. I stumble down the dark, narrow stairs and unlatch the door a crack, careful not to wake the Harkins family who live below us. There at the door stands a tall, stone-faced British soldier in a faded red uniform. A musket in one hand and a lantern in the other.

"I'm here for Mary Barrett, the midwife. Captain Pendleton asked that I summon Mrs. Barrett on a delicate matter."

"What delicate matter?" This isn't the usual frantic father-to-be, desperate for Mother's help.

"I'm not at liberty to say."

Now I'm desperately curious and not a little wary. "At least do the courtesy of telling me who you are."

"I am Lieutenant Daniel Pritchard, Captain Pendleton's aide."

I study his wooden-soldier stare for any clue. "I'll fetch my mother."

"Make haste!"

I traipse back up two flights of stairs to the attic, wondering why a tight-lipped redcoat needs Mother's services. True, she can set a broken arm or stitch a gash from the ax, but it's catching newborns that she does best.

Mother isn't perplexed at all. It could be the devil himself at the door, and she'd calmly dress, and gather the leather satchel with all her herbs and ointments for snakebites, fever, and birthing babies.

"Sarah, you stay with your brother, until I'm back." Ordinarily, I'd happily slip back into bed, but I'm dying to know what it's all about. "Mother, it's not wise for you to go alone into such uncertainty." She looks relieved and even a little pleased by my concern.

"Very well, we'll leave Benjamin with Mrs. Harkins."

I dress quickly, skipping the torturous whalebone stays, no need to squeeze my waist down to the size of a thimble. I'm already tall and thin, not in an unpleasing way. I slip on my gown and apron and jam my unruly red curls under a dark bonnet.

Mother must think I've had a change of heart about becoming her assistant. It's her fervent wish that I accompany her on calls and learn the trade. But I loathe everything about childbirth. I've already made it clear I'd rather dive into poison ivy than witness another "blessed event," as she calls them. The last one was so messy, so bloody, so ghastly that I vomited all over the floor and then fainted dead away, much to Mother's exasperation.

Yet here I am with Mother, about to follow a solemn redcoat to God-knows-where on a chilly pitch-black night. I wrap my wool cape tighter.

"Where are we going, at least tell us that," I mutter as we step into the dark, quiet street.

"Hush child," Mother whispers.

I hate being hushed, and I am not a child. I'm 17 and certainly possess enough wit to work for Livingston's *New York Loyal Gazette*, though Mother finds newspapers as dignified as whoredom.

I hold my tongue as we make our way over bumpy cobblestones, struggling to keep up with the soldier. His creaky lantern barely lights the way, but I make out the darkened houses on our road, the occasional farm, and wood. We pass loose chickens, and a cow sauntering down the road. We're barely a half mile north of Wall Street and the *Loyal Gazette*.

"We're going to the waterfront," Lt. Pritchard finally says.

"Why? No need for our services there," I ask.

More silence. Mother scowls at me as if I've just spoken ill of King George. She was thrilled when the British whipped General Washington's rag-tag army and took command of New York two months ago. Most of the city now backs the British, including my pompous, know-it-all employer, Jonah Livingston, and of course Samuel Mason, the man Mother believes is heaven-sent to marry me. That's enough for me to see the rebels in a shiny new light, though I'd never say so. I'm not an idiot.

The East River is only a few blocks away. Warehouses line the narrow streets, along with shops selling rope, sailcloth, tar, tools, and barrels. Soon I see huge cargo ships, the rigging on their tall masts clanging in the salty air. I have a bad feeling about this little adventure, but I'm curious to a fault, as Mother likes to say.

At the waterfront, the lieutenant directs us to a small rowboat tied to a dock in the shallows.

"We're going to the ship on the other side of the river," he says, as he sets the oarlocks in place. "No need to worry. It's a calm night, and I ply these waters daily."

Moments later we're rolling in the swells, my stomach lurching wildly. A pox on that smug Pritchard at the oars! Damn his boss Pendleton! And damn my curiosity!

It only gets worse when I inhale a stink so powerful, I gag. Worse than the privy on a blistering summer day. Then the old hulk comes into view. I look to Mother for some reassurance, and her wary eyes give me no comfort.

"Surely, there are no women in need out there," I shout over the creaking of the oars and the water slapping the side of the boat. The decrepit ship's mast is missing, along with its guns. The portholes are boarded shut. A handful of British soldiers lean on the rail. I feel dizzy, whether from the stink or the choppy waters, and I fight to hang onto the contents of my stomach.

"What kind of a ship is this? And what hellish mission have you brought us on?" I ask, cramming a lavender-scented handkerchief over my nose.

"No need to get huffy, Miss," Lt. Pritchard says as we sidle up to the battered old hulk's landing platform.

Huffy? He sounds like Samuel whenever I speak my mind, which is often.

An officer shouts down, "Thank you, good ladies, for aiding the Crown." He turns to the crew, barking: "Help them aboard."

We climb up the ladder, our skirts flapping in the wind. Terrible thoughts cross my mind: two women alone with the depraved crew of this shipwreck, far from help.

On board, a tall, portly officer bows slightly. "I'm Captain

Pendleton. Welcome to the *Defiance*, a proud member of the Crown's mighty naval force."

Proud? The deck is rotting beneath my feet, and the putrid air would choke a horse.

"She's a prison ship," announces the captain, whose white wig is perfectly coiffed with curls above his ears. "We have 500 rebel captives below deck."

A floating prison? I've heard rumors but it sounds impossible. He must sense my skepticism.

"We've no other choice. Our jails are full. We took nearly a thousand rebels at the battle on Long Island last summer."

"Are you saying I've been summoned to aid a rebel soldier?" Mother says, eyes wide with disbelief.

Pendleton nods solemnly. "We have no doctors we can spare."

Mother draws herself up to her full height, which is still a head shorter than me. I can see the disdain in her eyes. Mother hates rebels, savages, as she calls them.

"Sir! Rebels murdered my son. They burned down my husband's print shop, forced him into hiding, and ransacked our home. The rebels forced us to flee New Hampshire. Surely you can't expect me to help one of theirs."

"I am sorry for your loss," he says, seeming not sorry at all. "The situation we have is delicate. My good wife says you're the best midwife in New York, that your skill goes beyond birthing. Quite frankly, Mrs. Barrett, she insisted I contact you."

Mother blushes, his flattery working. "I will assist you as a favor to her."

"Bless you. And my dear wife says that you will be sensitive to the scandalous nature of the matter at hand."

My ears perk up. I love a delicious scandal. Pendleton leads us to the rickety ladder into the ship's dark, foul belly and directs a guard to take us below.

As I descend, the moaning hits me first. I struggle to breathe and when my eyes finally adjust to the dark, I make out a sea of scrawny, wild-eyed men dressed in skimpy rags and crammed so close there is barely room to lie down. A boy, barely my age, lies curled in a ball deliriously calling for his mother. I look away, embarrassed for the poor wretch.

"The pox," the guard says with nary a glance. "He'll be dead by morning."

As the men gape at us, it's clear they haven't laid eyes on a woman in months. "Ladies, come give us a kiss," a voice calls out. "I want more than a bloody kiss," another yells.

"Hold your tongues!" the guard brays. "Twenty lashes if you don't."

As we work our way through the tangle of bodies, arms reach out and I hear cries for water and pleas for scraps. The floor is slick with splotches of vomit and blood and who knows what else. Now I understand why Capt. Pendleton doesn't want to muck up his shiny black boots and spotless uniform. Finally, I can stand it no longer.

"Why must these men suffer so in this hellish prison?"

"Sarah! Mind what you say," Mother says, as if we're guests in someone's threadbare parlor.

The guard looks at me as if I'm daft. "They're traitors and deserve to die. Best you remember that. Mind you, the rebels don't treat their prisoners any different."

The scolding sounds like Samuel, and it sets my teeth on edge.

Finally, we arrive at a curtained-off area behind a storage bin. On a straw pallet lies a silent form writhing under a thin, stained blanket.

"Here we are, ladies. I'll leave you to your work." The guard hands me the lantern and is gone.

Mother and I look at each other searching for some further explanation. She gathers her skirts, kneels, parts a few rags, and uncovers a piteous boy, perhaps 15, with stringy blond hair tied at the back of his neck. Despite the cold, his face is sweaty, white, and gaunt, with not the hint of a whisker.

"Tell us where your pain is," Mother says.

"My belly," he whispers, his face contorted in anguish.

"Let me have a look." Mother kneels beside him. I watch, feeling helpless.

"Wait!" He looks at us both, eyes wide in terror. "Can I trust you?"

"Of course you can," Mother says softly. I think she's already forgotten he's a rebel.

His eyes fill with tears as another pain grips his belly. He looks so small and afraid. Then he whispers something neither of us can hear. We move in closer.

"I'm … I'm not a boy."

I am dumbstruck. I can't move. Mother goes straight into her midwife role as if we haven't just heard the most impossible news. "What is your name, my dear?"

"Sally, Sally Upton."

"And what has brought you here, Sally?"

She gasps for breath now. I feel her forehead; it burns like fire.

"My husband, Peter, joined the rebels in Boston. I couldn't bear it without him, so I cut my hair and bound my breasts. The rebels were happy to have another able body. At the Battle of Long Island, Peter was killed by a bayonet to the stomach." She chokes back tears. "I was captured. No one knew my secret until I got word to a guard."

She takes a deep breath and lets it out slowly as if the effort of telling us this crazy, fantastic story has sapped her of everything. I look at her with awe and wonder if I'd have the grit to do any such thing.

Mother digs through her medical bag. "I'll have a look. Sarah, bring the lantern near and lift the blanket."

As soon as I do so, I gasp at the sight.

"Oh, merciful God!" Mother says.

What we see is a small skeletal shape, skin stretched so tight we can almost see through it. She is all bones save for the small bump on her belly.

"You are woefully thin, my dear," Mother says.

I'm more direct. "Don't they feed the prisoners?"

"Just bits of biscuit, usually crawling with maggots. Sometimes rotten pork," Sally murmurs.

No one can survive on that. But I have no time to inquire more. Just then she draws up her scrawny legs, arches her back, and screams.

"Rest now child," Mother says, squeezing her hand. "The babe won't arrive for a while yet."

11

Mother always attends to her ladies with such tenderness and patience. I yearn for the same treatment. It had always been Father's gentle hand on my shoulder when I was afraid or confused. Perhaps Mother feels I'm hale and hearty and have no need for a loving touch.

She grips Sally's hand for the next two hours as the wrenching pains of childbirth come and go. She never runs out of Bible passages or soothing words of encouragement. I'll never be a midwife, not like her. My legs are cramped from sitting on the rough wood planks. My back aches something fierce. Mother shows no discomfort. I'm helpless to do anything and wracked by jealousy.

My self-pity is interrupted by a breathtaking scream from Sally.

"Sarah, be at the ready," Mother orders. "You know what to do."

I spread a cloth in my hands, but what comes out is a bloody mess and a baby so small I can hold it in the palm of my hand. I wait for a cry, the usual lusty wail of a newborn. No sound, not even the sound of breathing. Its tiny arms and legs are still.

"Mother! Do something!"

She listens for a heartbeat. "Poor thing is dead," she whispers, as I cradle it in my hands. It can't be dead. I will it to breathe, cry, move, anything. But there is nothing. Sally lies still, with her eyes closed.

Grief washes over me. I've seen stillbirths before, but none gripped my heart this way. I don't want to let go of this tiny soul. Finally, I lay the bundle on her chest, my hands shaking.

"Sally, my dear, you have a son, a fine son, but God has chosen to take him from us," Mother says.

Sally neither opens her eyes nor says a word. Her breathing has stopped. Mother checks her pulse and shakes her head. I can't believe it.

"Mother, can't you do anything?" I plead. I never wanted anything so much in my life.

"No, it's God's will."

"No, it's not," I cry. "It didn't have to happen."

"Quiet! Now pull yourself together so we can leave this hellhole."

I sniffle and I dab at my eyes, my anger building. Mother calls for the guard, and he makes his way to us through the sea of pitiful, stinking humanity on the floor.

"Died in childbirth, I see. The babe too." It's as if he's seen a dead dog and pup.

"No!" I say loud enough to turn a few heads. "Died of starvation."

"Sarah, please! Let us leave without incident."

The guard looks at me as if I'm an impudent child, deliberately trying his patience. I lag behind him and Mother as we head for the steps. I will myself to remember everything I've seen on this gruesome night.

"Sarah," a weak voice calls out. "Sarah, over here."

I stop. Who could possibly know my name in this miserable sewer? "Sarah Barrett from Essex?"

That voice, I recognize it. "Thomas? Is it you?" The laughing brown eyes and perpetual grin are absent. Instead, I see the gaunt, haggard face of Tom Jordan, the brother of my best friend Emma.

"Yes, it's me, though I've seen better days." He manages a weak smile.

Before I can say another word, the guard grabs my arm as if he's about to haul me to the deck and toss me overboard. I look back at Tom, then tear my glance away.

# Chapter Two

It's nearly dawn when we straggle home, exhausted. Mother falls asleep with her clothes on, but I'm too agitated by the horror I've seen. I light a candle, retrieve my diary, and try to remember each detail.

*One poor soul, with barely a rag for clothing, was gnawing on a shoe for sustenance. His legs were mere sticks, his eyes dark hollows. Another, no more than 15, sobbed pitifully for his mother. I wanted desperately to help them all ...*

I write page after page until the point on my quill pen breaks, spattering ink all over the page.

Seeing Tom brought back memories of home. He and my older brother Seth were always such good friends, getting in all kinds of trouble when they weren't out hunting deer or raising hell. They couldn't be bothered with me and Emma, shooing us away like mosquitoes.

Tom went off to fight with the rebels. Not long afterward, the whole town turned against us. Father and his newspaper supported the British, not the so-called patriots, and everyone needed to take their bloody revenge. That's how we came to live in a dismal attic in New York. And that's how I wound up carrying a dark secret, probably to my grave.

• • •

I wake the next morning to the sound of the Harkins' three-year-old son Peter banging a pot. My head throbs with every bang and I'm dog-tired, but it's no use trying to go back to sleep. The events of the previous night rush back to me, and I can't wait to tell my boss about the floating prison. This time I'm sure he'll let me write about it. Real news, instead of the drivel he usually throws at me. Last week it was something about the silly rivalry among rich ladies for the tallest hair fashion, complete with feathers, jewels, and even tresses cut off corpses. One foot, two feet? No, even higher. So idiotic!

Walking to the *Loyal Gazette*, I hurry past a cluster of British soldiers who eye me suspiciously, probably because I refuse to wear the red ribbon that signifies to the world my loyalty to the Crown. Truth be told, I haven't made up my mind on the war, though I keep my doubts to myself.

My thoughts return to the best way to approach my esteemed employer. Flattery is no use; he's wise to me on that front. I barely notice the usual hubbub on Wall Street as I walk up the stone steps to the print shop. The sign hanging by the door makes me smile: LIVINGSTON'S NEW YORK LOYAL GAZETTE, EDITOR AND PUBLISHER: JONAH LIVINGSTON, PRINTER OF LEAFLETS AND SELLER OF FINE BOOKS. Not spelled out in ornate letters are Egotist, Bigot, Drunk.

I lift the heavy brass latch and walk into chaos. Jonah is screaming at a cowering apprentice.

"You ignorant jackass," he sputters at the young man, who probably dared suggest a better turn of phrase in a sentence. "Leave it be and get back to work before I throw you out in the street."

A ridiculous threat. Short and squat, wheezy Jonah can barely swat a fly. He sees me and searches wildly for the spectacles on top of his bald head ... bald that is when it isn't covered by one of his pricey powdered perukes.

"You're late," he spits. "I should get rid of you too, troublesome hussy."

"And a lovely good morning to you too." I've found sarcasm to be cold water on his repulsive bluster. "I have news I think you'll find interesting."

"Speak up, girl! What have you heard? Something about that traitorous turd Washington?"

"Last night I was aboard the prison ship *Defiance*, the old hulk in Wallabout Bay. The men are crammed like sardines in the belly of the ship, starving to death, drowning in their own filth. It's awful. The British don't give a fig whether they live or die." Then I summon my courage. "I can write all about it. For the *Gazette*."

"You?" he bellows. "Don't be silly. It's no secret the ship is there, and others are on the way. And we've got more important news to give readers than your weepy account of how to treat prisoners of war. And for your information, the prison ships are the charge of Captain Pendleton, a fine officer, and my good friend."

"But it's wrong, maybe even against the law. At the least, it's inhumane. We don't treat dogs that way."

His eyes bulge to the point of near explosion, a sure sign he won't back down. I should have known he'd dismiss any criticism of his precious redcoats.

"I have far bigger news than your little tale of woe," he murmurs. He takes out his ornately engraved silver snuff box and inhales a wad of tobacco under his bulbous nose.

"What is it?" I ask, knowing it couldn't possibly be more important than what I saw on the ship.

"I know who set the town afire." A smile creeps onto his porky face.

The fire, a little more than a month ago, was a monstrous blaze that torched nearly 500 homes and buildings on the west side. A quarter of the city burned to the ground. It was the scariest night of my life as the flames roared within blocks of our home.

"It started accidentally at the Fighting Cocks Tavern," I say. "The raging wind drove it north. That's what everyone says."

"Not everyone," he grins. "I suspected from the start it was the work of Washington and his men; his parting shot after we sent his little boys a-packing. Now the British have rounded up nearly 200 rebel supporters to squeeze out the truth."

"But Washington denied it." I read so in the newspapers I pore through every day.

"Girl, you're so naive. You know nothing of war." He makes me want to scream, but I swallow my anger.

"Even Washington wouldn't do anything so heartless," I insist. That night thousands of people fled for their lives as the wall of flames consumed everything in its path. Mother, Benjamin, and I were among them. We all hunkered down in the Commons. Rich, poor, ladies, prostitutes, every last one of us gasping for air, certain we were at the gates of hell.

"I don't believe he did it." I know I've gone too far. He's practically foaming at the mouth.

"You ignoramus! You think I care about your opinion? Now get back to work. And stoke the fire. It's colder than frostbite in here."

I stew for hours. I'm not an ignoramus, and he knows it. I can write as well as he can, probably better, and I'm about 3,000 times more logical.

Finally, he heads for Hazen's Coffeehouse down the street, leaving me in peace. I hope "His Highness" returns in a better mood after his midday pork pie and a pint of rum.

I start to gather the sheets of printed paper that hang drying from every corner of the cavernous room, this week's paper, with Jonah's big news right below the British royal coat of arms: TRAITOROUS WASHINGTON ORDERED THE CITY'S DISASTROUS FIRE.

A bare-faced lie, an unproven accusation at the least. My "tale of woe" about the wretches aboard the prison ship is an eyewitness account, not the fantasy of a tipsy old man. Oh, things will be different at my newspaper. Of course, Mother would say I'm unhinged.

Jonah returns, reeking of rum. He hovers over me as I set the type for the final item. I can feel his hot breath on my neck, and it makes me furious. I'm going as fast as I can, grabbing metal letters from the drawer and laying out word after word—upside down and backwards—a mind-scrambling feat that I excel at. But it's not fast enough for the old goat.

"Girl!" he hisses. "You're slower than a three-legged mule. I rue the day I promised your father I'd employ you."

17

I fight to keep back the tears. I'd sooner die than weep. "Jonah, we're not late!" I know it vexes him when I use his first name. When he stops calling me "Girl!" maybe I'll address him with more respect. "And another thing, I'm as fast as any other typesetter in the city."

I could give him an earful, but as I said, I'm not stupid. I know as much as he does about the war because I've been in it. When the rebels took over the city and tore down the statue of King George, I was there, but Jonah wouldn't let me near the story. And when the British took back the city after a spectacular victory on Long Island? I even saw the fleeing rebels slam ashore in a flotilla of small boats. But, no—not a suitable article for a "troublesome hussy"!

Lest you think me a braggart, I should point out that I was setting type at Father's newspaper when I was 10. At 15, I was writing news accounts, such as the time a bear mauled to death a farmer planting corn. Mother thought it hardly suitable work for a young lady, but Father said he'd rather I turn a clever phrase than stitch a straight line.

Jonah has little use for my cleverness and tells me so every day. Yet I gladly accept the pittance he pays me if the alternative means working at Mother's side. Though today, he makes me think twice. The ink is too thick, the paper too thin, the fire too low—and it's all my fault. By the end of the day, I'm exhausted, filthy, and still mad that Jonah brushed off my account of the *Defiance*.

I'm about to go home when Samuel arrives unexpectedly, wearing a new purple velvet waistcoat, white silk stockings, and a new wig, freshly powdered and scented with lavender.

"I have a surprise for you, Sarah," he says. "I know you'll love it."

Ah, the day is not a total loss. "How nice, Samuel. You've saved me from misery." He's not stunningly handsome, though not unpleasant to look at. He's tall, a little gangly, and his shaggy blond hair gives him a boyish look he tries to conceal under his lawyerly wig. He's generous to a fault, always showing up with some bauble for me, ribbons for my hair, a comb, and even a fur muff once. I wonder what the evening holds.

It feels good to be pampered as he wraps my cloak around my shoulders. The sting of Jonah's foul tongue fades. A light rain falls as we walk along Wall Street arm-in-arm. The lamplighter is making his rounds, hauling his ladder to the lampposts that stand sentry on every block. Soon the shops will close: the candlemaker, the tea seller, the milliner with the flowery bonnets in the window, the chocolatier. The taverns are already doing a lively trade. The British with their muskets at the ready seem to be on every corner, standing statue-still for king and country.

Samuel won't tell me where we're going, only that I'll be thrilled. I hope it's Lowell's Bookshop, where they carry all the newest, most scandalous books. Samuel can be fun when he's not droning on about misdemeanors and legal precedents. He's studying to be a lawyer at Stoneham, Delancey, and Winston, big supporters of the Crown.

My hopes are dashed when we walk into Mrs. Brockton's Clothier Shop. "I want you dressed in the finest gown New York has to offer when you become Mrs. Samuel Mason," he says, grinning ear to ear.

"Mrs. ... this is so sudden," I blurt out. I haven't even accepted his proposal. I certainly haven't given a moment's thought to wedding attire.

"Sarah, I asked for your hand more than a month ago," he says. "We're hardly strangers."

True, we've known each since he apprenticed at Father's newspaper when I was a schoolgirl. He was bookish then and engaged Father in lengthy political discussions. His lips were the first I tasted. I confided to him my secret—what I'd done in Essex that fateful night—though he could scarcely believe it was a girl's doing.

At Mrs. Brockton's, it seems as if I have no choice. My course is set. Mrs. Samuel Mason. I gaze at all the bolts, satin, silk, linen in all colors, so many that my head is awhirl.

"Pick out any one you want," Samuel says. "I want you to look beautiful. I'll make a lady of you yet."

His words sting—what am I, a pitiful ragamuffin—but I hold my tongue. He need only point at my plain gown with its patches and ink stains, my wild, red curls. I'm tall and skinny, and small of bosom. Nothing he can do about that.

I settle on a royal blue satin because I've never worn satin before, only the wool and cotton gowns Mother stitches. That's another thing that Samuel will have to accept. I hate sewing. Just sewing on a button is torture. I have no talent for needlework. It's tedious.

We leave with the bundle of cloth wrapped securely against the weather. "How can I thank you, Samuel? You're too kind."

He laughs. "Become my dutiful wife without delay; that's how you can thank me."

I cringe. Dutiful wife? What does he expect of me? Must I be at his beck and call every minute of the day? Rush to his bed whenever his passion flutters? Surely, he doesn't expect me to keep my opinions to myself. That's asking too much. On the other hand, life with Samuel would be safe, predictable, and full of new dresses and bonnets. There would be plays, concerts, parties, and all the hat-tipping respect I could stand.

Mother would have me marry him today. Any girl would swoon with joy—her actual words—to wed a soon-to-be lawyer and loyalist. But I'm not any girl, and the idea of swooning over someone, even a lawyer, is just twaddle.

"I have good news," Samuel says as we walk home in the drizzle. "Mr. Stoneham raised my wages again."

"He likes the work you're doing." I know he's already impressed them. At the Crown's request, he composed a loyalty oath, demanding that residents pledge their allegiance to the King, or go to jail.

"Yes, he wants me to help interrogate rebel sympathizers about the fire. The British are certain Washington ordered it. We'll get the truth out of them. Tar and feather them if we must."

I shudder at the thought. In New Hampshire, I saw the steaming tar plastered on the bare skin of a preacher, a loyalist who dared praise the King. Rebels dumped armloads of feathers on the mostly naked, scalded, screaming man, then shoved open his legs, slammed him down on a wood rail, and paraded him through town. If it weren't for Mother's care, he would have died.

"Tar and feather … that's torture, Samuel."

"So be it. I'll stop at nothing to get these traitors."

His callousness startles and irritates me. "How do you know

Washington ordered the fire? Where's the proof?"

"I have my sources."

"But the wind that night—"

"Sarah, you needn't get worked up about this."

"I'm not worked up. I'm just asking."

"Enough! Leave this business to me."

"It's my business too," I insist.

He puts his finger to his lips. "Shhh! Not another word."

"But-"

"Hush!"

That's more than I can take.

"I will not hush!" I'm mad, and I don't care if I draw stares from passersby, even if it's embarrassing for Mr. Velvet Breeches.

He looks at me in disbelief. "Ever the feisty one. I can see I have my work cut out for me."

That doesn't help. "I'm not a child, Samuel, or some brainless twit."

"I didn't say that you were, but you must learn your place."

"*My place?*" I would have called him a pompous ass but he just doled out a week's wages for the bolt of satin. I change the subject.

"You're not the only one with news."

"What is it?"

"Mother and I visited the prison ship *Defiance* last night."

"Why in God's name did you go there?" The look on his face is pure horror, not what I expected.

I tell him about the baby and everything I saw. Everything except Tom. I'm not sure why, except Tom has been in my thoughts constantly. Besides, it's none of Samuel's business.

"I want to write about the trip for the *Loyal Gazette*, but Jonah won't hear of it." Hoping that Samuel will denounce my impossible boss is a fool's errand.

"You were there among those filthy traitors, so close they could touch you?"

I nod yes, swelling with pride.

But Samuel's eyes are filled with anger. "I would have forbidden you to go!"

"Who are you to forbid me anything?"

He stops and grabs me by the shoulders, his face so close to mine I can see spittle in the corners of his mouth.

"No wife of mine will mingle with those animals. Promise me you'll not do that again." His voice softens at the end, but I'm still angry.

I tear away from his grasp. "I won't do any such thing," I say, looking him straight in the eye. "You're not my keeper."

Now he's frustrated and red in the face. "Sarah, you have much to learn about marriage."

"And you have much to learn about me."

We walk home in silence. At the front door, he tries to kiss me goodnight as if nothing had happened. I turn my head away. My feet are wet and cold, along with the rest of me. With a pained look on his face, he hands me the bundle of satin. I take it without a word and walk inside.

# Chapter Three

It's anarchy as usual in the house. The two youngest of Mrs. Harkins' five children race around, screaming while she stirs a steaming pot on the hearth. The smell of onions is overpowering.

"Good evening, Sarah," she says over the din. "Your mother has made a fine potato soup for supper. There's plenty for you too."

With Mr. Harkins off fighting for the rebels, I know there isn't enough for her brood, let alone ours. Besides, it's not supper I crave but solitude, time by myself, to think about Samuel and his maddening outburst.

"Thank you, Mrs. Harkins, but I'm not hungry."

Mother, ever the defender of the British but also a practical woman, has made her peace with Mrs. Harkins. We have a roof over our heads, leaky though it is, and Mother works her magic in the kitchen, producing bread, stews, and puddings from whatever scraps she can find. She's also revived the scrawny vegetable garden in the backyard. As for their political differences, they simply don't discuss it. It's a feat I shall never begin to understand.

I trudge up to the attic and find Mother reading her Bible to Benjamin, who shows more interest in picking his nose. He leaps up when he sees me.

"Sarah!"

"Hello, little man!" He's not the least bit sleepy, and he tugs on my dress until I pick him up.

"What's in the bundle?" Mother asks. "More books?"

I dread her jubilant reaction after the quarrel I've just had with Samuel. At the moment, marriage is the last thing I want. I tear off the paper wrapping and spread the shimmering satin on the little wooden platform that serves as a desk and dining table.

"Oh, my. It's the most beautiful fabric I've ever laid my eyes on," she says. "This is Samuel's doing, isn't it? This is the dress you'll be wed in. Soon you'll be Mrs. Samuel Mason."

"You must be overjoyed, Mother." She gently runs her fingers over the satin, clearly not picking up my sarcasm.

I feel my world is out of control, racing toward the altar, and I'm powerless to stop it. I'm seeing a side of Samuel that infuriates me. Is he just another man who insists a woman can't possibly have an opinion of her own? That we're mindless pieces of fluff, empty-headed vessels for childbearing and nothing more? I thought he was more than that, more like Father. I can only imagine what he thinks about my dream of being a writer.

"It's the loveliest shade of blue, the color of your eyes," Mother babbles on, caressing the fabric. "I must start sewing straightaway. I'll need velvet ribbon and pearl buttons. It must be elegant and stylish … like Samuel."

The last thing I need is Mother telling me how perfect, even godly Samuel is. "I'm in no hurry," I say, knowing that will provoke her.

"Sarah, what is your hesitation? Is it fear of the marital bed?"

"No!" Besides, I heard from Emma that this "chore" is pleasurable beyond words, if her older sister can be believed.

"Then what is it?"

"Samuel can be an overbearing toad."

I knew I wouldn't get sympathy, but I had no idea she'd screech as if I were a thief making off with the family pig.

"Ungrateful child! How can you say such things? Samuel is the one who spent the better part of a year searching for you after we fled Essex."

"Hunting me down is more like it. I'm not some kind of trophy!"

"I thought you were fond of him," she says.

"I am, I think. That doesn't mean I'm ready to bed down with him … or take orders from him."

Mother scowls. "Such talk! I've prayed and prayed for this marriage. It's God's will."

"Maybe it's not my will, Mother!" I shout.

"You don't mean that, Sarah. You're being selfish and headstrong. You'd best do what's right."

"What's right for you; that's what you really mean. If I marry Samuel, your money troubles will be over. You're the selfish one!"

Mother's hand comes up so fast I don't have a chance to duck. She slaps my cheek so hard I bite my tongue, setting free a river of blood inside my mouth.

"I've lost everything in the last year," Mother screams. "Your brother killed, your father dead from the pox. We fled Essex with barely the clothes on our backs after you took matters into your own foolish hands."

I've never seen her in such a rage. It's frightening. Benjamin starts to cry.

And she isn't finished. "You'd best hold your tongue and be grateful Samuel wants you. Don't you see, this war is killing our young men! You may not have another offer of marriage this prosperous."

That is the final insult, the one that unleashes the tears I'm doing my best to hold back.

"You mean no one else can possibly want me!" I can't stand for her, or anyone, to see me slobbering like a fool. I storm down the stairs, collapsing in a heap on the landing. So, Mother thinks I'm no prize. And Samuel thinks he can turn me into a dutiful wife. Well, a pox on them both. I'll bloody well do as I please.

I fall asleep on the stairs, waking at daybreak to a stiff neck and aching back. I'm covered with an old quilt that Mother must have spread over me in the night. That's her way of apologizing. I'm not ready to do the same, yet. My cheek still smarts, and my mouth tastes like beef liver. And besides, I'm right. I don't regret a word I said to either Samuel or Mother.

In the kitchen Mother silently stokes the fire and stirs a pot of bubbling oatmeal hanging from a hook over the flame. I'm reminded of my hunger. Thankfully, the Harkins clan aren't up yet. She ladles out steaming bowls for each of us, with dollops of maple syrup. We sit across from one another, eyes down. Benjamin jabbers nonsense and spits oatmeal.

Mother finally breaks the silence. "Did you post a letter to Emma yesterday?"

I nod. "I told her about Tom, but not how gaunt and sickly he looks."

"That's wise. She'll be relieved he's alive."

Mother acts as if we haven't had the worst row of our lives, and it suits me fine. I have no desire to revisit my marriage to Samuel. I dreamed about Tom last night. He kissed my lips, my neck, and my breasts. Who knows what would have happened if I hadn't awakened with a start? Am I evil to dream of such pleasure when I'm all but spoken for in marriage? I don't think so.

"I have news," Mother says as she wipes Benjamin's face with a rag. "Captain Pendleton summoned me and paid handsomely for treating that poor girl on the ship." She takes the lid off her porcelain sugar bowl and shows me a handful of coins. "Pounds, not those worthless Continental dollars."

"Oh, Mother!" My mind flies to all the things we've denied ourselves lately, like books and chocolate.

"It will help me secure passage back to London with Benjamin, and you, too, if you're not wed by then."

I prickle at the mention of "wed," and stifle my disappointment that chocolate isn't in my future.

"Not London again," I moan. She's talked incessantly about returning to London ever since Seth's murder in Essex. Thousands of loyalists have already fled.

She ignores me. "I told Captain Pendleton about my garden—the carrots, turnip, corn, apples—and the few pence neighbors pay for them. He says his men on the ship would welcome fresh food and other goods, and so would those prisoners who have a few coins hidden away."

So that's where all the produce has gone: Now I know why there's so little food for us and the Harkins family. Mother has been stockpiling her profits for the ship's passage.

"I told the captain no, of course. One trip out to that miserable ship is enough for me."

My mind is spinning. Tom is on that miserable ship.

"But he kept insisting," Mother continues, "said they couldn't trust any man selling wares. Might be a rebel and try to poison the crew or sneak weapons aboard. But a woman, a loyal supporter of the Crown, would be acceptable."

I'm thinking only of Tom. "Mother, I think it's a fine idea. I can go with you." I know it sounds preposterous, putting my stomach through the tortures of roiling seas and the stink of that old ship. But it's a chance to see him. "How soon can we start?"

I can see she's pleasantly surprised by my suddenly agreeable nature. So am I.

"I don't have much left over from the harvest. A few apples and pumpkins, plenty of pumpkins. I have sufficient flour. I could bake bread."

"They'd pay dearly for that," I say, hoping my flattery works.

"I'll see what I can round up," Mother says, a hint of a smile on her face.

• • •

As I leave the house that morning, I imagine the fit Samuel will throw when he hears about our plan to return to the *Defiance*. And I don't care, not a bit. Let him call off the wedding. I feel on top of the world as I stride to the *Loyal Gazette*, past the garbage and horse manure in the street, past shops that are opening for the day's trade, past Hazen's Coffeehouse, one of the many spots where men gather to share news about business, the war, and who's bedding whose wife.

I picture Samuel there, smoking his pipe and gossiping about me, that brazen slut who dared to challenge his manhood. That's when it hits me, like a punch to the gut. Would Samuel be so blazing mad at me that he'd tell the world my most carefully guarded secret? Some would pay dearly to know—but who would believe it?

# Chapter Four

A week later Mother and I stay up late in the kitchen, filling baskets with what few wormy apples we can round up along with a pumpkin pie, three loaves of bread, and a pinch of tea, I convince Mother to part with. It isn't much, but it's all we can spare for our first trip back to the *Defiance*.

We wait until Mrs. Harkins and her brood are asleep. No use flaunting our goods when they barely have enough to eat. No one goes to bed with a full stomach these days. Feeding the armies of both sides puts a crimp in everyone's eating style, including the mighty, omnivorous Jonah, who complains that his beloved meat pies are on the skimpy side.

It's all I can do not to drag my finger through the pumpkin pie for a fleeting moment of bliss, but it's not worth raising Mother's hackles. We've been on such good terms lately. I steal upstairs to join her and little Ben in bed, but first I retrieve my trusty diary to sum up what's most urgently on my mind.

*I've thrown myself into Mother's money-raising scheme, though it's Tom I'm thinking about. I've kept to myself something else: King George will sprout wings before I sail back to London.*

Dawn is damp and frigid, but we've bundled up as best we can against the November chill. I curse the icy wind that cuts through my wool cape. Why on earth am I transforming myself into a human icicle? After all, in a matter of hours, I could be laying out my best gown for dinner with Samuel and his boss's family at their lavish mansion overlooking the harbor. That is, if Samuel had bothered to invite me, not that I care about such rot.

He's been cool toward me since the night we picked out the blue satin for my dress. I never apologized for my words that night—not that I need to—and we haven't spoken of our spat again. But it's still in the air.

Mother hasn't had a moment to sew my dress, and I'm relieved. I can breathe freely, and Mother, bless her, has stopped talking about Samuel as if he's destined for sainthood.

"Look, there's the boat," she says as we reach the waterfront. "And Lieutenant Pritchard. Such a fine young man for some lucky miss."

I know what she means, and I'm not that easily impressed. Waiting on the shore is the same tall, stern-looking soldier who rowed us to the *Defiance* before. Would it pain him to give us a smile or a warm word? He doesn't seem any happier to see us now.

"Step quickly, ladies," he says. "I don't have all day and the weather is likely to worsen. He tosses our baskets in the boat.

"Careful with those," I shout.

I'm glad Mother insisted we bring an old wool blanket. We wrap it around our shoulders and huddle in the chill as he rows in silence through the choppy waters toward Brooklyn. I command my stomach to behave, but each rise and fall of the boat brings me closer to losing the morning's porridge.

"Feeling a bit queasy?" Mother asks, yet another reminder of her cast-iron stomach and will. When she inoculated us both against the dreaded smallpox, I nearly fainted as she cut my arm and rubbed in a gob of festering pus from a poor soul already sickened. Afterward, she suffered nary a headache, while I puked and fevered for four days.

My stomach settles by the time the old ship appears, foreboding, dark, dismal, and naked without its mast and sails. Two chains hold her firmly in place, though she tilts to one side. Despite the cold, my hands are sweaty in my gloves, and my heart pounds. I haven't told Mother my plan. She'd fly into a rage if she knew.

As we approach, guards on the top deck wave. "What have you brung us?" one yells.

We pull up alongside the ship, where the lieutenant helps us climb onto the landing platform and up the gangway. Some of the guards and a few shivering prisoners crowd around Mother as she unloads the baskets.

All eyes are on her as she shows off one treasure after another. "Freshly baked pumpkin pie with bits of nutmeg and ginger, gentlemen," she crows. The pie nearly brings swoons, and a few of the guards pool their coins to buy it. The bruised apples will be a harder sell.

This is my chance and just as I planned, I slip away and find the ladder to the lower deck. As I descend, the smell seems worse than last time, and I briefly reconsider my crazy scheme. But I've gone too far to turn back now. My eyes adjust to the darkness, and I take in a sea of rail-thin arms and legs and faces pale as snow. The icy wind blows in through the portholes that haven't been completely boarded up. Most of the inmates are barefoot, and some are nearly naked, not a sight I'm accustomed to. Nor are they accustomed to skirts and bosoms. They stare at me as if I'm a freak. Oddly, I'm not worried about my safety, though you and the rest of the civilized world might think me foolish.

"Have you some water, a scrap of food," one pleads, his eyes sunken. "Rum?"

Wordlessly, I shake my head. What good can I possibly bring these men, these enemies of the Crown, as Jonah calls them? But something keeps me from turning back. As I make my way to the spot where I last saw Tom, no one steps in my way, they're too stunned. Then, I see a lump under a flimsy blanket. Am I too late?

"Tom," I cry. "Tom!"

Desperately, I shake the lump, pull the blanket down, and gasp at Tom's ashen face, his dark hair a matted mess.

"Sarah?" he whispers, teeth chattering.

"Yes, it's me." Reaching down around his shoulders to help him sit up, I feel only bones.

The men begin to crowd around us, and it makes me uneasy. Then a deep voice rings out above the din.

"Back off men. Give them some air. Have you not a shred of decency left?"

I look up to see a young man no older than myself, bare-chested in tattered pants that hang on his scrawny frame with a rope. The men back off, and I turn to Tom.

"Who—"

"Nathaniel," he says. "We look out for each other. They're good men, just desperate is all."

I wince. "I have something for you." I reach under my cloak and pull out a small apple. It was pitiful, but it was all I had.

His hand comes up like lightning, grabs it, and shoves it under the blanket.

"Can't let the others see."

"I understand." Though it's so tiny and so pathetic that I don't, really, not at all.

"I'm so glad to see you, Sarah. Tell me you're not a vision, I'm not delirious."

I gingerly clutch his hand and smile. "I've written to Emma to let her know you're alive."

"If you can call this living. Every day we haul up a dozen or so dead, sewn up tight in their blankets."

I want so badly to help him. Finally, I unwrap the thick wool scarf around my neck and shove it in front of his barely comprehending eyes. "Tom, take this."

He looks at it with wonder.

"You mustn't look too closely," I say. "I have no talent for knitting. I'm not Emma."

"It's the most beautiful thing on this dreadful ship. And I'm glad you're not Emma."

"Tom, I'll try to bring you Father's old jacket. You may find it a great comfort. He would write poetry and tuck it in the coat lining where he thought no one would find it."

For a moment I feel deliriously happy.

"You must go now," he whispers, lowering himself in an exhausted heap. "This ship is no place for a lady, Sarah. The men are filthy, and we all have lice. Lice everywhere, in our hair, in our rags, everywhere you can imagine."

Suddenly I'm gripped by the urge to scratch every inch of my body.

"I'll return. I won't forget you, Tom."

I hurry back on deck, hoping no one saw me go below. But Pritchard eyes me suspiciously.

"Where were you?"

My mind races. "I sought some privacy. My stomach is too delicate for all this." I wipe my face with a lace handkerchief, figuring that's what a lady would do if she were truly sick.

He shows just the hint of a smile. "So, you don't have the constitution for it."

I lower my eyes, stifling my urge to set him straight.

Mother is busy gloating over the dozen or more coins jangling in her hand. "We'll be in England soon at this rate."

"That's wonderful," I say. As we climb down into Pritchard's small boat, I see 10 blanketed bundles on the ship's deck.

"Today's dead," he says.

"Poor souls," I say. One day Tom will be among them unless I do something.

"They'll be buried proper?" Mother asks. Even she is appalled at the sight.

He snorts. "You could say that. We toss them overboard, each with a cannonball, to keep them sunk."

My stomach lurches. I think of Tom, already half dead. What a horrible way to end a life.

"The burial ground ashore is full," the lieutenant says, without a hint of compassion.

As we descend the gangway, a guard heaves one of the bundles into the water, leaving a trail of bubbles as it sinks.

"Bye, bye, damned rebel," he shouts.

# Chapter Five

Mother calls it a "mission of mercy," and I've come along because I want to stay on her good side. And it takes my mind off Tom's sorry state. It's early evening, and we pass a handful of people as we walk a few blocks to what everyone in town calls the "Holy Ground." There's nothing holy about it; it's where the prostitutes ply their trade, hundreds of them.

Mother takes it upon herself to treat these women with her medicinal wares and gives them a dose of scripture at the same time. It pleases me that she doesn't think them shameful, though she's warned me not to go near the Holy Ground, which is thick with rowdy taverns, cockfighting arenas, and gambling houses. I'm fascinated by these so-called "painted ladies" and what they do for a living. Samuel calls them filthy tarts, though he seems to know a lot about them.

"Go into any tavern, and you'll see them flaunting their wares," he told me. "Their services are plentiful, and their fees are like the price of a pint and meat pie. If they weren't disease-ridden and morally bankrupt, they'd be the perfect merchants."

As we walk down Broadway toward the southern tip of New York, it's a grim reminder of the fire just two months ago. Most everything west of Broadway to the Hudson River lies in burnt ruins. Only chimneys remain, or the occasional brick house of some wealthy merchant, curiously untouched by the blaze.

"Oh, my heart aches so," Mother says, as we come upon the charred remains of Trinity Church. Before the fire, she dragged me here every Sunday to sit straight-backed for hours while the pastor droned on. And the parishioners? She made a point of telling me (over and over) that they included some of the city's wealthiest loyalists.

"It was such a sacred place," she says.

Not hardly. Jonah told me the whole story, not without some glee. The church divided its huge plot into little lots and rented them out for cheap, inadvertently inviting in a slew of brothels and other seedy businesses. It sounds unbelievable, but I swear it's true. Mother despises the name, Holy Ground, though I think it clever.

The church is gone, but the brothels continue to churn out satisfied customers, thanks to the arrival of the redcoats. The women—and the men who prey on them—have cobbled together shanties with canvas, charred lumber, and still-standing chimneys and fireplaces. It's amazing to me that lust thrives in all that rubble.

We make our way to one such hovel where a young redcoat in a bedraggled uniform stands ill at ease outside, apparently awaiting us.

"Might this be the quarters of Lucinda?" Mother asks.

"Yes. I'm Matthew Porter. Thank you for coming, Mrs. Barrett."

His eyes dart everywhere, and I suspect it's not his real name.

Mother turns to me: "My apprentice and daughter, Sarah."

I can't help but notice that, with Mother, "apprentice" comes first.

"How long will this…treatment take?" the redcoat asks impatiently. "I must return to my quarters soon."

"It will take as long as the good Lord sees fit," Mother says without hesitation.

Inside the lean-to, it's dark and barely big enough for a straw mattress, battered little table, and charred chest, all crowded next to a miraculously intact fireplace. Once my eyes adjust to the dimness, I can make out Lucinda, and she's not at all what I expected. Dressed in a yellow satin gown, hair piled high, she's beautiful and about my age.

Her lips and cheeks are rouged cherry red.

"How can I help you, my dear?" Mother asks as if she's addressing the pastor's wife.

"I've not bled for two months," Lucinda says without a trace of embarrassment. "I would like the elixir to bring on a bleed."

I know this is part of Mother's services, ending unwanted pregnancies. But I've never been a party to one until now.

"Sarah, bring the parcel of herbs from my bag and stir the fire under the kettle." At last, I can be of some use.

Mother looks Lucinda in the eye. "My dear, I must ask you something important. Have you felt any kicks yet?"

"No, not a flicker," she says, eyes wide.

"That's a blessing." Mother looks greatly relieved. "You do realize, don't you, that after the quickening, it's against both God's law and the King's for anyone, midwife or not, to interfere. And while you might think you can dispose of babies whenever you please, I swear I would be struck dead by God Almighty if I should have any part of it once those kicks tickle your innards."

I don't think Mother would be struck down but when it comes to God, she's the absolute authority.

"Sarah! Is the water hot? I'll need a steaming cup of water." Totally in command, Mother suddenly softens as she turns her attention back toward Lucinda.

"My dear, how did you find yourself in such woeful circumstances?" It's as if Lucinda is already at the gates of hell for selling her services.

"It's not so bad, really," she says, as if her hovel were a cozy cottage. "Mother and Father died of the pox three years ago. It's just me and my brother, Will. He runs Black Horse Tavern. I worked there as a barmaid, then learned how I could earn a lot more money."

"Such a hard life for someone so young," Mother says. "Such a pity."

"Oh, you needn't pity me, Mrs. Barrett. "I can look out for myself, and Will stops by every morning for a cup of tea and to pick up his share of my nightly receipts."

The water in the kettle finally boils, and Mother pulls an assortment of dried herbs, plants, and berries from her bag.

"What's that?" Lucinda asks.

"Pay no mind," Mother says as she stirs the greenish heap into a cup of steaming water. She prefers to keep her own counsel when it comes to the trade she knows inside and out. She won't even tell me, her "apprentice."

Lucinda sips the tea slowly. Bits of the sodden pile inside rise to the top, emitting a strong unfamiliar smell. Her eyes fill with tears, and I assume she is having second thoughts, so I take her hand in my awkward attempt to comfort her.

"My dear, you must be strong," Mother says. She has such a way of wrapping a command in a blanket of tenderness.

"He said he would marry me, give the child his name. He said he loved me, as if I don't hear that every fortnight from fools who say anything in the heat of passion. This time, though, I was the fool — because I believed him."

"At least, he's paying for my medical services," Mother says. "Others wouldn't be so generous."

"Why did he change his mind?" I ask gently. She wipes her eyes, smearing her black eye shadow.

"He said his family would disown him if he married a whore."

I'm struck by his selfish excuses, the unfairness of it all. "You're better off without him!"

"My dear, it may take hours for the elixir to work," Mother says, flipping open her Bible as Lucinda, emotionally done in, sniffles. "I will find us some words of comfort and wisdom. Right here in the Book of Jeremiah, it says: 'Heal me, O Lord, and I shall be healed; save me and I shall be saved, for thou art my praise'."

Lucinda looks both comforted and trapped. I decide to get some air.

Outside, I'm surprised to see that the young soldier is still here.

"Lucinda is in good hands," I say. "Your little inconvenience will be over soon."

He gives me an odd look. "Are you lecturing me on morality?"

I put on my best innocent face. "Certainly not."

"She's just a whore. I could have left her high and dry," he says.

"Yes, she has much to be grateful for. But why did you fill her head with empty promises?"

"I can't risk a blemish on my family's good standing. You wouldn't understand." He looks chagrined, and I'm glad. We don't speak until I break the silence.

"This could take quite a while. Might be wiser to come back later."

He seems relieved to hear this. "I have a terrible thirst and a hunger to match. Perhaps I'll seek out a tavern."

"King's Tavern is just a short walk," I tell him, knowing full well that it's a rebel hangout where he'd be welcome as week-old fish.

He eyes me suspiciously. "Why would you send me there?"

"It's the closest one."

"I'm sure you know it's crawling with rebel sympathizers who'd tear me to pieces."

"I had no idea—"

"Spare me your false sympathies. I'll take my commerce somewhere I can lift a glass and drink to the King's health."

Without another word, he strides off, and I wonder if he'll raise a glass to Lucinda's health. I sit on the remains of a stone wall and wait for Mother as darkness closes in and a light snow falls. My hands feel numb, and I rub them together for warmth. The solitude gives me a chance to think about Tom. How long can he cling to life on that ship from hell? His dark eyes haunt me, and strangely enough, attract me.

I don't understand his zeal to beat the British at any cost. Surely, he doesn't think Washington's gang of ragtag rebels can succeed. Already the rebels are surrendering in droves to join the British, if I can believe anything Samuel says. But some part of me admires Tom's bravery and passion. And I'm jealous that his life has a bold purpose. Mine is destined to follow a predictable path of boredom, starting with marriage to, God have mercy, Samuel.

You would think he'd give up on me after my impertinence, as Mother calls it. But oh no. He apologized for shushing me. Even indulged my passion for chocolate. I didn't close the door completely on our nuptials, nor did I encourage him.

Finally, Mother emerges from Lucinda's shack. "Best to let nature take its course now. Either the elixir will work, or it won't. It's in God's hands."

We walk home quickly in silence. Mother is exhausted, and I'm struck by how much faith she has that God is in charge now that she isn't. When we get home, she falls immediately into the kind of deep, restful sleep that eludes me. I light a candle and open my diary.

*I must put into words a question that has been gnawing at me for some time. Does God really exist? If he is truly up there looking down, why would he allow the suffering and injustice that anyone with eyes can so readily see?*

# Chapter Six

The next morning as I trudge to the *Loyal Gazette*, a biting wind nips my face, and I think about the frigid, miserable night Lucinda must have spent in her shack. My own misery doesn't compare.

Of course, Lucinda doesn't have to deal with the likes of Jonah Livingston. As soon as I walk in, I know he's on one of his rampages. His wig teeters on his head, and his face is nearly purple.

Before I've even hung my cloak on the hook by the door, he thrusts a sheet of paper with scribbled writing at me. "Girl, I need you to set type! And make haste."

"Something about the prison ships?" I ask hopefully.

Jonah's eyes bulge with exasperation. "Why must you waste my time with questions about something you have no business meddling in?"

I snatch the paper from his hands. "Why must you be so cantankerous?"

He softens a little, as I knew he would. "If you must know, King George has made a generous peace offering to those damned rebel prisoners—not that they deserve it. If they pledge allegiance to the Crown and agree to take up arms for the King, they'll be pardoned for their treason. Even return to their homes and businesses without harm."

"This means all the prisoners could be set free!" He is momentarily stunned by my sudden enthusiasm.

"Jonah, I'll have it done by the time you return from the coffeehouse. Perhaps a biscuit would sweeten your disposition."

Still grumbling, he goes out the door as he does every day, mid-morning. I know it's at Hazen's where he gets much of his news and other bits of gossip, whether true or not. Once he printed a colossal lie that Washington was dead. It was at Hazen's that he learned why the church bells failed to ring an alarm the night of the fire: Washington's men had stolen them and recast them into cannonballs. Desperate for munitions, no doubt, but church bells?

I put on my leather apron and begin to pull the metal type from the drawers, setting the words letter by letter for the article about the peace offering. Jonah trusts me more and more each day, though he's never let on. He seldom reads the articles once I set them in type. A deliciously evil thought crosses my mind. I could change his words to mine, the newspaper would roll off the press and into the hands of thousands of readers. *King George Outlaws Pork Pies*, the headline screams. Jonah's eyeballs would sizzle. Smiling, I tuck away that bit of mischief.

There are other items to set as well. One is a letter praising the British troops for ridding the city of rebel soldiers. Hardly seems noble when so many are trapped like rats on the prison ships. Another relates to the death of Anna Morgan, wife of prominent lawyer Peter Morgan, who suffered the misfortune of being bitten by a rabid cat. And a performance of *Tom Thumb* at the Theatre Royal will feature British officers acting the parts, even Princess Huncamunca, Tom's true love, and her mother, the fat drunken Queen Dollalolla.

There is nothing about the prisoners and those foul ships. Nothing about the bodies piled up on shore and clogging the waters. I know Samuel won't listen to me, and Jonah goes into a rage if I mention it. It's all in my diary. But what good is it if no one ever sees it?

Surely General Washington must care. Does he even know how

awful it is? If I could get a letter into his hands, would he even believe the blathering of a witless girl, as Jonah, in his infinite wisdom, puts it? It's a long shot, but Lucinda's young soldier has given me an idea.

After Jonah goes out for his beloved rum and meat pie, I find a scrap of paper and dip my pen into the ink.

> *Dear Gen. Washington,*
> *I'm writing this letter to tell you about the dismal conditions aboard the prison ship Defiance. Your men are starving and sickly, dying by the dozens every day in the frigid cold. I saw it with my own eyes. Surely, this is not acceptable under military rules of war. I beg you to do something.*

I make no mention of Tom. Too risky. Nor do I sign my name. I sign the most dramatically influential name I can think of: Mrs. Charlotte Eloise Vandervoort Pierpont. I hurry to fold it and seal it with wax. Jonah will return soon, tipsy, and utterly unpredictable.

If King's Tavern is such a hotbed of rebel intelligence, maybe the owner can help me. Jonah has told me about him. "A skunk, that's the most charitable thing I can say about Jack Morton, or 'Black Jack' as he likes to call himself."

As soon as I stand up to put on my cloak my knees feel weak, my face flush, and my stomach queasy. I stuff the letter inside the fur muff that Samuel gave me and walk as quickly as I can to the tavern, keeping my head low and covered by my hood. I pass people going about their business, and no one seems to notice me.

Walking up the stone steps of the three-story brick tavern, I hear men's voices and laughter from inside. Mother would pray hard for my soul and then faint if she knew where I am. I could turn around and no one would be the wiser. But I take a deep breath and unlatch the heavy front door, stepping inside to dim light and the warmth of a fireplace.

All the talking stops, and I feel every eye on me. Even the two men playing billiards stop to stare. Then a tall, thin Negro in an elegant green velvet waistcoat walks over to me.

"May I assist you, Miss?" he asks in a French accent. He guides me back toward the door as if I'm a troublesome beggar.

"Are you a friend of the Crown?" I ask, my voice shaky.

He waits several seconds before answering. "I am not. Why do you ask?" He eyes me suspiciously.

"I must get a letter to General Washington. Might you have a way of doing that?" I look into his eyes for any sign he thinks I've lost my wits.

He stares at me for a full minute. I begin to squirm, wishing I hadn't come.

"And who are you, Miss?" A hint of a smile creeps onto his face, and for a moment I think he sees me as a child. I stand taller and lower my voice.

"No one of any importance. I'm simply delivering the letter for someone else. It's most urgent."

He takes it and looks at me with a kind of grimace. "I'll do my best to see that he gets it. Now you must go."

He opens the door for me, and I step outside, forgetting to thank him.

Racing down the steps, I finally calm down and turn the corner to walk back to the *Loyal Gazette*.

I almost bump into Samuel coming from the other direction. I suddenly feel as queasy as I did in the wave-battered boat going out to the *Defiance*.

"Why Sarah, what brings you over here?"

"Nothing in particular," I stammer. "Just taking some air. Jonah is in one of his foul moods."

"It's cold and windy. Why would you choose today for a walk?"

"I might ask the same of you."

"It's my business," he says with an air of importance. "I like to take account of who goes in and out of King's Tavern. Best to know as much as possible about the enemy."

I flush and begin to sweat. Did he see me come out of the tavern? I fight to keep calm.

"Don't concern yourself, Samuel. I'd never associate with those rebels." I smile at him, but he doesn't smile back.

43

"Where is your red ribbon?"

"I forgot it."

"Sarah, how thoughtless. You know it's for your own safety. It lets everyone know you're not a bloody rebel."

Too bad I hate wearing the damn thing. Too bad I feel less loyal to the Crown every day.

"Samuel, I don't need you or anyone telling me how to dress. Now I must return to the *Loyal Gazette*. Good day."

"So charming when you try to act professional! I like a little fire in a lady," he says, not appearing to like it at all.

Fuming, I whirl around and walk away before he can say anything else. I'm certain my letter to Washington is already in the fire, and the man in the elegant green vest is regaling his patrons with a hilarious story about a serious young woman who is as stupid as she is pretty.

# Chapter Seven

I wait weeks for some sign that Washington received my letter. I feel foolish about what I've done, wishing I'd never set foot in King's Tavern.

Heavy snow and bone-chilling winds make it impossible to go out to the *Defiance* with our goods. This morning I awake to find my ink bottle frozen. We cover ourselves with every scrap of clothing we own, and if it weren't for the copper bed warmer, filled with embers from the fireplace, we'd be frozen solid in the morning.

At breakfast, Benjamin coughs and feels feverish. Mrs. Harkins finally takes pity on us.

"Tonight, you'll bed down in the kitchen by the hearth where it's warmer. I won't have you freeze to death up there. Not with a sickly one." Mrs. Harkins is a saint. Her stack of firewood is dwindling, just like everyone else's. At least we're not forced to burn furniture for warmth. And food is in short supply too. Whatever happens, the British army mustn't go hungry, despite the American families starving in their homes. I wonder how Lucinda will ever make it through the winter. And Tom? I'm certain he's dead. No one on that ship could survive the cold, day after day. I feel awful that I didn't do more to help. I dread giving the news to Emma.

Mother isn't encouraging. "Best you put that boy out of your mind," she tells me tonight over a scant helping of porridge and bread. She has no idea how deep my anguish goes.

Part of it, I suppose, is that for all my loathing of the privileged British, I can't resist a sumptuous meal that comes my way. Samuel's invitations keep arriving, and I find myself accepting them, whether out of boredom or a need to be pampered now and then. There are sleigh rides through the city under bearskin robes and ice-skating parties with his loyalist friends, all followed by lavish dinners of turtle soup and roasted pig. I'm not ashamed to say that I slip some scraps into my muff for Mother and Benjamin. Whenever he can, Samuel manages to surprise us with a chicken or firewood. His generosity touches me, and I'm beginning to think that marriage might be tolerable. His kisses are pleasant enough, though not swoon worthy.

I fight the cold and snow to walk to the *Loyal Gazette*, my shoes soaked through. Believe it or not, Jonah's blustery outbursts are a respite from Mother's scrutiny. She abhors laziness and insists that I spin wool until my hands bleed or I fall asleep at the wheel.

Samuel seems to have a new respect for me, but he still can't stand the idea of my working at the *Loyal Gazette*, or for that matter, anywhere else. And he still pressures me to marry him soon. I'm running out of excuses. Perhaps marriage is my fate, and I should just accept it.

By early spring more prison ships stand sentry in Wallabout Bay, all full to the brim with captured rebels, according to a gleeful Jonah. Mother can't wait to resume our trips out to the *Defiance*. But without my almost-certainly-dead Tom, the whole prospect sounds dreary.

Mother pesters me and finally, when the weather is bearable, we start making trips into Wallabout Bay to sell what little we can scrape up: tobacco, needle and thread, bread, biscuits, the last of the apples. It's always under the watchful eye of the lieutenant, and I dare not slip below deck to see for myself what I already know in my heart.

As soon as the ground thaws, Mother and I plant her garden anew, with help from Samuel. "It will be bigger than last year's," she tells him. "I'll likely turn a good profit."

"No doubt." He smiles at me as I keep Benjamin occupied drawing pictures in the dirt with a stick. Samuel even softens up about our trips out to the ship after I tell him we sell only to the British officers and guards. He doesn't need to know every detail of everything I do.

"You seem to have a spring in your step these days," Mother remarks after he leaves one Sunday. "Thank the Lord you've begun to see the good sense of marrying that wonderful lad."

"Maybe I'll marry him, but I'm in no hurry so please stop nagging me about it," I say as we put the garden tools away.

"He won't wait forever, though he clearly adores you."

"Samuel is not the perfect man you think he is. He's bossy and claims to know more about everything than everyone else on the planet."

Mother laughs at me. "Once you're married, you'll become accustomed to his likes and dislikes and demands."

"What about my likes and dislikes? And my demands."

"Nonsense, child!"

"Marriage sounds like prison."

Her scowl is the last word.

After our supper of fish chowder, Mother works on my wedding gown. Lately, she takes it up whenever she's not needed for a birthing or tending the ailments of the Holy Ground's prostitutes. There are pieces of blue satin scattered all over the attic. Samuel has offered to pay for a dressmaker to hasten the process, but I insisted Mother's feelings would be hurt. If he suspects I'm just delaying the "happy day," as he calls it, he doesn't let on.

Sometimes I lie awake for hours, troubled by what I've gotten myself into. Samuel can be so kind and charming. Even Jonah thinks he's too good for me.

"A better loyalist you'll not find," he tells me. If I find fault with anything about the Anointed One, Jonah calls me a twit who doesn't know good fortune when it lands in her lap.

Tom's fate consumes me. I'm not sure what else I could have done but I feel somehow guilty and must find out whatever I can about his demise. I owe it to Emma.

I'm so desperate that I cajole Mother into going to the ship before we have enough goods to sell.

"I have a stack of newspapers," I tell her—not just the *Loyal Gazette* but all the others that come into our office. The British guards onboard are happy to pay for any scrap of news about the war, especially glowing accounts in the British-leaning journals.

"Captain Pendleton is so pleased with our visits," I say. "Didn't he tell you how much they lift the men's spirits? And it's no bother for the lieutenant, since he makes several trips a week across the river. I think he enjoys the exercise." If she's suspicious of my motives, she doesn't let on.

Three days later we're in his boat, and sweat is rolling down his face. It's a hot, muggy morning, more like summer than early May. Mother gushes about her new watermelon plantings and her larger corn patch, and even her hopes of being in London, or at least Nova Scotia by year's end.

I've heard about the droves of loyalists who've already fled the colonies for friendlier British soil. Mother grew up in London and often yatters on about the elegant gardens, lavish mansions, and more civilized populace. It all sounds terribly stuffy. Even so, I dread telling her I won't be going with her.

The lieutenant pauses in his labors and, oddly, smiles. He's been unusually companionable this morning, but actually smiling is unheard of.

"Pleasant breeze right now," he observes with unnerving friendliness. "But a storm's growing in the east, and we'll have a downpour by tonight."

"Praise the Lord," Mother says. "My garden needs a good drenching."

"My family has a fine garden in London," he says. "I miss it and I miss them."

His life story tumbles out: He was educated at Oxford and chose the military rather than the family's prosperous shipping business, now in the hands of his brother. "He's an agreeable chap and my best friend, but better at playing the ponies than minding the books. Still, we've had some good times."

As he resumes rowing, he hums a lively tune. This is a pleasant side of the lieutenant I've not seen, and it makes me wary.

I wonder if Tom had a chance to feel a pleasant breeze before he died. Just the thought of his poor body heaved over the side makes me wish a tortured, deathly pox on his captors.

We pull up next to the *Defiance* and climb the ladder to the top deck. Pritchard even lugs our basket of goods. "We are pleased to see you tonight, ladies," a guard says. "It's been weeks since we've been ashore."

"What do you have for us?" a grimy prisoner asks, thrusting a couple of coins toward Mother. Something about his voice stops me. I've heard it before. I look closer and realize it's Tom's friend, Nathaniel.

The guard shoves him. "Stand back and wait your turn."

I try to catch Nathaniel's eye, but he's staring intently at Mother's goods as she rummages through her basket for bread, tobacco, and apples. Finally, I ask him whether he'd want an apple. He gives me a slight nod of recognition.

"Yes, Miss. Thank you kindly." He hands me a coin and I fetch the best of the wormy lot.

I lower my voice. "Can you tell me anything about Tom Jordan? Did he suffer much at the end?"

He looks at me startled. "Suffer much? He's not dead, at least not yet."

The guard pokes Nathaniel with a club. "Move along scum, or I'll see that you don't live to eat that apple."

Not dead? I'm stunned. My heart is soaring, and I'm overwhelmed by an urgent need to see for myself. But I stop myself from dashing to the stairs that lead to the horrors below.

Mother nears the final prize: a custard pie topped with bits of nutmeg, that the guards ogle with naked lust. Then I notice that Pritchard is nowhere to be seen. Opportunity awaits. In a flash, I concoct a bold lie.

Tugging on the guard's sleeve, I say. "Sir, I think you should know, I saw some white object moving in the water as we approached the ship. At first, I thought it was a big fish, but then I'm sure I saw a beard. Might have been a prisoner escaping."

A flash of anger fills his face. "I'll see to that right away," he says and disappears.

I dash for the ladder to the lower deck, knowing I don't have much time before he returns empty-handed and foul-tempered. Quickly stepping down, I'm crushed by a wall of swampy heat. A cluster of men crowd around a boarded-up porthole, struggling for fresh air.

I find Tom in the same spot, pale and skeletal, and wearing the same ragged pants. I stifle my shock.

"You're a sight for sore eyes, Thomas Jordan. I thought you were dead."

"Some days I swear I am." He sits up slowly. "Sarah, I'm ashamed for you to see me like this."

"Never mind me. I'm not the one near starved to death."

I hear the commotion above me, likely boats being lowered to look for the "escapee." I could pay dearly for the little wild goose chase I've started, but I don't care.

Running out of time, I pull a biscuit from under my cloak and give it to Tom. In a majestic display of willpower, he quickly hides it under his foul blanket. If he's saving it for Nathaniel, I can only wish him to be as selfish as I am.

I want to give him more, but I have nothing. Then I remember the comb I carry everywhere, though God knows why. It's a pathetic offering. "This may come in handy for all sorts of things, least of all taming that unruly hair."

He laughs, then breaks into a fit of coughing. "Seems to me you know something about unruly hair."

Immediately my hand goes to my head, and I stuff a few loose strands back under my cap.

"No need to get all fancy with me. I like the way your red hair is wild and free. Kind of like you."

I can't stop the warm blush creeping over my face. Abruptly, I change the subject. "Tom, I have exciting news. The King has promised freedom to rebel prisoners who apologize, pledge allegiance to the Crown, and fight alongside the British."

His smile is gone. "We have nothing to apologize for. And I would rather die than take up arms for the King."

"You likely *will* die," I plead. "At least give it some thought."

"I'll do that for you. But I'll not change my mind."

I'm stricken. How could he be so stubborn? Who cares which side you're on when so many are suffering so needlessly?

Just then a loud bell clangs three times, startling me. "Prisoners, haul up your dead!" a voice commands.

"Happens every day," Tom says. "We must search among ourselves for those who died that day. Then we bundle them in their blankets and haul them on deck to be disposed of like so much garbage."

Suddenly, I feel nauseous and dizzy. "Tom, I must leave before I'm missed." I jump to my feet and clamber up the steps. Once on deck, I gulp the fresh air until my head clears. Then a low voice startles me. It's Pritchard.

"Miss, are you feeling sick? Would you like to sit down?"

"No!" Did he see me go below deck?

I look out over the water and see a flurry of small boats. "They're searching for a foolhardy prisoner who dared try to escape his fate," he says. "Even if he makes it to land, we're sure to get him in the woods." I'm certain he knows about my lie; certain I'll be in chains soon.

"I've just come from the captain's quarters. You know he serves as Provost Marshal, in charge of all New York's prisoners, on both land and sea," he says.

My heart pounds as I await my death sentence.

"The captain is pleased with your mother's visits. Says they build morale. He hopes that you'll visit us even more often."

I'm astonished. I can't utter a word.

"Very well then. Your mother is ready, so we'll take our leave before the storm rolls in." My heart doesn't stop thumping until we're in the boat, and I hear him whistling that old tune again.

51

# Chapter Eight

I'm thrilled Tom is alive, and I don't need to write Emma the letter I'd been dreading. But I can't stop stewing over his stubbornness. He'll die for certain in that hellhole. Even worse, I can't help but think his pigheadedness is also a rejection of me. Just to see him, I've lied to the British military, lied to my mother, and risked my life in a small boat, not to mention the risk of getting the pox, or at the very least a raging case of lice.

That's my cheery mood as I walk into the *Loyal Gazette* this June morning to face Jonah's latest insult.

"Someone tipped off Washington about the 'poor' prisoners," he screams at me. "Told him they were starving to death. Now the damned general wants to see for himself."

I do my best to react as if he'd said something about going to the coffeehouse or reading a church bulletin.

"He's coming to New York?"

"No, silly girl. He's trying to send one of his men. He knows better than to show his face here after the fire. And he wouldn't risk another assassination attempt. We nearly got him last time."

"We?" It's the first time he's admitted he had a hand in the plot to kill the general nearly a year ago. It seems like half the city's important people knew about it. One of the general's guards was in on the plot, and when Washington caught wind, he ordered the young man, Thomas Hickey, hanged from the gallows. I saw it myself, along with thousands of others.

"Never mind that," he snaps.

"Who would have told him the prisoners were starving?" I ask, trying to control the quaver in my voice.

"It wasn't exactly a secret, but whoever did it is a damn traitor, and we'll find him."

I should be worried, scared out of my wits, but truthfully, the excitement of what I've done thrills me.

Jonah quickly scratches out an item for the newspaper, ruining two quill pens in the process. He makes it sound as if someone has spread the basest of lies about the condition of the prisoners. Certainly, he writes, the men are fed just as well as the British officers. Certainly, they are clothed against the cold. Of course, they drink plentiful amounts of fresh water.

After he shoves the paper at me, the ink still damp, I set the type, hating every lie, wishing I could set the record straight.

While I'm working, a horse and rider pull up to drop off a bundle of mail for the city's residents, as he does once a week. (Postmaster is Jonah's newest title.) The horse is foamy with sweat, and the weary rider is caked in mud. Among the letters is one addressed to me, and I know instantly by the tiny, precise writing that it's from Emma.

> *Dear Sarah,*
>
> *Your letter arrived on the post at Mr. Bascomb's general store, and he discreetly passed it on to me, just as we planned. He's the only soul I trust to keep secret your whereabouts. He wishes you well.*
>
> *I am so grateful Thomas is alive, though held captive. I pray that this miserable war ends soon and that he comes home. Mother is faring well, though having a difficult time keeping up the farm without more help. Seems like all the men have gone off to war and left the farming to the*

*women. I help her when I'm not teaching school.*

*I've not married. With a shortage of men, it seems near impossible, not that I haven't tried. I fear my heart still belongs to your brother Seth, and I think of him every day when I walk past the cemetery on my way to the schoolhouse.*

*I was so happy to hear from you, dear friend. Have you and Samuel married? If not, you'd best hurry. He is a good man, and there aren't many left. It's not too late to learn how to make the perfect pie.*

*Please write back and tell me more about Thomas if you are able.*

*Your dear friend,*

*Emma*

*PS: Your cat Ezekiel has turned into a fine mouser. Mother keeps count.*

The thought of Ezekiel tears at my heart. I had no choice but to leave him with Emma the night we fled New Hampshire. At least he's making a name for himself.

Emma's letter puts me in a better mood. And even though Jonah's words make me ill, I feel certain Washington will raise hell and make conditions better for Tom and the other prisoners … maybe even secure their release. I'm proud of what I did. Honestly.

• • •

The theater is full when Samuel and I walk in. It's the most elegant place I've ever seen. Twinkling crystal chandeliers light the stage and the seats are covered in red velvet. All of them are filled by British officers and their wives, who, at this moment, don't seem the least bit troubled by the war.

Samuel's invitation was a surprise, accompanied as it was by a new satin bonnet, bedecked with ribbons and lace and tiny silk roses. How could I decline?

My best yellow cotton gown—the only one without ink stains—is no match for the flowing satin and silk gowns the other ladies wear.

Mother helped me pile my wild hair into a mound that stays put with what seems like a hundred hairpins. She tightened my stays to the point of suffocation before she deemed me presentable.

She said she barely recognized me when I went out the door. I feel different too, like a woman, not a mere girl. Pretty and elegant. Samuel even tells me so as we take our seats.

"Sarah, you've made quite a transformation. I'm proud to walk by your side." He looks handsome in his new breeches and royal blue waistcoat, white lace cravat, and white silk stockings. His thick blond hair is completely covered in a new wig, this one made from horsehair and dusted with flour. He says it gives him an air of dignity and maturity. That must be why he's recently taken up smoking a clay pipe.

We sit next to Samuel's boss, Mr. Stoneham, and his beautiful young wife, Caroline, whose mountain of curls towers over mine. I pity the person sitting behind that monstrosity.

"Mr. and Mrs. Stoneham, allow me to present Miss Sarah Barrett, the young lady I've told you about," Samuel says. "Sarah has agreed to marry me, and we'll wed soon, perhaps later this summer."

I'm thunderstruck. Wed? Later this summer?

"Congratulations," Mr. Stoneham says, his portly frame squeezed into the seat. "Our best wishes to you both."

Mrs. Stoneham turns and smiles sweetly at me. Her flowing silk gown is cut so low her bosom looks as if it will flop out with any sudden move. A pearl choker rings her long neck. Like a goddess, she's enveloped in a cloud of rosewater perfume.

"I'm so happy for you, Sarah," she says.

I force a smile. "Thank you" is all I manage to mutter. So now I'm officially engaged to wed before I've even officially said yes. And the blessed event will be this summer. I want to put up my hand and say, "Stop!" I feel I'm in the path of an avalanche gathering force as it hurtles downhill. And I'm powerless to stop it before it smothers me.

"If it would please you, we'd be honored to host the wedding at our home," Mr. Stoneham whispers as the curtain rises.

"Summer is a lovely time for a wedding," the goddess says.

"How kind of you and Mrs. Stoneham," Samuel says. "Thank you."

Samuel beams at me and squeezes my hand. I manage a weak smile. Now it's all arranged. We'll be wed in a matter of weeks in one of the most elegant mansions in the city. Maybe I should be thrilled and thankful, but I can't feel anything except suffocation.

I fume during the performance. Judging by the laughter, it's riotous as British soldiers take to the stage in a farce about Washington's defeat in the city. The poor general is portrayed as a timid little man, afraid of a mouse. It might have been funny a year ago, but Tom's life is hanging by a thread and Washington is his only hope.

We ride home in an elegant, enclosed carriage that Samuel has hired for the occasion. On the way, he gushes about the Stonehams' offer. "Wait until you see the mansion. The staircase winds up to a balcony overlooking the Hudson. It's so big I want to invite everyone we know."

"Samuel, slow down … it's too much for me to take in."

He laughs as if I've said something hilarious.

I try to picture myself stepping daintily down the staircase in the dress Mother is making, but I see a red-faced clumsy girl tripping on her skirts and falling headfirst into a crowd of exquisitely dressed strangers who find it amusing.

"We shall set the date soon. Surely your mother has finished the dress. She's had more than enough time." I've never seen him so excited.

I finally gather my wits. "Why must we rush?"

"Because I'm tired of waiting," he says, raising his voice. "I can provide for you handsomely. You'll have the finest gowns in New York. And you'll have no need to dirty your hands at that newspaper."

I feel defeated. A lump rises in my throat. "But—

"Sarah! Why aren't you filled with joy about this? I know you love me, though you've not said so. We're good together, you and me. You'll not find a man better suited to your independent spirit. We can be happy."

I must confess, it's a persuasive argument. I'm close to giving in.

"If that's not enough, consider this. You're about to marry a man of sharp intellect, a man who will improve your social ranking. Look at you … you have nothing. This is your chance to rise in society."

That ruined everything. Now I'm low class and growing madder by the second. "Perhaps," I say sarcastically, "you would be happier with a lady from your own station in life."

"I don't want to marry anyone else," he says. Then he takes a deep breath. "I love you. You're smart—too smart for your own good—and pretty when you put some effort into it."

"If that's a compliment, you've failed miserably." I look away. How could this evening turn so miserable so fast? The silence is filled by the *clop, clop* of the horses, and the occasional squeak of the carriage.

"What I mean to say, is you're beautiful when you smile. Your blue eyes sparkle." He smiles shyly. "Is that better?"

"Only slightly."

"Sarah, you dazzle me with your beauty and wit," he says, faking sincerity. "Better?"

I fight to hold onto my frown. He has a way of brushing aside my anger with charm, which only makes me madder. We arrive home, and he kisses me tenderly on the forehead. I give him a quick goodnight.

Mother and Benjamin are fast asleep when I tiptoe into the cramped attic. I light a candle and gaze upon the dismal sight … the two of them curled up on the tattered mattress, a threadbare quilt barely covering them. Mother has fallen asleep sewing a pearl button on my wedding dress. My anger dissolves into exhaustion. Perhaps Samuel is the best I can do, and I should be grateful.

# Chapter Nine

"Today is the day," Jonah says, as he prances into the *Loyal Gazette* after his mid-morning coffee at Hazen's. "Washington's men will tour the prison ships, the sugar factories, churches, anywhere those so-called patriots are in custody. They'll see that all this fuss about starvation and overcrowding is a big lie concocted by some rebel sympathizers." I've never seen him this happy.

"We'll have some news for certain," I say, only it won't be what he expects. Finally, the truth will come out. I can't wait to see the crestfallen look on his face then.

Hours later Jonah is so edgy and bothersome, I urge him to stroll over to the waterfront and poke around for any news of Washington's men. As soon as he's out the door, I pull my diary from my bag. Every page is filled to the edges with tiny, jammed-together words that are barely readable. I need more paper and getting some will be near impossible, with the paper shortage throughout the colonies. Jonah even publishes a notice every week seeking "clean cotton and linen rags" that can be turned into paper at the nearest mill. He guards his dwindling supply like a hawk, but I take as many sheets as I dare and stuff them in the back of my diary.

After an hour, he swaggers back in. A bad feeling wells up inside me.

"I chatted with Captain Pendleton. Washington's men were given a tour of the *Defiance* all right. They even talked with some of the prisoners, who were eating a hearty meal of pork, potatoes, carrots, and buttered biscuits. They came away convinced the men weren't starving or abused in any manner."

I gulp. Not at all what I expected. I feel my face flush. "So, the letter to Washington was … a lie, a trick? Is that what people think?"

He smiles broadly. "Pathetic, isn't it?"

My stomach churns, and I taste the morning's oatmeal and cider. What went wrong? I know what I saw. It's no lie.

Jonah writes the account of the prisoners' feast as if it were the first Thanksgiving. He chuckles as he works, making it impossible to think. One thing is certain. I must visit the *Defiance* as soon as I'm able.

• • •

Another week passes before Mother and I scrape together enough goods to warrant a visit to the ship. Soon the garden will be bursting with fruit and vegetables but today we haul a basket of biscuits and dried apples, though they're barely fit to eat. I hide a biscuit under my skirts, along with a chicken thigh from Mother's stew.

She must suspect that I'm sneaking off to see Tom, but she doesn't lecture me, thank the Lord! I think she can't bear his suffering. Though a rebel, he was my brother Seth's best friend, and that means something to her.

It starts to rain as we hurry to the waterfront at first light, and the wind picks up.

"We'd be smart to turn around and try tomorrow," Mother says. "No use getting drenched."

"No! It's just a shower. It'll be over in minutes." I'm determined to see Tom and sort out why my letter failed.

"Have it your way. Samuel must have the patience of Job to put up with such a strong-willed girl."

"He doesn't complain." If only she knew. I wonder when he'll say he's had his fill of me, and look for someone more eager to please him, someone less headstrong. It seems the more I push him away, the more he fights for my hand.

"In fact, the wedding will be at the Stonehams' mansion," I say. "They offered it the night we saw them at the play."

Mother gasps. "And why did you wait until now to tell me? That's wonderful news."

"Because I knew you'd fly into a feverish pitch of preparation and hound me with questions."

"And why not? It's any mother's hope to see her daughter marry into distinction and wealth. When is the wedding?"

"This summer, if Samuel has his way."

"So soon. So much to do. I must finish your dress."

It's exactly the fuss I'd hoped to avoid.

The rain is a steady drizzle when we reach the waterfront, and I'm soaked to the bone. Lt. Pritchard is waiting and none too pleased to see us. Our added weight will mean more work for him.

"Wind is picking up," he shouts. "Won't be a pleasant trip, I fear."

If he's trying to dissuade us, he's wasting his time. I gather my skirts and leap into the boat, a move I can now accomplish with some grace.

As he rows against the wind, the boat rocks back and forth with every wave. The bow rises high and then slams down so hard my innards jam against my throat. Nausea sweeps over me. Mother just glares. Just when I think I can't hold out any longer, we bang up against the *Defiance*.

As the lieutenant lifts the basket of goods aboard the landing platform, he turns to me and asks, with a half grin: "Are you feeling fine, Miss?"

"Just perfect, thank you." I hate for him to know the truth: The stink from the ship is more sickening than the churning waters. Even cramming my lavender-scented handkerchief up my nose can't stop the volcano in my stomach. I reach the railing just in time to spew over the side of the boat.

When I finally raise my head and wipe my face, Pritchard is smiling. "Quite a spectacle for someone who's just perfect."

I'm too rattled and embarrassed for a smart reply, and I sense a softness in his voice. He takes my hand and gently helps me up to the deck. Mother is already there, laying out her goods.

Oddly, only British officers greet us, no prisoners. "We're always happy to see you ladies," one of them says. "You bring us good cheer." I steel myself to be pleasant.

"I have a pint of rum," Mother calls out. "Who's the highest bidder?"

Just as before, I slip below deck. Even before my eyes adjust, I hear it: "Brung us some bread?"

Sadly, I shake my head. Before he can say more, I catch sight of Tom who is helping a young man with a blood-encrusted head wound wrap a dirty bandage around the foul mess.

He ushers me behind the huge copper kettle that holds the day's ration of gruel.

"Tom, I brought you some food."

"I figured as much. Didn't want to start a brawl over a few crumbs."

As discreetly as I can, I reach under my skirt for the chicken thigh, biscuit, and dried apple I tied to my petticoat.

"You are a saint," he says, stuffing the whole biscuit in his mouth. "They've cut our rations in half and bring in a boatload of new prisoners every day. We've had nothing but sour oatmeal for two days. There are hogs in pens on board that are better fed than us."

"Surely, they feed the meat to the prisoners."

"No, it's only for the Brits. I've seen men pick through the slops heaved out for the pigs."

"Tom, I wrote to Washington about the horrible conditions."

"They inspected … if you can call it that. The captain rounded up the healthiest of us and offered up a feast if we lied about what we're going through. Everyone else was too afraid to complain. The inspector never saw the lot of us jammed together in the belly of this stinking beast."

I don't know what to say. "Tom, I'll think of something we can do."

"If I ever escape this hell or get set free, I'll repay you for all your kindness."

I shake my head. "Just stay alive."

I join Mother and we climb down to the rowboat and our waiting oarsman. The trip back is smoother. When we arrive and Mother is fussing with her baskets, the lieutenant leans over to me.

"I've been watching you," he whispers. "I know that you go below deck to help one of the prisoners."

I freeze. "What are you going to do?"

"Nothing, just yet."

"Sarah, come along," Mother says. "It's late, and we must get home."

# Chapter Ten

The lieutenant's words scare me senseless. People have been shot or hanged for aiding the enemy. Mother didn't hear, thank God. Of course, I can't tell Samuel. He'd be leading the mob to the gallows.

As Mother and Benjamin sleep, I write to Emma, hoping it will settle my nerves. I want to tell her the whole truth, that neither Tom nor I stand much of a chance of living out our natural lives. But that seems needlessly dramatic, so I take a more cheerful tone.

> *Dear Emma,*
> *I've seen Tom and he's faring as well as can be expected. I will continue to offer what little I can to ease his confinement. Be assured that if there is any way to rescue him from this horrible ship, I will find it.*
> *I'll wed Samuel this summer. He's most anxious for it to happen. I'd sooner wait longer, but I don't think he'll stand for it.*
> *Sarah*
> *PS: I've decided I will never master a decent pie. Samuel will have to do without.*

. . .

The next morning Jonah is strutting around the print shop like a rooster when I walk in. He doesn't even notice I'm late again.

"It'll be a grand day, June 4," he bellows.

"What are you prattling on about?" I'm in no mood for a guessing game.

"The King's birthday celebration. Haven't you heard?"

"No. His Highness must have forgotten to tell me about it," I say, as I put on my ink-smudged leather apron.

"Girl, your arsehole comments will land you in trouble one day. If you care to know, the celebration will be quite an affair, bigger than in past years. Huge fireworks show."

"Doesn't the King know we're fighting a war here?"

He lights his pipe with an air of smug satisfaction. "Not in New York. The British are firmly in control here. They'll soon stamp out this little rebellion."

That should be cheerful news. It's what everyone in New York wants, and Mother, and of course Samuel. I thought I did too. It's what Father would have wanted—an end to the fighting. But honestly, I'm beginning to see the rebels' side of things. They're fed up with the British taxing everything to death and ordering everyone around. The nightly curfew is the least of it. It's the treatment of the prisoners— dogs on the street fare better—and the all-too-vivid examples of Tom and his mates that fill my head with doubts.

Jonah is blathering on. "And the mayor wants to put on the most lavish, elegant celebration New York has ever seen to send a message that the Crown is still at the helm."

"This hardly seems the time," I say. "A quarter of the town has burned down and still lies in ruins. People are starving."

Jonah gapes at me in disbelief. "It's not that bad. I see people eating heartily in taverns. They go to plays, dressed in the best finery." Then his eyes narrow. "Didn't you and that boy go to the theater all fancied up recently?"

"That's different." I feel my face redden. "We were guests of Mr.

Stoneham and his wife. He's Samuel's boss."

"Girl, you'd better have a change of heart. Your Mr. Stoneham is working with the mayor on the King's birthday celebration. The grand ball and dinner will be at his mansion."

I barely have time to take in this bit of information when Jonah announces, "Enough small talk. We have news to print."

. . .

Mother talks of little but the upcoming wedding. You would think she's the one marrying Samuel. She's insisted we invite him to dinner, likely to pepper him with questions that I'm tired of answering. When the day arrives, I drag myself from bed to discover she's already spent hours preparing a fish stew with the first of the vegetables from her garden: parsnips, peas, onions, and radishes. All that, after spending the evening at the Holy Ground in a shack where she guided a prostitute through a difficult birth. She should be exhausted, but no, she's cheery, humming "A Mighty Fortress Is Our God." It's maddening. All I can think about is the next time I'll see Tom—if I see him at all. The look on Pritchard's face is seared in my mind. Will he turn me in? Will he try to blackmail me? At the very least, it could be the end of our trips to Wallabout Bay.

I keep Benjamin out of Mother's hair all morning; it's the least I can do while she makes a custard pie. I tell him stories as fast as I can make them up.

"And then the boy went off to pick blueberries. When his bucket was full, he started to walk home. But he lost his way. Then a giant bird with beautiful red and blue feathers appeared out of nowhere. 'Hop atop my wings,' the bird said. He did just that and the bird flew high above the treetops back to his mother's house. And that's the end."

"No, it's not," Benjamin says. "Tell me the rest."

Children can be so tiresome. Yawning, I continue. "Then the giant bird disappeared, and the boy searched for him—"

Thankfully, Samuel arrives, presenting Mother with a gift, a chunk of chocolate that nearly makes her faint.

"Thank you," she gushes, gazing at him with adoring eyes. I muster a smile, not at all close to adoration.

"Sarah, I have something for you too," he says, grinning broadly.

"What is it?" I'm hoping for a book. Maybe the half-century-old "Gulliver's Travels" that I've raved about to Samuel.

"We're going to the King's birthday celebration. Mrs. Stoneham is in charge of the invitation list. The mayor and all the dignitaries will be there. Everyone except the King and Queen of course."

Mother covers her mouth and gasps. "Oh Sarah, you are a lucky girl, rubbing elbows with the city's finest."

It sounds unbelievable, me, mingling with aristocratic ladies in their elegant gowns and bonnets, chatting with the city's nobility. Samuel would fit in just fine. Even today he's wearing his best lavender-scented wig and green velvet waistcoat.

"That is good news. Don't you think so, Sarah?" Mother prods.

It sounds like a fairy tale, and I imagine ginger tarts and seven-layer chocolate cakes. "Yes, it is, but—"

"But what?" Samuel says. "I thought you would be excited and grateful for such an opportunity."

"I am." My mind darts back to the scolding I've just given Jonah, and guilt sets in.

"It seems wrong to celebrate when people have so little right now." I cringe when I hear my words. I sound so self-righteous. Samuel hears it too.

"The celebration will go on whether you like it or not. So you might as well get off your high horse and enjoy it."

That takes me aback. His gruff tone irritates me, and I dig in my heels.

"If you saw the misery I witnessed on the prison ship, you'd find it difficult to fill your belly with fine food and drink."

Samuel falls ominously silent. Mother knows a fight is brewing, and she throws herself into the fray.

"She'll come to her senses. Of course, she'll need a proper gown and bonnet. And shoes."

"Certainly. You can't go as you are," he says, eying me up and down. "These are important people!" He lights his pipe, and the smell of tobacco fills the air, offering the illusion of maturity. He seems to think it's all settled, but I'm not done.

"What's wrong with the way I am?" I know I'm provoking an argument, and I'm in no mood to stop. "Must you pretty me up before you can be seen in public with me?"

Samuel sighs wearily. "Look at yourself, Sarah. You still have an ink smear on your face. Your clothes are all stained with ink. The smell of ink is in your hair, which looks like it hasn't seen a brush in days. You work in a print shop with rough characters."

"Jonah, a rough character?" I laugh. "At least he's never complained about how I look."

With his attempt at a tender look, Samuel takes my hand. "I'm only saying that a little sprucing up would make a big difference. After all, you are going to be my wife and I want to be proud of you."

I'm still mad, but Mother rushes in between us. "Enough. Let's sit down and have some stew before it gets cold."

I'm not the least bit hungry, but I grudgingly sit down at the big table in the kitchen. Fortunately, the Harkins family is away for the day. But without the commotion of children running about, the awkward silence is deafening.

Mother makes up for it with dreary chatter about wedding details. "The cake must be a spice cake with dried fruit and nuts." Samuel nods approvingly.

I hate spice cake. It seems like he and Mother have my wedding and my entire life planned out. Next, they'll tell me what I can and can't say. I can't let go of my anger.

Mother says grace, offering thanks to God for the "paltry meal" we are about to eat. It's all for Samuel's benefit. We haven't eaten such a lavish meal in months. Sitting through it all will be torture.

"The stew is delicious," Samuel tells Mother before he's even had a bite. "Where did you find clams and oysters?"

"Payment from a fisherman. I removed a fishhook from his hand and bandaged it up. I never know what my services will yield. Sometimes it's a meager offering, a slab of cheese or stale bread."

"Not always, Mother," I say. "Captain Pendleton's wife was most generous, offering a shoulder of mutton after her last child was born." I should leave it at that, but I can't. "Who knows where it came from?"

I know exactly where it came from. British officers are keeping the best of the provisions allotted to the soldiers and prisoners. I heard it from Jonah, who thought it only right that the men in the least peril eat the best meals.

Samuel scowls at me. "You're not suggesting others are going hungry because—"

"Sarah! You'd best show more gratitude for the bounty on our table," Mother says with a stern look.

There it is; the tone she has used since I was five. I hated it then, and I loathe it now. I feel ugly and ungrateful. I know how much effort she put into making the meal, and I should be thankful. I try to make amends.

"Mother, the stew is delicious."

"Oh, it's hardly fit for consumption," she says, coyly looking down for Samuel's benefit.

"It's as good as any we'll likely be served at the King's birthday," Samuel says, knowing just how to please Mother. "I've seen the menu Mrs. Stoneham is putting together. Dozens of dishes: venison, veal, pork, beef, fish of every kind, and puddings and pies."

Mother is awestruck. "Sarah, you are so lucky to partake in such an affair."

"I know I am," I say, trying to keep the irritation out of my voice. "But it must cost a fortune for all that food, the orchestra, the fireworks."

"Sarah, don't trouble yourself about that," Samuel says. "The city is wealthy, and the Crown wants us to make a big fuss."

"It's not right," I say. "Since the fire, hundreds of people are still living in tents on the Common with little to eat. I see them when I walk to work. Even the British soldiers barely have enough food. And the prisoners on the ships are starving to death."

Samuel rolls his eyes. "Sarah, stop beating a dead horse. Enough about the prisoners. They eat as much as you or me, and if they die, where's the loss?"

I gasp, spilling soup down the front of my dress. "How can you be so heartless!"

"When did you become so high and mighty?" Samuel's face is beet red. "Those men deserve to die for what they did. Showing sympathy for these bloody fools makes me question your allegiance to the King and why it is we're even together."

"I've been questioning that for months, not that you've ever listened!" Nothing can stop me now.

"Sarah!" Mother says. "Samuel is right. Listen to him."

"No, I won't!" I stand up, overturning my chair, and run to the front door.

The last thing I hear is Mother's pleading voice: "Samuel, she'll change her tune, don't worry. At the least, she owes you an apology. You've been so patient."

Apology? That just stokes my anger as I flee the house with no idea where I'm going. I walk toward the Common, passing a wagon piled high with belongings, including a grandfather clock. Crammed among the blankets, chests, and furniture is a family of five. Trailing the wagon is a bellowing cow. Another rebel family fleeing, afraid to stay in this loyalist-held city. As fast as they leave, British officers and their families move into the homes they just left. Soon everyone will be toasting the King's health. Mother will be pleased, and Jonah too. And, of course, Samuel will be over the moon. Everyone will be delighted, except Tom and the starving legions. And me.

# Chapter Eleven

For days I hold onto my anger and refuse to see Samuel. Not that he wants to see me. I know I was rude, but I don't regret a word. And I don't care a whit about going to the King's birthday celebration.

Mother pesters me every day to apologize to him. She says I acted like a spoiled child. I stand my ground—politely, of course—until I can't stand it anymore and tell her maybe she's the one who should wed Samuel. She raises her hand to slap me but stops short. I probably deserved it.

At any rate, she's a blubbering mess and I feel awful. I know Samuel's pride won't allow him to take me back so, just to calm Mother down, I write him a half-hearted apology.

> *Dear Samuel,*
> *Please accept my apology for the unkind words I said about the King's birthday celebration. I will attend the gala with you after all.*
> *Sincerely,*
> *Sarah*
> *PS: I will still need suitable attire for the evening.*

I nearly choke on every word. The next day I receive a note at the *Loyal Gazette*.

> *Dearest Sarah,*
>
> *I accept your apology, and I'm pleased to see that you now understand your place. Let's put this behind us and move forward toward a happy and proper union.*
>
> *I'm looking forward to attending the celebration with you, and of course, you shall have the finest attire New York has to offer.*
>
> *With deepest affection,*
> *Samuel*

I'm stunned. What will it take for him to cast me aside? On the contrary, he arranges for me to have a silk gown made by the best seamstress in town. The best milliner will make my headdress, and it will tower over the others. I know it will all cost a king's ransom, and I don't see how he can afford it. But I don't ask.

Even after my "apology," Mother keeps trying to shame me into being nicer to Samuel. "Father would be appalled at your childish, ungrateful behavior." That hurts, but I also realize that it's partly for him that I'm risking my freedom when I secretly detail the misery of prisoners aboard the *Defiance*.

· · ·

A week later, Jonah's invitation to the King's birthday celebration is delivered to the *Loyal Gazette*. He won't stop crowing about it. Everyone who enters the shop to gossip or buy a newspaper gets an earful.

"Feast your eyes on this," he boasts to a well-dressed man placing an advertisement offering $3 for the return of his runaway slave, a "gregarious" fellow with a missing front tooth.

"They say there will be a slew of elegant dishes served," he tells the man, who evidences no interest at all.

Nor do I escape his gloating. "Hazen has invited me to share his carriage for the ride to the ball. I'm having a new waistcoat and breeches sewn."

"You need them because you're bursting out of your old ones," I say, knowing it will get a rise. "Too much pie."

"You'll be wise to tend to your work and not my girth."

I smile to myself. The old goat is seldom in such a good mood. He's writing his third article about the upcoming celebration, with more details about who will attend and what they'll dine on. He drools over every dish listed. It's a pathetic display.

"Chocolate cherry cordials." He looks at me as if I should swoon at their very mention.

I make a face that conveys I'd rather drown than eat one. Truth is, I've never eaten a cherry dipped in chocolate and can't imagine its wondrous taste. I keep it to myself that I too have been invited to the glittering affair. Let him be surprised when he spies me at the ball. Oh, the shock on his face will give me such pleasure!

Just as I settle in to set type, the print shop's big oak door creaks open slowly, and a boy no more than six or seven years old, slips in. He thrusts a note sealed with a glob of wax under my face.

"Miss Sarah Barrett?" he asks. I nod and take the letter. The boy is out the door before I look up.

I break the seal and unfold the paper:

> *British Commander Charles Laurence is pocketing untold money intended for the American prisoners held on ships and elsewhere. As the manager of supplies, he orders food for the men. When one of them dies, he fails to record it so money for those rations continues to come in. But it goes straight to Laurence. He is getting wealthy while the prisoners die.*
>
> *Do what you wish with this information. I trust you'll do the right thing.*

I fold the letter and tuck it into my sleeve. Outside, I look up and down the busy street, but the boy is nowhere in sight. Who sent it? And why me? Is it even true?

I spend the rest of the day pondering what I should do. Jonah never takes anything I have to say seriously. He'd look at the note and say it was a ruse, the work of a scoundrel. But if it's true, surely the British command will want to know. They'll want to punish this Mr. Laurence. After all, it's the Crown's money being stolen. Even worse, he's starving his own prisoners.

When Jonah heads out to his tailor's shop for a fitting, I copy the letter word for word, then fold it carefully and tuck it into the bodice of my dress. I'll need it later for my diary. I feel like a spy with a big secret, and the excitement is making me jumpy.

The day drags on. Jonah wants this, he wants that, and then he changes his mind. I feel like I'm going mad. And the shop is bustling with people wanting pamphlets printed or copies of Thomas Paine's *Common Sense*, the rebel rant that blames every wrong in the colonies on Britain. Jonah calls it "barbaric nonsense," though he's happy to take their money.

By the end of the day, I decide to show the letter to Samuel. You might think it odd when we're not on the best of terms. But he knows people high in the British command. He is an excellent lawyer who will surely see the crime committed against the Crown. (Or, closer to my heart, the crime against the prisoners.) To be completely honest, I want to be back in his good graces, at least temporarily. Not because I feel guilty over the money he's spending to make me presentable for the King's birthday celebration, and not because I'm curious about the chocolate cherry cordials and the stream of fancy dishes that will be trotted out. The truth is this: Being in his company, I may learn some useful information about the prison ships and Tom's fate. Does that make me an exploitive user of men? Does it make me a spy? I have to say the notion excites me.

At closing time, I leave the *Loyal Gazette* and hurry toward the rooming house where Samuel lodges. It's on a narrow cobblestone street, lined with elm trees. Mother would never approve of me visiting unannounced, but it seems the quickest way to show him the letter.

At my knock on the door, a tall thin old woman with beady eyes opens it a crack.

"Yes?"

"I wish to see Samuel Mason." I use my most polite tone, then turn my head so she can see the red ribbon on my bonnet. It's a last-minute addition I knew would please him.

"I see you're a loyalist," she says, as she opens the door. "Down the hall and to the left." If she thinks it scandalous for me to visit a gentleman's quarters, she doesn't show it.

I'm curious to see where he goes every night, where he sleeps, where he hangs his coat, and the books he brags about reading. I knock on the door softly. Soon he swings it open with a big smile that vanishes when he sees me.

"Sarah? What are you doing here?"

"I have something to show you."

He looks about the room nervously, then gestures for me to come in.

"This is most unusual," he blurts out, hurriedly adding, "but I'm happy you came nonetheless."

He doesn't seem happy in the least.

I look about the room. The bed is neatly made. The papers on his desk are orderly. He is dressed in a clean, pressed shirt, breeches, and white stockings. A fire burns low, heating a black iron kettle with something that smells like beef stew. On a small table, a wine bottle stands open next to two glasses.

"I hope I'm not interrupting you," I say, certain I've done just that.

"No." He seems impatient and ill at ease. "Now what is it you want to show me?"

I hand him the letter and watch his face as he reads it. Furrowed brow, pursed lips. Finally, he looks up at me. "Who gave you this?"

"A boy who ran off. I thought you might know the proper person to give it to. Someone who can make sure this Charles Laurence is stopped."

"Sarah, do you know who Charles Laurence is?"

I shake my head.

"He works directly under General Howe. He's a most important man, a friend of my boss, Mr. Stoneham. He'll be one of the guests of honor at the King's birthday celebration."

"And he's stealing from the Crown."

"The King doesn't care that the prisoners have enough to eat, General Howe doesn't care, Charles Laurence doesn't care, and, frankly, neither do I."

"They have a right to be kept alive, Samuel!" This isn't going the way I expected. None of it.

Then the patronizing tone. "Sarah, my dear, you did the right thing by showing this to me. Let me handle it."

"Are you at least going to show it to Captain Pendleton? Won't he want to know someone is stealing right under his nose?"

"No. You simply don't understand how these things are managed. Laurence isn't the only one benefiting from this war. You are so smart about some things but so naive about others."

Before I can say anything, he tosses the letter into the fire, and it takes only a second for the flames to consume it.

"You had no right to do that!"

"Now, forget about it."

"I won't!"

"Without it, no one will believe the words of a hysterical child."

"So you think, Mr. Attorney-at-law. I have a copy and it's in a safe place. You'll never find it."

"Don't toy with me, Sarah." He grabs my arm tightly. "You'd best tell me where—"

Just then someone raps on the door. Samuel lets go of my arm. He opens the door, and I expect to see the same beady-eyed woman, complaining about the racket we're making.

But it's not her.

In glides Mrs. Stoneham, elegantly dressed in a red velvet gown, her ample bosom on display. Every blond curl is perfectly in place under her ribbon-strewn straw hat.

"Am I interrupting something?" She smiles sweetly.

"No, Sarah was just leaving," he says, practically shoving me out the door before flinging it shut.

I want to scream. The wine and cozy fire are all for Mrs. Stoneham. Are they lovers? Of course they are. I'm not naive. How long has this little tryst been going on behind my back? Have they consummated their affair right there on the neatly made bed I've just seen?

I start walking aimlessly, going over again what happened. I hate Samuel, hate his lavender-scented wig. Hate that he deceived me and embarrassed me. I despise her too, her beauty and elegance and her mountainous breasts. He isn't at all the gentle, studious boy I knew in New Hampshire back when we both helped Father print his newspaper. He's a monster, cruel and unfeeling. My arm still throbs. No one has the right to hurt me. Ever.

Before I realize it, I'm at the Holy Ground. The taverns are full by now with boisterous drinkers and gamblers. Somehow, I feel safer here than anywhere near Samuel. I'd rather dance on rats' teeth than go to the ball with him. And if you think I'd still marry this human stain, you must be insane.

I tear the red ribbon off, toss it on the ground in disgust, and storm off.

"Miss, you dropped something." I turn to see Lucinda bounding toward me. I haven't seen her since that unfortunate night. She's wearing a rose-colored silk dress with a matching choker. Her hair is piled high in ringlets, and her lips and cheeks are their standard cherry red.

She doesn't recognize me until she hands me the ridiculous ribbon. "You're Mrs. Barrett's daughter, the midwife's apprentice." She smiles warmly.

"I'm Sarah." I wipe the tears from my face with my sleeve. "You seem to have recovered well, Lucinda."

"Thanks to your mother and you."

"Me? I did nothing except get in the way."

She laughs, a big jolly laugh, throwing back her head. This is not the distraught young woman I tended to that night.

"You told me I'm better off without my soldier."

"I'm sorry, I didn't mean to speak ill of him."

"I'm glad you did," Lucinda says, still smiling. "I told him to never darken my door again, and he was all too happy to oblige."

I didn't expect this news. "You mean you're not providing services at the Holy Ground?"

"Unfortunately, that is not the case yet. I must save some money—a lot of money—before I can leave the business behind me for good."

She looks at me with concern. "You've been crying. Can I help?"

"You already have." I manage a smile. "Lucinda, I was right when I said you're better off. Men are such pigs."

I'm clear-eyed and resolute as I walk away. Samuel will never darken my door again.

# Chapter Twelve

It's late when I slip into the nearly empty King's Tavern. Men are huddled around a small table drinking ale, playing cards, and talking in low voices. In the corner, two are playing billiards.

They stop their chatter and stare as I motion to Jack Morton behind the bar.

He walks over smiling. "Another letter from Mrs. Pierpont?"

I shake my head no. "This one came to me anonymously," I whisper. "I thought it might be of use to General Washington. It says that Charles Laurence is stealing from starving prisoners."

He reads the letter and then looks squarely at me, the smile gone. "How do I know this isn't a trick?"

"Sir, it's no trick." I return the look.

"Miss, how can I trust you?"

"I've seen it."

"You?" He seems incredulous.

"I've boarded the prison ship *Defiance* several times. My dear friend is held captive there. He's near death from eating moldy, rotten scraps of food, and so are most of the others."

"What is your friend's name?" He's still dubious, and it's maddening.

"Thomas Jordan, from Essex, New Hampshire."

Then his eyes narrow. "How do I know you're not a damn Tory working for the British? The city is crawling with them."

"If I were a Tory, would I accuse a British officer of stealing? That wouldn't be smart, would it? My friend Thomas is as loyal a patriot as George Washington. Would you be so kind as to pass the note to him?"

"A smart reply indeed," he says. "Something about you suggests I can trust you, and I hope, for your sake, that I'm not wrong. I'll see that the general receives this note."

I'm curious about this dignified Negro. "How do you know General Washington, if I may ask?"

"It was I who foiled the plot to kill him," he says. "That is all you need to know. Now you must go."

I'm desperate to know more, but I don't want to press him. "Thank you kindly, sir." I turn and leave as quickly as I can. Sauntering down the front steps, I feel good about what I've done. And there is nothing Samuel can do about it.

But the thrill fades as I walk home. The streets are dark and deserted. I should be keeping a watch for beggars and drunkards and thieves, but I'm distracted. I've given aid to the enemy. Again. But who is the enemy? I'm not sure anymore. Father would be furious with me if he were still alive. Mother would pray for my doomed soul ... if she isn't already. The war makes no sense to me.

When I finally arrive home, Mother is in quite a state.

"I imagined you dead in an alley. What kept you so long?"

I tell her about Samuel's betrayal but nothing about the letter. I'm beginning to sense that she wants to hug me but can't quite bring herself to do it.

"What possessed you to visit a gentleman's quarters alone?" she asks.

"He's no gentleman! And she's no lady. And Mother please, I'm old enough to do what I wish."

"I'm still your mother, and you'll do as I say under my roof. I care about your safety. As for Samuel, I say good riddance!"

"I don't want to hear his name again. Now, I'm going to sleep!" I lie in bed, my face to the wall, and let the tears stream down silently. I feel ugly and awkward and stupid. I'm no match for Mrs. Stoneham.

• • •

Emma's letter arrives the next day at the *Loyal Gazette*, and I tear it open hoping it will cheer me up.

> *Dearest Sarah,*
>
> *I have the best news. I'm coming to New York. I want to be there when Thomas is let go from that awful ship. He'll need care and help to return to Essex. I suggested it to Father, and even he thought it was a good idea. Can you imagine?*
>
> *Mr. Bascomb says he'll let me accompany him and Mrs. Bascomb when they next go to New York for supplies for their store. I don't know when that will be, so I might just appear on your doorstep.*
>
> *As for other news, Ezra Johnson, the owner of the sawmill, wants to marry me. He's already talked to Father, who loves the idea because he makes a good living and owns a brick house with six fireplaces and a featherbed. But he's old and crabby and has bad teeth. I'd sooner marry a wild boar.*
>
> *I can't wait to see you, Sarah. Of course, Father has no idea you're in New York. He still thinks you had something to do with the events of that night. He would die if he knew I helped you.*
>
> *Until then,*
> *Emma*

Emma was right. It is the best possible news. I'm so happy I nearly kiss Jonah.

"What's gotten into you today?" he says, almost as if he cares. "You came in bad-tempered as a mule, and now you're happy as a lark. Must be something about that boy."

I smile, wearily. "No, it's not about that boy." As I clean the printing press, I feel giddy knowing that Samuel will no longer tell me how to think, what to wear, and what I can or can't do. I'm so preoccupied that I don't hear the door open. Suddenly, he's there and looking like he's about to cry.

"Sarah, I must talk with you."

"Don't waste your breath." The mere sight of him makes me sick.

"Please hear me out. Please."

Jonah looks over at us, straining to hear every word.

"If you must," I mutter. "Not here, outside."

His face brightens a little. "Of course."

I take a deep breath of air, a relief from the heat and stink of the print shop and Jonah's prying eyes. People hurry by, paying us little mind. Carts rumble past, loaded with produce and firewood and barrels of rum.

Samuel tries to take my hand, and I yank it back. "Say what you need to say, then go."

"Sarah, I'm sorry about last night. I think you misunderstood—"

"Which part of last night? The part about you seeing a married woman or the part about me discovering it?"

"Mrs. Stoneham was there to finalize the preparations for the King's birthday celebration. Perhaps it was wrong to meet with her in my quarters. I promise you that won't happen again." His lip quivers. I don't care.

"Do you take me for a fool? I know what I saw. Samuel. Don't call on me again. And don't ever lay a hand on me again."

He looks stunned. "Surely you don't mean that."

Such arrogance. "Of course, I mean it! Did you think you could insult me, and I'd just forget it? If you'll excuse me—or even if you won't—I'm going back inside."

His hurt, pitiful look is gone, replaced by a sneer. He grabs me and turns me around so fast I nearly trip.

"I forgave your childish behavior earlier, Sarah. Certainly, you can do the same for me. It was just one silly mistake. Surely you can forgive me."

"It was the worst possible mistake," I say, not caring that people are slowing down to stare as they walk by.

"But you've agreed to marry me. Plans for the wedding are underway. I've already paid handsomely for your hand in marriage: dresses, bonnets, shoes."

"You should have thought about that when you took up with Mrs. Stoneham."

"I didn't take up with Mrs. Stoneham. I won't let you go. Not without a fight."

"Fight?" None of this makes sense. "Why must you persist? It's no use. Find someone else to marry you; perhaps someone easier to control." I mean every word of it and expect him to skitter away like the lizard he is. But, oh no.

"You're making a terrible mistake," he says in a haughty tone. "I'm a man of the law. You're lucky I even bother with you."

That condescending, bitter ass! "So, you think I'll never have another chance to marry? You think no one would stoop so low?"

He sticks out his chin and purses his lips. "Yes, that's exactly what I think. You're wearing a filthy apron, and you smell like horse piss."

I laugh. "I can't help it if we use horse urine to clean the press. Besides, I've grown rather fond of it."

"No wife of mine will smell like horse piss. Why is it so difficult for you to act like a lady and do what's expected of you?"

"I'd sooner eat nails than do as you say!"

You would think he'd finally get the hint and leave. But he glares at me, hatred in his eyes. "Sarah, my dear, you forget that I know your deepest, darkest secret. I know all about the flaming arrows you shot into the armory back in Essex. I'd love to know what the rebels will do with you when they somehow get their grubby hands on that little tidbit."

My heart is in my throat. "You wouldn't …"

"Wouldn't I?" Like the villain in one of the melodramas staged by the British troops, he turns and storms away.

# Chapter Thirteen

I'm glad about the trip to the *Defiance*. It takes my mind off Samuel's threat. It's nearly dusk, and the night is hot and humid, but the breeze on the water makes it bearable. Sweat rolls down Pritchard's face and wet splotches appear on his uniform as he strains at the oars. With his straight, aristocratic nose and high forehead, he's a handsome man, a fact I never took note of until now.

He's said nothing to me, except, "Evening, Miss." I watch him closely, looking for any sign of what he might have in mind for me. One word to Pendleton and he could expose me as a traitor who has repeatedly stolen onto a British prison ship to comfort the enemy. They'd hang me, and maybe Mother too.

Pritchard pauses for a moment to wipe the sweat off his face. "Ladies, I don't know how much longer the captain will allow your visits to the *Defiance*."

"Why? I thought he was pleased about our visits," I say. "Buoyed their spirits, you told us."

"Things have happened." He resumes his rowing. "A fight broke out among the prisoners. They killed two of their own and beat up one of ours pretty bad. The guards stopped it … smashed a few heads in the process. The captain's patience is wearing thin."

"He can't just stop our visits," I say.

"He can, and will, if need be," he says.

All I can think about is Tom. Please, God, let him be safe.

"Looks like a hearty load you have tonight, Mrs. Barrett," the lieutenant says.

"Yes, I expect I'll reap a fair sum for my trouble." Beside Mother sit two baskets piled high with fruit and vegetables, along with a pouch of tobacco and a clay pipe with a broken stem. I found it under a desk at the *Loyal Gazette* after Jonah heaved it in a rage.

I'm certain Mother is as rattled as I am by Pritchard's news. She's counting on more trips to build up her little cache of money. Now that the wedding is off, she again talks endlessly about sailing back to London, the three of us, Mother, Benjamin, and me. As usual, I don't let on that I'm not going.

She's happy about Emma's visit, perhaps thinking Emma's manners and charm will wear off on me. Mother gladly offered to put her up in our attic. Space will be tight, but I don't care. I must see Tom today if only to tell him Emma will be here soon.

We finally dock at the *Defiance*, which now has the company of three more prison ships nearby in Wallabout Bay, all just as dismal. I'm terrified that the lieutenant is laying a trap for me, hoping to catch me in the act of aiding a rebel.

He helps Mother onto the loading platform, and then me. We lock eyes for several seconds. Nothing! There might have been a faint hint of a smile but it could just as easily have been a trick to let my guard down, a bit of bait in the trap.

On the ship's deck, Mother lays out her treasures to a small group of officers. Three soldiers holding muskets stand guard. Was this for my benefit or because of the rioting below deck? I'm wary of making the wrong move.

"I'll take over for you if you'd like to survey the goods," Pritchard tells the guards.

He stares straight at me, and nods, ever so subtly. His gaze drifts to the steps leading below deck. Is he signaling me it's all right to go below, or is he closing his trap? He turns his back, and I inch toward the steps, hoping I've guessed right. In one quick move, I slip into the dark pit that seems worse with every visit. I expect to hear footsteps behind me ... the guards coming to arrest me. But there is nothing, only the suffocating heat, sucking my breath away.

In the dim light, it looks like a battlefield. Filthy men with bandaged heads and bruised faces lie about, some moaning, others still as death. A boy, no more than 14, rocks back and forth, staring into nothingness.

Suddenly, one of them grabs me from behind, and then another, nearly naked, tears at my skirt.

"Where's the bread? We all know you have some," he says, ripping my skirt. I scream, and in one swift move kick him squarely between the legs. He crumples and looks back at me with hate.

"Why do you come down here in your fine clothes and fancy ways?" he moans. "Just to pity us?"

"No!" Now I've drawn a crowd of emaciated madmen, like rats around cheese. Tom barges into the fray, his head covered with a blood-soaked rag, and guides me out of the throng.

"Tom, you're hurt!"

"Never mind. It's too dangerous down here. Go back."

I stand my ground. "I want to know what happened?"

"A guard whacked my head with the butt end of his musket. Started when the bastards threw a moldy, bug-filled hunk of bread into our midst just to see us scramble for crumbs. They do it for cheap entertainment."

"Let me have a look at your head," I say, but he brushes my hand away.

"Some weren't so lucky as me. They suffered the sharp end of the bayonet. At least two bled to death in the night."

"I'll go but let me give you one piece of good news. Emma is coming to New York. She wants to be here when they free you from this dungeon. The war can't last much longer."

"I pray I'll live that long," he says, his voice hoarse.

"I'll see you soon," I say, pressing into his hand the small leather pouch I've been clutching in mine. Inside, are a candle and a small knife. "You need these now more than ever."

"Go now, my love."

My heart swells as I race through the maze of starving, broken bodies. Hurrying up to the top deck, I take a huge gulp of fresh air and spot Pritchard eying me. Surely, he knows I've been below. But he does nothing. He's helping to load two hogs onto another boat to be taken ashore. The skittish animals are squealing in terror.

"Where are they taking the hogs?" I ask, hoping to distract him from me and my whereabouts. "What are they doing here in the first place?"

"They'll be slaughtered and roasted for the King's birthday banquet." There is nothing cheery in his response and his grim bearing suggests displeasure. He's a conundrum, this tight-lipped redcoat, though I must admit I've grown slightly fonder of him.

Back in the boat, he takes the oars, and we start across the river. I feel different, in a pleasurable way. Tom called me "my love." I know it sounds preposterous, dazzled by the stray words of a starving, half-crazed man in rags. Maybe the stench has gone to my head.

"A successful trip for you, Mrs. Barrett?" the lieutenant says, snapping me back to my senses.

Mother is ecstatic. "Yes!" She jiggles a pouch jammed with coins.

"And you Miss, was it a successful trip?"

"Yes, I suppose it was. And you may call me Sarah."

He smiles wide. "Sarah, you may call me Dan."

• • •

It's after 9 o'clock when we arrive home. The house is stifling hot, and even worse in the attic. I throw open the window to catch a breeze. Mother goes straight to bed, after scooping up Benjamin from Mrs. Harkins. I can't sleep. I'm puzzled by Pritchard's friendly behavior.

I light a candle and open my diary.

*Was Pritchard flirting with me? Is that why he's giving me free rein? Honestly, I enjoyed his attentions…"*

I write down everything, sparing no detail. *The British lords and ladies will feast on hogs intended for the starving prisoners. Samuel and his lady friend, the righteous Mrs. Stoneham, will toast them all. Let them stuff their bellies with pork, Yorkshire pudding, and their idiotic chocolate cherry cordials until they're sick as dogs.*

*One final thing. I fear Tom won't survive this macabre ship from hell. Am I delusional to think that I could rescue him?*

# Chapter Fourteen

It's another steaming day, and Jonah is livid when he returns to the *Loyal Gazette* after coffee at Hazen's. He slams the front door and growls at a smirking apprentice. I fear the worst.

"We have a spy in our midst," he rails, sweat dripping off his face.

"What are you talking about?" I say as I haul down a drawer full of type to be cleaned.

"Someone has written to that turd Washington claiming Charles Laurence is pocketing ... stealing ... money intended to feed those lousy prisoners on the ships and in the jails."

"Is it true?" I ask as if I couldn't care less.

"No! So what if it is? So what if the prisoners don't get their bellies filled every day? This is a war for God's sake, and the prisoners were the ones stupid enough to get caught."

I know better than to rile him up with facts about bothersome things like basic human decency.

"No matter. We'll have our culprit soon. It's time we had another hanging."

I try to keep my voice even as if I'm reading aloud from a long, boring property record. "They know who wrote the letter and passed it on to Washington?" I try to keep my voice from quavering.

"Not yet, but the Stoneham law firm is mounting an investigation. And you'll be happy to know that your young man … Samuel, is it … has come forward to lead it."

I so despise him that I can barely breathe. "Samuel?" I choke out.

"It appears he's a rising star within British intelligence. Mr. Stoneham sings his praises and so does Charles Laurence. You're lucky he's taken a shine to you."

I groan. "Samuel is not 'my young man'. Not anymore. He's lower than dirt."

Jonah backs away as if I'd spewed fire. "Well, I wasn't expecting that. What could that boy have done to give you such a change of heart?"

"I don't care to discuss it with you."

Jonah's eyes narrow. "And why does it matter so much to you that these prisoners fill their bellies every day? Even our soldiers don't get their full rations."

"They aren't starving."

"Sounds like Samuel was put off by your curious concern for rebel prisoners. I'm starting to see why he took his affection elsewhere. Mrs. Stoneham perhaps?"

It takes every ounce of self-restraint not to explode. "You couldn't be more wrong."

. . .

For days, I stew over what Samuel's investigation of the Charles Laurence letter means. Does he think I passed it on to Washington? Did he follow me to the tavern that night? What, if anything, will happen to the real crook, Charles Laurence? I have to know; it's killing me.

Finally, I dash off a note to Samuel, saying that I wish to see him, though nothing could be further from the truth. "We have some things to discuss about our engagement," I say, figuring he'll view it as a sign I've decided to marry him after all. My hope is to pry loose from him whatever information I can about the Charles Laurence matter, all in the course of pleasant conversation. Then I'll tell him that the reason for the meeting is to formally decline his marriage proposal in case he still thinks I'd ever, in a million years, assent to marry a rabid dog like himself. Of course, I wouldn't say it quite like that.

His reply arrives within the hour.

> *Dear Sarah,*
> *Your letter took me quite by surprise. I didn't expect to hear from you again. My first impulse was to toss it away. Then I thought better of it. Perhaps you are ready to apologize for your dreadful behavior. And perhaps you've come to your senses about a lady's place in marriage. After careful thought, I've decided a meeting with you might bring some good. Why don't we meet Saturday at noon at the gardens by the Common?*
> *Sincerely,*
> *Samuel*

He took the bait!

. . .

A heavy rain Saturday morning finally cools the air, giving the city a break from the relentless heat. The sun is breaking through the clouds as I walk to the gardens. As usual, Tom is on my mind and I imagine the worst; his head wound has festered into a massive pool of infection, and he's delirious with a fever. Maybe he's even dead.

I'm wearing my nicest dress, a blue cotton gown that I've managed to keep free of ink blotches and horse piss. Few people are on the streets, mostly British soldiers and their wives or other loyalists. How different from a year ago when the city was jammed with Washington's troops! Now even the rebels' supporters have long since fled, and loyalists are trickling back. It's not the same city, though. Rebel troops made a mess of things with all the barricades and trenches they built to fend off the British. Then, too, the fire left so very much of the city in rubble.

The garden is like a sanctuary, away from the mud, the stink, the noise, and the constant reminders of war. Today it seems half of New

York has decided to while away a pleasant summer day walking the orderly paths curving amidst the park's flowers, shrubs, and trees.

Outside a tavern, a string quartet is playing a rousing selection when Samuel strolls in. He takes my hands and kisses my cheek. I find it repulsive but hold onto the pleasant look plastered on my face.

"Sarah, you look lovely." It's as if our last fracas never happened.

I took a little extra care dressing this morning, even lacing my stays so tight my eyes nearly popped out. A new bonnet sits on my well-brushed hair. Lately, I've discovered I can make myself somewhat attractive without much effort. My thick red curls are shining. A little rouge gives me a glow, at least that's what Mother said. I feel like I'm in disguise on a clandestine mission, and the whole idea excites me.

As we sit under the shade of a giant elm, I get straight to the point. "I hear you've been assigned to investigate the Charles Laurence letter. That's quite an honor. Mr. Stoneham must have a lot of faith in you."

"Yes, he does," Samuel says, puffing up with pride.

That's just the reaction I'm aiming for.

"Do you know yet who wrote the letter?" I ask.

"You mean the rat who betrayed him?"

"Well, yes."

"We have a pretty good idea, but surely, we can talk of more pleasant things, Sarah."

I smile sweetly, and it feels like my face will crack. "But I want to hear all about your success. Mr. Stoneham must be confident you can get to the bottom of things."

"He does seem to trust me more than the others. I've already made great strides in the investigation. The Charles Laurence affair has stirred up quite a hornet's nest."

"So he *is* stealing from the Crown," I say as calmly as I can.

"I wouldn't call it stealing. Open your eyes, Sarah. That's the way things are done. But that's not the point of my investigation. I want to catch the traitor who wrote the letter and make him pay for it with his life. And the same fate awaits the one who put it in Washington's hands."

I hope some giant crows in the trees start shrieking so Samuel can't

91

hear the thumping of my heart. "So you have a suspect, the rat who informed on Laurence?"

"We do."

"Who is it?"

"Can't say just yet. I will tell you that he's fairly high in the British command, someone connected to the prison ships. And he might have been aided by some stinkin' rebel, trying to get himself a better lot."

"Captain Pendleton … that's who it is!"

"You know I can't tell you."

"What about the person who tipped off Washington?" I ask.

"Nothing yet, but I know we'll find the culprit."

"I'm not a suspect, I hope." I try to sound indignant.

"No, of course not," he chuckles. "You're just a girl."

"Of course," I say with sincerity.

I barely have time to take in all this news when Samuel stands and reaches for my hand.

"Enough of this war talk. Would you care for some tea?"

I want to dig deeper, so I put on a cheery face. "Yes, thank you." I watch him as he goes to order the tea. He could be considered handsome. He isn't as skinny as those days in Essex. He's filled out in a muscular way. He seems more at ease with his tall frame; more confident. I see why Mrs. Stoneham finds him appealing. Compared to her own aging, portly husband, Samuel is a god. But I can tell you, he's no god.

When he returns with the tea, he's all smiles. "You'll never guess what everyone is standing in line for."

"I haven't a clue." I'm impatient to get back to the letter.

"Strawberry ice cream!"

"No! I've read about it in London and Paris. But here in New York?"

"I say we try some," Samuel urges.

I can't say no; not to something that sounds so impossibly delicious. We stand in line like giddy children waiting. I know this isn't part of my plan, but how can it hurt?

Finally, he hands me a dish of pink mush, and I take a spoonful. It's cold, creamy, and sweet, and slides down my throat like custard. Little bits of strawberry linger in my mouth. I lick the spoon clean and would have licked the bowl if I'd not been in public.

"That is the best dessert I've ever tasted," I blurt out. For a time, I forget about why I'm here, forget about Tom and the starving prisoners. It's all a pleasant dream, listening to a minuet and watching well-dressed couples strolling the paths, far from the ravages of war. The flowers are in bloom and a cool breeze blows off the Hudson.

"We could have more days like this, you and me," Samuel says with a tenderness I haven't heard in months. "I still love you and want you to be my wife."

Under the spell of strawberry ice cream, it would be easy to put aside all the nastiness of the past few months and consent to become Samuel's wife. But I'm not an idiot. I know exactly who Samuel Mason is, and no amount of persuasion—or strawberry ice cream—will change my mind.

"Why, Samuel? Why do you want to marry me? I haven't an ounce of tenderness in my heart for you. We nearly came to blows the last time we met. That's why I wanted to see you, to tell you officially I won't marry you. Not now, not ever."

His eyes are full of hurt. Does he hate losing me, or does he just hate losing?

"I want you, and no one else. You have a natural beauty you're not even aware of. You're feisty and quick-witted and smart as a whip, and I like that."

"Do you?" I look at him in disbelief. "You must be joking."

"I know I haven't shown it lately."

"That's because you don't believe it yourself, Samuel. Find someone else." Then, I can't help myself. "What about Mrs. Stoneham?"

His face reddens. "I was a fool, Sarah. Please accept my deepest apology."

It's a performance worthy of the Theatre Royal.

"I'll accept your apology, but I won't marry you," I say firmly and without hesitation.

After an awkward pause, he appears to shrug off his run of bad luck with me. "I'm disappointed but I understand. Will you at least consent to a stroll around the park?" He offers his arm and I take it, only because I hope to squeeze more information from him. We walk past roses, lavender, rhododendrons, and statues of animals. I'm relieved that we'll at least part on good terms.

We stop in the shade of a giant elm, shielded from everyone else. Samuel suddenly draws me close and kisses me hard.

I push him back. "You haven't heard a word I've said!"

The tenderness in his face is gone. "If your father were alive, I'd surely have your hand in marriage. I am not a man who takes 'no' for an answer. When I set my sights on something, I don't give up."

"Are you persisting simply because you can't bear rejection by a woman?"

"Of course not. Sarah, your head has been turned by events. And there's your obsession with the *Loyal Gazette*, not to mention your devotion to bringing food and God knows what out to the prison ship."

"How dare you imply such a vile thing! Thomas Jordan is a prisoner on that ship, Thomas from Essex, my best friend Emma's brother. I won't abandon him."

Now he's showing his true colors. "So, you have affection for another man, and after you criticized me for seeing Mrs. Stoneham."

"No, you have it all wrong. Tom is just a friend. How can I not help Emma's brother?"

Samuel isn't having any of it. "So, you care more about a stinking rebel than me?"

"When did you become so spiteful?"

"Just how much of a friend is this, Thomas Jordan?"

Now my voice is booming with disgust. "He's skin and bones from lack of food, sick with dysentery, and still not willing to save himself by pledging allegiance to the Crown. He's twice the man you are."

Samuel glares at me with contempt. "You might as well pledge allegiance to the damned rebels yourself."

"Maybe I will."

The look on his face is pure hate. "I can make life unpleasant—no, intolerable—for those who defy the Crown, especially those who give aid to the enemy. And I haven't forgotten about your little secret.

People are hanged for less."

My hand comes lightning-fast as if it isn't a part of me. I slap him so hard it knocks him backward and into a prickly rose bush.

"You'll be sorry you raised a hand to me," he mutters as he pulls himself together and straightens his wig.

"You don't scare me." The slap felt good, at least on my end. "Don't forget, Samuel, I know all about you." For the first time, I see fear in his eyes. "Mr. Stoneham, your esteemed employer, would be none too pleased to find out about you and Mrs. Stoneham."

# Chapter Fifteen

Certain that Samuel is out of my life, I feel free and strangely happy. Even Mother agrees Samuel is despicable, despite his fancy clothes and manner. I think she's proud of me for walloping him, though she'd never say so.

Emma is due in New York any day, provided Mr. Bascomb's wagon can get past the British soldiers who stop everyone entering or leaving the city. Their hunt for rebel spies is relentless. They even tore apart a farmer's load of freshly picked vegetables, convinced the poor devil was smuggling a message to the rebels tucked inside an ear of corn.

I can't wait to tell Emma about Samuel and the infamous slap. She'll be shocked, then break out in raucous laughter. She'll be shocked by something else too. My flat-as-a-pancake breasts, which she hasn't seen in at least a year, are now ample enough to draw looks from Lt. Pritchard on our trips to the *Defiance*.

Tonight, we're baking cornbread loaves for tomorrow's trip. Mother has gleaned the garden for the last of the raspberries, radishes, and turnips. My offering? A perfectly good shirt that Jonah tossed out when he couldn't squeeze into it.

The Harkins family went to bed early, giving us full rein in the kitchen.

With Mr. Harkins home from the fighting, you'd think life would be easier for them. But the loyalists and redcoats refuse to do business with a rebel cobbler, choosing shoemakers more aligned with their politics.

You'd think Mother would sooner be homeless than live under the same roof as Mr. Harkins. But she keeps her opinions to herself, especially after he made new shoes for her, complete with silver buckles. He doesn't talk much about the fighting he saw, but I know he has nightmares about it. I've heard him yelling in his sleep.

"Sarah, set aside some cornbread for the Harkins' breakfast," Mother says. "They'll surely be pleased in the morning."

Before I can do so, there's a loud rap on the front door.

"At this hour, it can only be someone for you, Mother." Babies always announce their arrival at the most inconvenient of times. Trust me, I know about this.

But when I crack open the heavy oak door, I see only Mr. Harkins' young apprentice, Abe. His face is tear-streaked and he's out of breath.

"I came as quick as I could," he gasps. "The redcoats…they broke into Mr. Harkins' shop."

"Mr. Harkins," I yell from the stairway. "Come quickly!"

Moments later, he's bounding down the stairs with his wife right behind.

"What's happened, Abe?"

"The redcoats. They smashed in the front door. I was sleeping in the back." He catches his breath. "When I refused to tell them where you were, they ran me out at the point of their bayonets."

"It's all right, boy," he says. "What happened then?"

"They stole all the leather, buckles, tools. Then they smashed everything else to bits."

Mr. Harkins suddenly turns to his wife. "We can't stay here. It's not safe."

"Where can we go?" she asks, in shock.

"We'll head for my brother's place in Connecticut, where it's safer. Now dress the children quickly and gather a few provisions. I'll fetch the wagon."

"Must we go tonight?"

97

"Yes, woman! Now make haste, before they return for me."

The next hour is a blur of frantic activity and children crying. Before I can object, Mother gives them the basket of food we've prepared for the *Defiance*. Our trip tomorrow—my chance to see Tom—is dashed. It hardly seems the time to wallow in self-pity.

Mrs. Harkins packs up bedding, clothes, and the family Bible, and hauls her spinning wheel and loom from the hallway. Her husband arrives in time to load everything into the wagon in the pitch black of the moonless night.

It seems unbelievable that we were baking cornbread just hours ago, and now we're huddled in the dark saying goodbye to an entire family that took us in without a thought as to whose side we're on. Even I get teary as they climb into the wagon.

"I don't know when we'll return, God willing," Mr. Harkins tells Mother. "Stay as long as you like. I'd be grateful if you looked after the house and its furnishings."

"Of course." As they rumble off into the night, Mother is sad.

"The house will seem so empty," she says.

Suddenly, it dawns on me. We'll no longer be relegated to the cramped attic with its leaks, dust, and abominable mice.

"Mother, look on the bright side. We'll have the entire house to ourselves. Isn't that wonderful?"

"Sarah! Their beds are still warm, and you've already moved in. How can you be so selfish?"

I feel ashamed, but only for a second. "You'll have free rein of the kitchen."

Even Mother can't hide it: "The Lord does work in mysterious ways."

I fall into bed, exhausted, but sleep doesn't come easily. I'm too excited, making plans. There are three bedrooms on the second floor, one for each of us including Emma. Benjamin, of course, will stay with Mother. I'll go to sleep, in a real bed, without Mother snoring in my ear. I'll sleep in my clothes if I feel like it. I can write in my diary without Mother peering over my shoulder. Privacy at last.

Best of all, there will be room for Tom once he is freed. The only dark spot in my fantasy is Samuel. Now that he knows about Tom, he could order us hanged, but I don't think he'd risk my exposure of his affair with Mrs. Stoneham. I'm not going to let his threats stop me. I imagine what else I can sneak onto the ship: shoes, one of Jonah's meat pies? Why not? But I try not to dwell on the fact that I have no idea how to go about his rescue.

. . .

Days later I'm sitting on the front steps shelling peas with Mother and Benjamin when a wagon, drawn by two horses, pulls up. I leap off the steps, spilling the peas.

"Emma! I thought you'd never arrive."

Old Mr. Bascomb helps Emma out of the wagon, and she hugs me so tightly we nearly fall over giggling and laughing.

"You thought I'd never get here? I thought I was going to the ends of the earth to get here!"

She's the same jolly Emma I remember from Essex, the only person who can make me laugh so hard I wet myself. She looks just the same: shorter than me, rounder too, with silky blond hair and rosy cheeks. Unlike me, she is perpetually smiling and popular with everyone.

"Come inside everyone," Mother says. "You must be hungry and thirsty and in need of a good rest."

"Thank you kindly, Mary," Mrs. Bascomb says. "I've missed you so."

"And I you." Mother gently pats her arm.

"Essex has suffered for a midwife since you left." Mrs. Bascomb is a homely woman with warm brown eyes.

Mother puts together a feast in minutes: clam chowder, greens from the garden, and a big bowl of strawberries and blueberries. She's at her best making people feel at home. She soaks up all the news about Essex from Mr. Bascomb, whose store is thriving so well that he needs to make frequent trips to New York and Boston for supplies.

Meanwhile, I show Emma to her room, but as soon as we close the door, she grows serious. "What news have you of Tom? Tell me the truth. Don't spare my feelings."

I don't know how much to tell her. He could be dead as we speak.

"He's in better shape than many of the men." That isn't a lie if you consider how many were at death's door on my last visit. I hold back details of how very frail he is and the awful living conditions. Emma isn't ready for that.

I tell her about my ventures out to the *Defiance* with Mother. And about hiding food under my skirts for Tom.

"Sarah, you devil!" she laughs. "I wish I'd seen his face when you lifted your skirts."

"He asked what else I had hidden under there." I feel a blush coming over me.

Emma breaks into gales of laughter. "I think he cares for you, and in a very special way!"

"Don't be insane!" I plop on the bed.

"I mean it. When you and your mother treated his leg in Essex, I could tell he had great affection for you," she says as she unpacks her bags, neatly folding everything into a pine chest at the foot of the bed.

"Well, he never showed it. He was quiet, angry about his leg, and furious that loyalists were patching him up."

"He was a fool, never one to show his true feelings," Emma says, "even as a boy."

"Unlike you, Emma," I laugh. "You couldn't possibly hide your feelings. Or keep a secret. It spills out all over your face."

"I kept your secret, even though Father threatened me with the strap if I or anyone I knew had anything to do with the explosion."

"And I'm grateful you kept mum," I say. "I realize now I put you in a terrible spot."

I tell her what happened with Samuel, sparing no details about the slap and his most undignified fall into the rose bushes. I even act it out with dramatic flourishes.

"You're too good for that pompous rat."

"And what's become of the old man who wants your hand in marriage?" I ask.

"I told him I'd sooner marry a toad. He decided I wasn't fit to be his wife."

I think I'll die laughing. Is that even possible?

# Chapter Sixteen

Mother doesn't waste any time putting Emma to work. After a word with Mrs. Pendleton, she's hired to care for the captain's children, a fortuitous development. Of course, she can't reveal her brother is being held captive on the very ship he commands.

"You'd best keep your opinions about the war to yourself," Mother cautions her.

"If I have to, I'll wear the beastly red ribbon," Emma says.

Later, when she and I are alone in my new room, I can't hold back my excitement.

"You'll be in a good position to hear any news about the *Defiance* and the prisoners."

"Yes. I suppose so."

"Don't you see what this means?" Emma can be maddeningly naive at times.

"You want me to be a spy."

"Spy is a strong word. Just observant," I say.

"Are you insane? Did you learn nothing from your treacherous little escapade in Essex?" Now the perpetual smile is gone. "Forget it! I barely survived your last harebrained scheme."

"Don't you care about Tom?" Instantly, I regret my words.

"How dare you say that to me! I'm his sister."

"I'm sorry, Emma. I didn't mean it the way it sounded."

"I'll wait until Tom is released," she says, brushing her thick, blond hair. "It can't be much longer."

Then the smile returns, as she holds up an elegant yellow gown she's unpacked. "What do you think? I stitched it myself, even the lace trim. I can't wait to wear it. Surely there are balls and …"

"Emma!" She's completely unaware of the danger Tom is in. "I haven't been completely honest with you about Tom and the ship."

She looks confused. "What are you talking about?"

"The prisoners call the old tub 'Hell's Ferry,' and there's a reason for that. Who knows how long he can survive starvation and torture?"

Emma turns white. "You never said anything about starvation and torture."

"I didn't want to worry you. It's much worse than I let on. Now there are a half-dozen prison ships in Wallabout Bay. Thousands of prisoners are living in hell. The British don't care if they live or die, and, believe me, dozens die every day."

"And Tom? How is he really?"

"Skin and bones, though I slip him whatever food I can smuggle in. Like the others, he's hardly ever allowed on the top deck for a breath of air. The men are jammed below in an airless pit that reeks of vomit and urine and you can imagine what else." I spare her the lice, smallpox, and yellow fever.

Emma's face twists in anguish. "Poor, poor Tom."

"We have to do something," I say. She nods in silent agreement.

• • •

Tom's fate appears even more uncertain when Jonah greets me one morning with a list of orders.

"Girl, mix a batch of ink, bring me a new quill pen, and make sure every piece of type is spotless." He barely looks up at me from his paper-strewn desk, right below a glowering portrait of King George III.

"Yes, sir! May I do anything else for Your Highness?"

"Don't rile me, girl! I'm in no mood."

"What's so important?"

"Last night those prisoners set fire to their ship. Destroyed the old hulk."

"Which ship?" My heart is pounding.

"I don't know. What does it matter? They say the fire was deliberately set by one of the prisoners. Could have got his hands on a candle or stole the coals from under the cooking cauldron."

"A candle?" My mind leaps to the candle and flint I smuggled in for Tom. I feel a flush of panic.

"What happened to the prisoners?"

"Don't know. I hope they burned to a crisp."

My anguish comes out as a nervous laugh.

"Serves them right. Setting a fire to engineer their escape," he says.

I want to knock him senseless, this cold-hearted wretch. "Don't you at least want to find out what happened to those on the ship, Jonah?"

"Why? If they're dead, saves us the trouble of hanging them," he says without a second thought.

Something in me snaps. "Maybe they set the fire to put themselves out of their misery. Did you ever think of that?"

"Girl, watch what you say! You could be mistaken for a rebel."

"I don't care."

Jonah leaps up. "Enough! I'm not paying you for your foolish opinions. I rue the day I promised your father I'd employ you. He never said you were such a troublemaker."

I stalk away, furious at the old ignoramus and scared for Tom. I'm desperate to find out more and plot excuses to stroll by Hazen's Coffeehouse in the million-to-one hope that I might hear a tidbit of value. But Jonah beats me to it and announces he's headed there himself.

"While I'm gone, make yourself useful and set type for this item about the ship fire. And don't change one word," he growls as he leaves.

He must know how much I crave rewriting it to show how desperate the men are. I leave it as is, even keeping his misspelling of the word treason, "treeson." That, at least, gives me the last word.

The rest of the day is agonizingly slow. There are advertisements to be set, including a new one for the "Suretravel Stage," offering overland passage from New York to Philadelphia, along with the usual ads for ground coffee, "exquisite snuff," and "the finest linen in New York."

Fortunately, Jonah drinks too much at Hazen's and comes back only to fall asleep at his desk. His wig falls off his head and onto the floor. His cheek rests on the newest addition to his bookshop: "The Expedition of Humphry Clinker."

I slip out early, figuring he won't miss me when he finally wakes. I rush home to see if Emma knows anything about the fire.

I burst in the front door. "Emma!"

She comes running into the hallway, her hands covered in flour. "Is Tom—"

"It wasn't the *Defiance* that burned," she says. "It was the *Eagle*. I overheard the captain telling Mrs. Pendleton."

I'm relieved for a second. "What about the prisoners…and Tom?"

Emma takes a breath. Her voice is shaky. "Many died in the fire. Some were captured. And some escaped."

"It must have been awful."

"Pendleton was furious and said the dogs would make short work of those who escaped."

I picture burned bodies floating in Wallabout Bay as howling dogs hunt down skeletal convicts in nooks and crannies along the shore. It seems more urgent than ever to rescue Tom, but I'm not ready to share that with Emma. That will have to wait, but not too long.

• • •

I decide not to tell Mother either. She would say we have no business meddling in such affairs. And she'd insist any rescue plan is too dangerous and could land us in prison, or the graveyard. Of course, that's all true.

I have an idea. She's exhausted from delivering babies, tending Benjamin, cultivating the garden, and leading our weekly voyages out to the *Defiance*. After supper tonight, I test the waters.

"Mother, why not let Emma go out to the ship with me? We can sell whatever we can and give you the money. That will give you a chance to rest."

She looks at me with suspicion. "And why do you care so much about your poor mother all of a sudden?"

"I can see that you're tired. I want to help you." I try to sound convincing but follow it up with a huge lie: "Emma would enjoy it."

"Doesn't seem proper for two young women to be in the company of all those men." I can tell she's considering it but needs just a bit more convincing.

"We're not so young, Mother. I'm old enough to marry."

"That you are." She was silent for a moment. "I'll ask the captain."

I'm so happy I hug her, nearly knocking her over. "I'm sure he'll approve it. Emma tells me the children love her and she gets on well with Mrs. Pendleton."

• • •

Emma takes more convincing than Pendleton.

"I'm not climbing into a boat and venturing out on the open sea," she insists, as we husk corn for Sunday dinner.

It's another sweltering day, but on the front steps where we sit, there's a slight breeze. From here we can eye passersby, mostly British soldiers, sailors, and the occasional loose chicken.

"It's not the open sea," I say. "And Lieutenant Pritchard is a good oarsman."

"I don't care. What if a storm comes up? I'm terrified of the water."

"The water is always calm," I lie. "And it's just a short distance. I can't swim either." Another lie. My brother Seth taught me to swim in the pond near the farm in Essex. Of course, Mother never knew. Nor did she know he taught me to shoot an arrow sure and straight.

I know it's wrong, but I resort to guilt. "You care about Tom, don't you?"

She glares at me. "You know I do."

I take another tack. "Lieutenant Pritchard is even more handsome than Seth was." She stops husking for a second. "His eyes are bright blue, and his smile is dazzling. And he's quite the conversationalist."

Preposterous lies. "I think you'll find him pleasing to the eye." Finally, she reaches her limit.

"All right, Sarah! Stop nagging me. I'll go. Once."

That's all I need to hear.

# Chapter Seventeen

Lt. Pritchard is waiting for us at the dock when we arrive with our baskets just after dawn. Something is different. He's not pacing, not irritated that we're a little late.

"Good morning, ladies," he says, removing his cap. "Welcome aboard, Miss Jordan. Captain Pendleton speaks highly of you." I've never seen him so gallant. His thick chestnut hair is tied with a bit of leather at his neck, his red uniform spotless. Emma's spirits perk up, as soon as he takes the immense summer squash she's lugged from the house.

"The water is calm. We'll be there in no time," he says, giving her a dazzling smile.

Emma starts to relax but as soon as the first little wave rocks the boat, she draws a sharp breath.

"Not to worry, Miss. You're in good hands."

He seems enchanted by Emma. I'm glad, though a tiny bit jealous. Perhaps he'll be so taken that he won't notice me slip below deck to see Tom. You might think me foolhardy to venture back into that pit after my last encounter with wild-eyed, desperate men. But I'm desperate to know more about the fire.

As we approach the *Defiance*, Emma seems uncomfortable. "That smell! It's worse than you told me."

I spare her the sordid details but they're in the air. "You'll get used to it."

She doesn't seem reassured. She looks as if she might be sick. She gives me a hostile look as she lets Lt. Pritchard help her board the *Defiance.*

"Miss Jordan is helping the Barrett ladies sell their wares," he tells the men. "I expect you'll treat her with the same courtesy."

After I help her unload the baskets, I slip down the ladder to the hold while Lt. Pritchard talks to the guards.

It's even more jammed than last time. Before I can search for Tom, I feel a massive hand clamp onto my arm.

"What do you think you're doing?" a guard bellows. He's a tall, beefy-faced hulk of a man.

I freeze. I can't utter a word.

The brute tightens his grip, and I feel searing pain. "Woman, what are you doing down here?"

"Nothing! Just looking around."

"Don't toy with me, you hussy. I want the truth."

He twists my arm until I cry out. "That is the truth. Let me go!"

"I know what you were doing," he sneers. "You're a prostitute, a dirty whore. Trying to make some money off these poor devils."

"I am not! Let go of me." He towers over me and stinks of rum.

"Since you're so willing to service these poor wretches, maybe you'd lift your skirts for a real man," he says.

"Never!"

"A feisty one you are. See how you like this." He rips the front of my dress, and when I push him away, he locks his arm around my neck. I struggle to breathe, and with my last gasp, I jab him in the eye.

He yelps like a wounded puppy. I feel like every eye in the hold is on me. Where is Tom?

"We'll take her off your hands," one of the prisoners yells. Seconds later there's a swarm of them around me and the guard.

"Get back, you stinkin' rebels," he roars, "or you'll feel the sharp end of this bayonet."

For a moment no one moves. Then, one by one, they back off. I barely have time to catch my breath before he shoves me up the ladder.

Once on deck, he resumes his death grip on my arm and marches me over to Pritchard. "Look here, lieutenant, look what I found offering her services to those filthy wretches."

"Not true," I shout. I'm scared to death and look at the lieutenant with pleading eyes.

He takes in my ripped gown, my missing bonnet, and tangled hair. "Thought you could sneak around and sell your wares to these men?"

"No!" What's wrong with him? He knows I'm no prostitute.

"I suppose your "friend" here, Miss Jordan, is a colleague."

"Me?" Emma shrieks. "I'm not—"

"Do you know what we do with whores?" he hisses.

Now I'm terrified, as I try in vain to cover my partially exposed bosom.

"We throw them in a cell with all the other whores! How do I know you're not a spy, working for the damned rebels?"

"I'm no spy," I say meekly, wondering where all his previous good cheer has gone.

"Guard, I'll take care of these 'ladies' myself." He grabs my arm and prods me down the gangway to the boat that will take us ashore. Then he gives the same rough treatment to Emma, whose face is frozen in horror. She will never forgive me for this.

Once in the boat, Pritchard barks another order at me, loud and clear. "Now sit quietly or I'll be forced to lash you to the boat."

We're halfway back to shore when Emma finally speaks to me.

"Prostitute?"

"Don't be ridiculous, Emma. Do I look like a prostitute?"

I look at Pritchard for some sign of sympathy. "I was just looking around below deck. I was curious. That's all."

"I know what you were doing down there," he finally says.

I can't say a thing. Am I on my way to some vermin-infested prison to die of starvation or the pox?

"And what did you see?" he asks in his sternest voice.

There is no point in lying, and by this time I'm numb with anger. "I saw men crowded together so close they couldn't lie down. I saw men who were nothing but skin and bones. I saw the worst kind of suffering. I saw a place that can only be described as hell."

Emma winces. I figure my goose is cooked. I'm silent, pondering my fate until we're nearly at the dock. Finally, I can't stand the uncertainty anymore.

"What are you going to do with us, lieutenant?" My eyes well up.

"Us!" Emma cries. "I had nothing to do with this."

He doesn't say a word for nearly a minute allowing me to imagine hanging on a gallows before a crowd of angry men hurling garbage at me.

"Lieutenant?"

"I'll need to consult with Captain Pendleton."

That is not the message I'd hoped for.

• • •

"You've made everything worse," Emma yells at me as we walk home from the dock. "I hope you're satisfied."

"I'm sorry, I didn't—"

"And a prostitute of all things! I'll lose my employment for certain."

"Is that all you care about, your job and your precious lieutenant? I saw the way he looked at you."

By now the streets are busy with seamen headed to the wharves for the day's labors, and I feel their stares. It's no wonder. I'm half naked and look like I've been in a fight, and Emma, sweet, very proper, schoolteacher Emma, is on a rant.

"I should have known better than to get involved. We might just wind up in some filthy prison. And who knows what they'll do to Tom."

"What about me? I'm the one in this even deeper. One word from Pendleton and I could be hanged as a spy."

That grim possibility is just beginning to sink in. Would there be musket-toting redcoats kicking in the door later today, come to take me away in chains? Maybe I should flee while I have the chance.

We're nearly back home, and Emma is still at it. "I've had enough. I'm ready to pack my things and return to New Hampshire where—"

"Hush Emma. We're being followed." I noticed him near the dock, an older man, neatly dressed in black breeches and a white shirt, black hair tied back. His face is sunburnt with deep lines, suggesting a fisherman.

"He's followed us at a distance since we passed the sailmaker's shop. I'm sure of it."

"What now?" Emma whispers. "You're the one who got us into this mess, you have to get us out of it."

My mind is frantic, until I spot Mariners Tavern, a few steps away. "We'll lose him in here," I say as I push Emma through the doorway.

Although it's barely the middle of the day, the place is packed with men, mostly dockworkers, drinking, gambling, and smoking. The noise is deafening, and for a moment no one takes note of our presence. Then a sailor in canvas breeches approaches and removes his cap.

"Would you ladies care to join us for a pint of ale?"

"No, we're just leaving," Emma says, tugging me toward the door.

"That would be lovely," I say.

"No, it would not!" Emma yells. "What's the matter with you?" She grabs my hand and pulls me out the door.

Outside, I look around for the man following us and see no one. We walk home in silence. It's no use trying to reason with Emma.

I go straight to my room, close the door, and take out my diary. *I've made a mess of things. But worst of all, I have no one to talk to. I feel embarrassed, dirty, and violated by that animal below deck on the Defiance. He ripped away a piece of me when he practically tore my dress off. Is it my fault that it happened? That's what Samuel would say.*

# Chapter Eighteen

When I leave the house the next morning, Emma is writing a letter to the Bascombs to see when she might accompany them back to New Hampshire. She barely says good morning to me, but at least she didn't blab to Mother about what happened. I've apologized 20 times to no avail.

On my walk to the *Loyal Gazette*, I keep a sharp eye out for the man who followed us yesterday. He looks like everyone, and he looks like no one. I'm puzzled why anyone would bother tailing us. Could it be Samuel's doing?

My day only gets worse. Jonah is in agony when I walk in. He's taken off his shoe and is massaging his big toe, groaning in pain.

"What have you done to yourself?" Pathetic fool that he is, I hate to see him suffer so.

"It's the gout. Woke up in the night with a pain so fierce I thought I would soon die."

I wince in sympathy. Jonah's foot looks like it has eaten a watermelon. It's a huge, red-purple ball.

"Feels like an army of rats is gnawing on my toe." He looks like he's about to cry. I can't help but pity him.

"What can I do for you?"

"You can bring a bottle of port wine. That eases the pain. And one of Madame Rousseau's sausage pies."

I know that won't help his toe, but it may improve his mood. "Mother says it's all your fancy food and drink that brings on the gout."

"I don't need a lecture on what ails me," he growls. "We've got work to do. The birthday celebration last night was quite an occasion. I must finish writing my piece about it."

"I suppose you ate and drank your way through the evening with all the British nobility and military might."

"I did," he boasts. "Twenty different kinds of wine, roasted pig, venison, and beef. There must have been a hundred puddings, pies, and ice cream with chocolate sauce."

I know I should be scornful of such excess, but he's got my mouth watering.

"I had a nice chat with your boy, Samuel."

"He's not my boy," I say, tying on my leather apron.

"He spent most of the evening on the arm of Stoneham's lovely young wife."

"I don't care."

"You'd better care about this," he bellows as he rubs his foot. "He says you're the one who wrote that so-called anonymous note about the director of the prison ships pocketing money intended for prisoners' food."

"I did no such thing. What an outrageous lie!" I wish Samuel and his lady friend a slow, painful death.

"He says he'd know your handwriting anywhere and can prove it."

"Jonah, I don't know who gave me the note. I copied it because I feared Samuel would destroy the original. And he did just that."

"Girl, I don't know who's telling the truth, but you best hope he doesn't spread the word among the British. I'm beginning to question your loyalty to the Crown."

"So am I."

Suddenly, Jonah is gripped with a fierce pain and lets out a yelp. "Now get me some port before I pass out from the agony. And set the type for this item about the banquet. And when you're done, write something nice about the new royal portrait of Queen Charlotte by Benjamin West."

I try to stay out of Jonah's way the rest of the day. Still, it gives me no peace. I fume over Samuel and his big mouth, and panic at what the British might do if they think I've turned in the czar of the prison ships. And I'm already in trouble with Capt. Pendleton who thinks I'm a prostitute. Let's just say I'm doomed on all counts.

With nothing to lose, I march straight for Samuel's quarters after work. I won't let him get away with spreading lies about me. I barely notice the people strolling the streets, the wagons loaded with lumber and fish. I'm steaming mad and want to make sure he knows it.

How did I ever care for such a despicable man? I must have been out of my mind. He and Tom Jordan cannot be more different. Sick and skinny as death itself, Tom still has something that attracts me. Maybe it's his sly smile and silly jokes, even in the belly of the beast. I feel closer to him than I've ever felt to Samuel. He makes me feel pretty and smart. I like that.

It's starting to get dark as I turn onto Samuel's street and notice a man behind me. I speed up. He does the same. I'm in no mood for games. Finally, I whip around.

"Why are you following me?" I see now that it's the same older man with the weathered face. "And you followed us yesterday."

He takes off his cap. "I'm sorry I frightened you."

"You didn't frighten me. Who are you? And what do you want? If you're a friend of the Crown, I forgot to pin the vile red ribbon to my cap this morning."

"I'm not a friend of the Crown," he whispers, looking about warily. "Quite the opposite."

I'm starting to feel uneasy. "What do you want with me?"

"My name is Matthew Kittridge. I'm with General Washington's operations."

I didn't expect that. "Then you know you're not safe here."

"Yes, I'm well aware. But I want to talk with you. I know that you and your mother have been bringing food and supplies to the men on the *Defiance*."

"Which they pay us for so we can eke out a living."

"I also know that you have been slipping below deck to give aid to one Thomas Jordan."

Now I'm terrified. "How do you know that?"

"I also know that you have witnessed the horrible state of our men on the ship, that you have tried to draw attention to the miserable conditions."

I'm stunned. "What do you mean?"

"Never mind. I'm not here to expose your secrets."

"Then what do you want of me?" Now I'm as curious as I am scared.

"Miss Barrett, you are in a unique position to help the patriots."

"Why would I do that?"

"We know you care deeply about this Thomas Jordan and the others."

"We?"

"Lower your voice! We're putting together a plan to rescue as many prisoners aboard the *Defiance* as we can."

My heart leaps.

"We can't do it without your help."

"How can I possibly help you? I was caught last time I tried to slip below deck to see Tom."

"We need you to bake a loaf of bread and bring it with you on your next trip to the ship."

"What?" Does he know I've never made an edible loaf of bread?

"Inside the bread, there will be a message about our plan so the men can prepare for the escape."

"Let me guess, you want the bread to go to Tom, so he'll find the message and spread the word to the men."

"Yes. He's steadfast in his support of our cause. He's resisted every attempt by the British to change his allegiance and leave that hellhole. He's convinced others to hold off as well."

"I didn't know … not surprising." I take a deep breath. "Even if I wanted to help you, how can I deliver the bread to him when I can't go below deck."

"We have that figured out. Will you help us?"

The thought of rescuing Tom excites me. But can I trust this stranger? What if it's a trap? My loyalty to the British is being tested. Also, if the escape fails and the British catch wind of it, I'll be hanged. Jonah will hang me himself. Still, it may be Tom's only hope. The more I think about it, the more I hate the British.

"Yes, I'll do it."

Matthew smiles for the first time and breathes deeply. So do I. Suddenly the gloom of the day lifts.

"I'll deliver the note to you within the week," he says. "Plan on taking produce out to the ship next Sunday."

"All right." I turn to leave, then I stop. "How do I know this isn't a trick? How can I trust you?"

"How can I trust you? Don't you work for Jonah Livingston's *Loyal Gazette*?"

I look deep into his eyes for any sign of ill will. "Tell me how you know about Thomas Jordan."

He eyes me carefully. "I shouldn't disclose this to you but Lieutenant Daniel Pritchard, your oarsman, told me."

"That can't be. He's a British officer."

"Yes, but his heart lies elsewhere. You must not breathe a word of it to anyone. If he's found out, you're both dead."

The lieutenant, a spy? It takes me a moment to fully understand what I've just heard. But then it all makes sense. No wonder he overlooked my visits below deck to see Tom. As I finally see the light, I realize he won't turn me in to Pendleton for "whoring" below deck.

"Why did you follow us yesterday?" I ask.

"Lieutenant Pritchard asked me to see that you arrived home safely after the unfortunate events on the ship. He said to tell you he is sorry that he treated you and Miss Jordan so roughly, but it was necessary to keep up the act."

"I see. You may tell him I will keep his secret." My mind is scrambling to put all the pieces together. "So he's the one who'll slip the bread to Thomas. Am I right?"

"You're always one step ahead."

"Why can't Pritchard pass the note to Tom himself? Why do you need me to bake bread?"

"We can't take a chance on him being caught. You are a trusted and familiar face on the ship. It wouldn't look out of place."

"I see. And if I'm caught?"

He looks me in the eye. "I'm not going to lie and tell you it's not dangerous. You're too smart for that. If you want to back out, I wouldn't blame you."

That's all I need to hear. "No. I'll do it. I want to do it."

"Good." He turns and slips away in the dark.

I walk straight home without stopping at Samuel's boarding house. Now that I have something much more important to occupy my thoughts, the need to set him straight has faded.

# Chapter Nineteen

Emma is speaking to me again, but I certainly can't tell her what I've agreed to do. She'd say it's further evidence I've lost my mind. Maybe she's right, but if it helps Tom, she'll be thankful in the end.

I can't sleep. I keep wondering what the plotters' plan is. Will they try to set the ship ablaze? The timbers are rotten enough to hold a flame. But even if some prisoners escape, others certainly would burn to death.

*Maybe I should leave well enough alone,* I write in my diary. *Maybe Emma is right, and Tom will be released soon anyway. But I feel driven to do this, and I've already given my word. A thought keeps nagging at me: What if it's the thrill that appeals to me more than the rescue? Am I as selfish as Emma says?*

I lie awake, waiting for sleep to put me out of my misery. But all sorts of bizarre thoughts creep in. You may find this preposterous, but I worry that I'll fail at the very task every woman is able to do blindfolded: make bread. My previous attempts were so miserable, Mother relieved me of ever attempting it again.

"Sarah, you are clever as anyone I know, but your bread making is deplorable," she once told me.

After that, I never tried it again, grateful that she prides herself on baking, roasting, and cooking anything edible. That means we sometimes eat some strange concoctions, like dandelion jelly and octopus turnovers.

In the morning, I casually mention I'd like to make bread for Tom. Mother and Emma look at me as if I've lost my senses.

"The boy's condition is already dire enough," Mother says, drawing ripples of laughter from Emma.

"Thomas has captured your heart," Emma snickers. "Why else would you dip your hands in flour?"

"Laugh all you want," I stammer. "It can't be all that difficult."

* * *

When I arrive at work, Jonah is still in agony, limping around the print shop in his bare feet, his big toe still a bulging mass of red.

"Morning, girl," he says with a sweep of his arms. I can tell straight away that he's stinking drunk.

"It's not even 8 o'clock and you're beyond help."

"No, I'm not," he slurs.

"Jonah, there's no point in denying it."

Then he looks chagrined. "Port is the only cure for pain."

"It's not a cure. It just dulls the pain and makes you a half-wit."

He glares at me. "Nothing worse than a simple girl who thinks she knows it all."

"I don't know it all, but my mother does. She gives people with gout an herbal remedy. It makes the swelling go down."

"I don't believe in herbal remedies when a bottle of port will do just as well."

"Well, I won't get any more port for you," I say, pulling out a little leather pouch. "And I've brought you some of Mother's herbs. I won't go to work until you've had some in tea."

He's useless. He leans on me as I help him to the back room where the apprentices sleep. He slumps on a cot while I put the kettle on the fire and take a pinch of the stinging nettle Mother has given me for tea.

He puts up a fuss but drinks it. Then he falls sound asleep, snoring like a bear. I know he'll be out of it the rest of the morning, so I set about putting the next day's newspaper in order.

His desk is piled high with papers, an item he's writing about the volunteer fire department, another about the garbage in the streets. I look for his list of articles and advertisements for the next issue, but I can't find it in the mess. I start pulling open all the drawers in his huge mahogany desk.

An envelope catches my eye. Father's distinctive script. I listen for Jonah's snoring, then unfold the letter inside.

> *My dear friend,*
> *I haven't long to live. The pox will send me to my grave soon. I have one last favor to ask of you. My daughter Sarah will need employment when she arrives in New York. She has a keen mind and a clever way with words, you'll not regret taking her on. One word of caution, though. She's not afraid to speak her mind.*

It sounds so like Father, and I can feel his presence. I read on.

> *You are the only person I can trust with this information. I have a formula for ink that disappears once it dries on the page but reappears with heat from a candle.*

My hands start to shake, and I feel sweaty and cold all at once. Father did indeed refine a formula for invisible ink. When he fled Essex to escape the rebels, he took it with him. He sent Mother and me letters with hidden messages between the lines. I thought the formula was lost forever when he died a year ago. In the letter, he explains its key ingredients include vinegar as well as some substances more obscure.

> *If you can put this to good use, take care not to burn the paper or yourself!*
> *Perhaps it can be a vital aid in advancing our common cause. God save the King.*
> *B.B.*

Benjamin Barrett: Father's name, and the name of my little brother. The letter brings back a wave of memories. Father's print shop in Essex where I played with metal type on the floor before I could read. Where I met Samuel and fell in love. Where Father wrote his articles against the war that turned the town against our whole family. Especially after Seth was killed by the rebels, the whole lot of us would have been tarred and feathered if we'd stayed. Others were, and I can still hear their screams.

I tuck the letter back in the drawer, but not before I take pen to paper and copy it. Why did Father give the formula to Jonah? Did Jonah already hand it over—or more likely sell it—to the British? Does Samuel know about it? Is that why he pursued me, because he thought I have the secret formula tucked away somewhere? I slip the formula into my bodice and wonder how I might make use of it.

Jonah awakes from his drunken sleep, not quite as ornery as before. Mother's herbal tea eased the pain.

"Get me my pen and ink, girl. We have much to do."

"I took care of everything. The newspaper is ready to go," I say, hoping for a scrap of praise or at least a proper thank-you.

"What! I didn't tell you to do that. It's probably all a holy mess."

"See for yourself," I say, at last weary of the prickly old man.

Though he can barely stand without help, he examines everything and picks it apart for no reason. Then he leaves it just as I've done it. Of course!

I'm exhausted by the time I leave the print shop. Walking home, dodging piles of garbage in the street, I hear a low voice in the alley behind Sheffield's Tavern.

"Sarah!"

It's Matthew Kittridge. I slip into the alley, hoping no one saw me.

"I was beginning to wonder if I'd see you again," I whisper. "I was afraid you'd played a cruel trick on me."

He smiles. "No. What we're doing is too dangerous for games. Are you still willing to help?"

"Yes. I've thought of little else since we talked." That is certainly the truth. I've slept fitfully all week, often waking in a cold sweat from nightmares.

"I have the letter for you to put inside the bread." He reaches into his coat pocket and pulls out a tiny piece of paper, barely a half-inch square, that has been folded a dozen times. "The note instructs Thomas to destroy it as soon as he reads it. That way it won't be traced."

"Will you at least tell me what the rescue plan is and when it's to happen?"

"No. And don't unfold the note and read it. It's safer that way. Then you can honestly say you didn't know anything about it if we fail."

"You won't fail. You mustn't fail!" I've not let myself dwell on that possibility. For Tom, failure means death.

"It will be in God's hand," he says, which doesn't ease my worry much. "Be at the waterfront at dawn on Sunday with the bread and whatever else you sell to the men. Lieutenant Pritchard will be waiting for you. And tell no one."

Before I can answer, Matthew has slipped away. I walk home clutching the folded note.

# Chapter Twenty

It's Saturday afternoon, and I'm exhausted. I woke at dawn to start the fire in the bake oven in our big kitchen fireplace. Mother has told me over and over how long to tend the fire to heat the oven. She must think I'm a child.

While the oven heats, I mix the dough—flour, water, yeast, and salt—exactly as Emma said. I knead it until my hands ache, but it still doesn't seem right.

"More flour," Emma instructs as she races after Benjamin. She is minding him while Mother is out awaiting another newborn.

I dump more flour into the sticky mess. That makes it impossible to knead.

"How much flour did you put in?" Emma asks, looking over my shoulder as Benjamin nags her to play hide-and-seek.

"I don't know, maybe a cup."

"Too much. It would take a team of oxen to knead that lump."

Sweat is trickling down my face. I'm ready to heave the mess into the fire, but I know I can't do that.

"Help me, Emma! Please! I can't do this."

She looks at me, perplexed. "Why are you so riled up over a loaf of bread?"

"It's not just a loaf of bread," I mutter, stopping myself from telling her the truth.

Emma smiles at me with sneaky eyes. "I see. This is for Thomas, and it must be perfect. So, you do care for him. There's no use trying to hide it. I know all your secrets."

"Not all of them." But I don't press it. Let her believe that I'm so lovestruck I'll do anything for a man, even bake him some bread.

"Let me help you," Emma says, handing Benjamin over to me.

She's a flurry of motion as she sprinkles more water on the dough, dips her hands in flour, and works the lump until it's the right consistency. She looks like she's done this a hundred times.

She sets the loaves, three altogether, so we have enough for the week, under a damp cloth to let them rise.

Meanwhile, I tell Benjamin a story about a fish that befriends a beaver and helps him build a home of sticks at the water's edge. Mercifully, he falls asleep. It strikes me as oddly interesting that I'm much better at beaver dams than bread.

Emma and I work in the garden, picking blueberries and raspberries, squash, and carrots to prepare for the morning's trip to the *Defiance*. I can't stop thinking something will go terribly wrong with the escape. I nearly drop an apron full of blueberries.

"Do you think Lieutenant Pritchard finds me attractive?" Emma asks as we haul the produce inside.

"How can you think about something so idiotic at a time like this."

"Pardon me, Miss Prickly Puss. What has you so agitated?"

I can't tell her the truth. I take a deep breath. "I'm sorry. I'm worried about Tom." At least that's not a lie. "And Emma, since when do you care about the affections of a redcoat?"

"Who says I do?"

Emma has a maddening way of brushing things off with a question. For once I'm glad to drop the subject.

When the oven is hot enough, I clean out all the wood and ash, then put the loaves inside, closing the metal door tightly. If I were the praying sort, I'd ask for divine intervention. While they bake, I write more in my diary.

*I feel guilty keeping such a huge secret from Emma. We've always confided in each other. Well, almost always.*

"May I read it," Emma asks, leaning over my shoulder.

"No!" I cover the paper with my arm.

"Why not? Are you writing about your undying love for Thomas?"

"Don't be silly. This is serious, and one day maybe it will see its way into print. Everyone will know the truth about the prison ships."

"And you'll be famous. That's what it's really about."

"No, it isn't!" Of course, Emma, as usual, is exactly right. I want more than anything to be a writer, a famous writer. But I'm wracked with doubt that I'm good enough.

• • •

I sleep little that night, worried the bread will somehow land in the wrong hands, or that Tom will be too weak to survive a rescue. Am I in love, like Emma says? But how can that be: We've never held hands, much less kissed. Yet I've never cared so much about anyone else.

When dawn arrives, I've already been awake an hour. I slip downstairs to the kitchen and quietly grab a sharp knife. I cut a slit, an inch long, in the bottom of a loaf. I start to nudge the tiny, folded message into the slit. But the urge to know what it says is too great, so I carefully unfold it and spread it out:

*Tell the prisoners to be ready at dawn on Wednesday for rescue.* The details spell out how Washington's men will seize control of the *Defiance. Make a ruckus to distract the guards so they won't hear us arrive.*

I carefully refold it and gently push it into the bread, far enough so that it doesn't show. I'm terrified and excited about what will soon unfold.

"Emma, wake up," I whisper. She opens her eyes for a second, then falls back asleep instantly. I shake her awake and listen to her grumble until we leave the house. Mother and Benjamin are still sleeping.

The sun is rising, and it looks to be another scorching day, yet another thing for Emma to complain about.

"Why must we be here so bloody early?" she whines.

"At this hour the water will be calm, and you won't have to worry about losing your breakfast," I say as we walk to the waterfront along empty, narrow streets.

"What breakfast? You were in such a rush I only had time for a crust of bread."

She perks up immediately when Pritchard is in sight on the dock.

"Good morning, ladies. A fine morning to be on the water."

"Yes, I do love the morning," Emma says, smiling broadly.

"Since when?" I hiss.

The lieutenant barely looks at me as he helps us into the boat. I watch him for any sign he is a spy, but I don't have a clue what one might look like. How can he be Pendleton's right-hand man and an agent for the enemy? Is Pendleton one too?

He says little during the boat ride, despite Emma's attempts to engage him. I'm too nervous to say anything.

As we pull up next to the ship, panic seizes me. How will I get the bread to Tom? I can't go below deck. He won't be on the top deck. He has no money to buy any of our wares. What if someone else buys the bread? One of the guards? Matthew Kittridge said they've taken care of that little detail, but no one told me exactly how.

The usual buyers, mostly guards, are in their usual frenzy to see what we're offering.

"Have you any tobacco? Rum?"

"Be patient men, and give the ladies the respect they deserve," Lt. Pritchard says. "And I would like to buy that fine-looking loaf of bread," he says, staring me straight in the eye.

The other men grumble as he takes the loaf and hands me some coins. "Damn officers take the best for themselves," one says, drawing a stern look from the lieutenant.

I finally let myself breathe as he heads below deck. Tom will surely have the loaf soon. Hopefully, he'll read the note before he doles out pieces to the others.

The rest of the goods are gone by the time the lieutenant returns to the top deck.

One of the prisoners, who has a stash of money, is badgering Emma to bring him a shirt next time. "I can pay you handsomely."

"That's enough men. Clear the way," Pritchard orders. "These ladies must return to shore."

On the way back, Emma counts the money and pronounces the trip a success. "Mrs. Barrett will be pleased. Better than last time."

Pritchard and I lock eyes without saying a word. He doesn't have to. I know the plan has been launched, and he knows that I know it. There is no turning back. Does this mean I'm now a rebel?

# Chapter Twenty-One

What have I done? For two days I worry myself sick. Every knock at the door sends me into a panic.

At the *Loyal Gazette*, it's the same. Every time Jonah returns from Hazen's Coffeehouse, I expect he'll burst in with "dreadful" news about how the traitorous prisoners have escaped, or "delicious" gossip that the evil plot has been foiled.

At the end of Wednesday when I leave the shop, I've worked myself into a ceaseless cycle of anger and worry. At home, one look at Emma's tear-stained face tells me something has gone wrong.

"What happened?"

"General Washington's men tried to take over the *Defiance* and two other ships and rescue the prisoners."

"And?"

"They failed." Emma wipes her eyes. "One of the prisoners ratted to a guard, and the British knew just when and how it was supposed to happen. I'm so afraid for Tom."

I'm staring into a bottomless pit.

"It was awful. Some of the prisoners were shot to death when they raced up to the top deck. Washington's men were forced to turn back under fire when it turned out they were so outmanned and outgunned. That's what Captain Pendleton told his wife."

"What about Tom? Do you know anything?" I'm already afraid of the answer.

"I couldn't ask Pendleton about him. He doesn't even know my brother is a prisoner. He thinks I'm as loyal to the British as your mother is. Do you know how hard it is for me to keep up this charade every day?"

"Yes, I do." I don't really, but I don't want her to go to pieces and quit her employment. "But we must find out about Tom."

"It won't be easy. All the prisoners are being kept below deck night and day. And rations have been cut again."

"How can they feed those men any less?" Tom must be practically a walking corpse by now, but I keep that worry to myself. I need Emma to keep her wits.

"Why would one prisoner betray all the others?" Emma asks, handing fussy Benjamin to me while she stirs the simmering clam chowder.

"Someone who wants more rations or some special treatment. Maybe even a few shillings. Whatever it is, I hope he didn't turn in Tom." As soon as I say it, I wish I hadn't.

"Why would he?" Emma eyes me suspiciously. "Sarah, did you have something to do with this? Do you know what's going on? You better tell me the truth."

Benjamin won't stop fussing. I grab a carrot and stick it in my nose. Mercifully, he finds it amusing. Then I breathe in deeply and look Emma in the eye. "The bread I made for Tom wasn't just bread. I slipped in a message about the rescue plan so he and the men would be prepared."

"You did what?" Emma's eyes are full of fury. "How did you even know about the plan? And why didn't you tell me?"

"I couldn't."

"And why not? We're supposed to be best friends. Tell each other everything."

"I'm telling you now if you give me a chance. But you must swear to me that you won't repeat what I'm about to say."

"I swear, but I don't like it one bit."

"Lieutenant Pritchard is a spy for General Washington. He made sure Tom got the bread with the secret message."

Emma looks at me as if I've said I'm Joan of Arc.

"A spy? A patriot?" Emma's world has turned upside down.

"Was Pritchard caught?" I fear the worst.

"He rowed Captain Pendleton back to shore today, so he probably wasn't suspected," Emma says. "But the captain is livid. He told Mrs. Pendleton he's got a 'viper in the ranks.' Someone in the military who's working with the rebels."

Emma's eyes fill up again. "We don't even know if Tom is dead or alive. And we have no way of finding out."

She's right, but I find it all curiously thrilling. "If Pritchard can still row us to the ship to sell our goods, we can find out."

"What!" Emma explodes. "How can you think about going back out there? It's too dangerous for Tom, the lieutenant, and especially us. Have you forgotten: We're both accused prostitutes, and now you're a spy too. And I'm furious that you didn't tell me all this before. You tricked me."

"You wouldn't have gone to the ship."

"That's right! And I won't go again. I can never trust you again." Emma whirls around, and I all but fall to my knees.

"Please Emma, don't be mad. I did it for Tom."

She glares. "No, you did it for yourself, so you could play the heroine."

*   *   *

Days pass before Emma will even look at me. It's as if I don't exist. She chats with Mother, plays with Benjamin, and goes off to work every day caring for the Pendleton children.

I feel so alone. I'm plagued by nightmares that Tom perished in the bungled escape. I decide to go back out to the *Defiance* on Sunday by myself; provided Pendleton will allow it. Mother would ask him, I'm sure. With the proceeds from our trips, she has nearly enough for passage back to England.

Mother has treated the captain's indigestion with herbs and chamomile tea, and he values her medical advice over that of any physician. When she asks him about returning to the ship, she sweetens the arrangement with more tea and a basket of produce from the garden. When she finishes, she has his word that Pritchard will be awaiting me again at dawn on Sunday.

Saturday night I gather what I can from the garden and add a few odds and ends I think Tom can use: Father's old jacket, candles, and more flint. That is if he's still alive. Finally, I toss in a chunk of maple syrup candy I took from Jonah's stash.

If Tom is dead, then I'm to blame, at least partly. My dreams bear out my guilt. Before dawn, I wake in a cold sweat. If he's alive, I must get him out of there. With summer nearly over and excuses for trips to the *Defiance* fading, I don't have much time. That's when I make a momentous—you may call it insane—decision. I write a note to Tom, telling him about the invisible ink and how to hold the letter over a flame to read a secret message between the lines. I say I'll write again soon with a rescue plan. What it will be, I haven't exactly figured out, but an idea is starting to take shape in my mind.

I need to hide the letter, and I look over the few offerings I have for Tom. I caress the tattered wool coat Mother made for Father all those years ago. At least it will keep him warmer in the coming winter months.

The coat still gives off the tobacco scent from Father's pipe. As I fondle the blue wool, I notice the buttons Mother covered in velvet to give it an elegant flair. Then it comes to me, a way to hide the letter. I remove the velvet on one button, fold the letter down to a tiny square, and replace the velvet on the button with the letter under it.

I lay awake until just before dawn, worried that Tom won't find it, or worse that he's caught with it. My hands shake as I dress silently and leave the house. At the dock, it's still dark and the water is calm. Even the dockworkers haven't arrived yet for their labor. I think about turning back, but then I see Pritchard approaching in his red uniform.

"Is Tom alive?" I search his face for some sign.

"He is ... barely."

"What does that mean?" I set down my heavy basket.

"What happened? Tell me, please."

"I will, but first I must tell you that I can't let you go out to the *Defiance*. I won't risk it for either of us, not after what happened last time. But I'll tell you this: The mission failed, badly. One of the prisoners warned the guards, and they were ready for our men. We lost four to gunfire, and a half dozen prisoners died or were beaten to death."

"And Tom? Did he get the message?"

"He certainly did."

"What do you mean by that?"

"I went below deck with the bread and put on quite a show of playing the brute. I singled out Tom first, yelling, 'Rebel bastard! If you're so hungry eat this!' Then I ripped off a chunk of the bread with the message and shoved it in his mouth. I threw the rest out to the rabble."

"Well done! So, the traitor didn't finger Thomas?"

"No, but Captain Pendleton ordered half rations for the prisoners until the ringleader is turned in."

"They can't survive on that. It might as well be a death sentence."

He looks up and down the dock. Workers are just starting to arrive.

"The guards have been merciless," he says. They beat the prisoners for sport, betting on who will survive."

"Was Tom beaten?"

"Of course."

"If only I could go below, at least slip him some food."

"No, Sarah! Don't be a fool. It's only a matter of time before Captain Pendleton finds me out. Then I'll hang for sure."

I look at him curiously, this spy. "Why do you do it?"

His face brightens and his eyes come alive. "This is much bigger than me. This is about freedom, freedom for everyone. Don't think that I'm the only one risking his neck. There are plenty of others, people like Black Jack Morton at King's Tavern. Not only does he sneak messages to General Washington, but he also smuggles food, clothing, even money to the prisoners."

"I had no idea," I say.

"Sarah, I must shove off. I'm sorry I can't take you."

"Will you at least do one thing for me?"

"Of course."

I hand him the little bundle for Tom. "Would you see that he gets this? He desperately needs the coat for the coming autumn."

"Of course. Captain Pendleton has asked me to interrogate each of the prisoners about the escape plan. I can give it to him then."

"And please tell him to take special note of the buttons on the coat. Mother was especially proud of them."

# Chapter Twenty-Two

When I return home, Emma is on the stoop husking corn with Mother. She leaps down the steps and rushes toward me.

"Have you news of Thomas?" she cries, nearly knocking me over.

I'm not expecting her to even look at me, much less talk to me.

"Is he…alive? Tell me!"

"He is." I look at her curiously. "You're not still angry with me?"

"Just tell me, Sarah. Can't you see that not everything is about you?"

Stung, I tell her the little that Pritchard said, leaving out some of the details about Tom's perilous state.

She seems to look straight through me, but Mother can't wait to ask questions of her own.

"Was it a successful trip?" She eyes the pouch that usually jangles with coins after our trips.

"No. I didn't go out to the *Defiance*." I can't tell her the truth. "I felt ill at the last minute, might have been the bacon." Another in my growing stack of lies.

Mother looks at me suspiciously. "Where is the basket? It was piled high."

"I left it all with Lieutenant Pritchard. He'll see that the prisoners get it."

"Thoughtless girl! I could sell it at the Common or in the neighborhood. There are good loyalists here who would pay a pretty penny. More are moving back to the city every day."

I have sudden regrets about my fleeting moment of generosity, but I bite my tongue and take the verbal thrashing.

Emma comes to my rescue. "And how is Dan…the lieutenant?" she says, cutting off Mother's rant.

"He seemed fit as ever. Why do you ask?"

"Oh, I don't know." Emma looks flustered.

I knew she'd taken a liking to Pritchard, even before he revealed his patriot sympathies. After all, he is pleasing to look at, and ever since I discovered he's a spy, I've found myself viewing him in a different light.

"He asked after you this morning," I say, recalling the twinge of jealousy I felt at the time.

"Oh, he did, did he?"

"Emma, you could do a lot worse than the lieutenant for a husband," Mother says. "Such a fine British soldier, he could have a real future."

Mother has no idea. For a heartbeat, I worry that Emma will blurt out the truth about him. But she doesn't. I take it to mean our friendship is back to normal, even if she isn't exactly saying so.

"Emma, come help me pick blueberries in the garden."

"Don't tell me you're going to make a pie," she says. "That would be a terrible waste of good berries."

As we head into the backyard, I whisper: "I need to talk with you."

In the far corner of the garden, we find a bush bursting with berries. We pick them by the handfuls and put them in our aprons.

"What's so important that you have to pretend you want to make a pie?" Emma asks.

I move closer, putting my finger to my lips. "I know how we can help Tom escape."

Emma's face clouds up. "Not again. Whatever it is, it's too dangerous. The war will end eventually, and Thomas will be released."

"No, it won't end soon, I fear. Neither side is giving up. And Tom may not last that long."

"What do you mean?"

"I didn't want to tell you, because I knew you'd worry."

"Tell me what?" Emma looks like she's ready to shake the truth out of me.

"It's worse than half rations. The guards use any excuse to beat them."

"And Thomas?"

"Yes, him too, that's why we can't just let him rot there."

Emma looks right at me. "You must be in love with my brother. Why else would you risk your life on some imbecilic plan that's bound to fail?"

I only hear the word "love." In all honesty, I feel something different, something special about him. "Perhaps I don't think of him as a brother like you do," I say slowly. "He's kind and funny, and passionate about the war."

"That's it?"

"No. He makes me feel smart and pretty and important."

"As usual, it's all about you."

"That's not so. I do have feelings for Tom."

"So, you admit it." Emma grins as if she's trapped me. "I never told you this, but back in Essex, he told me he fancied you, despite your obsession with Samuel."

"I was a silly, ignorant girl." It seems like a hundred years ago.

"Do you love Tom?"

Emma is leading me to a place that seems hopelessly confusing and murky.

"How do you know if you love someone?" I ask. "There ought to be a test or some clear indication, like bleeding blue, so you don't make a mistake."

"Mother says all this talk about love is nonsense," Emma says. "A good husband works sunup to sundown without complaint. That's all that matters."

"So, I should look for a workhorse to marry?"

Emma rolls her eyes. "I've suspected you cared more for Thomas than you were letting on."

She always claims to know more about me than I do. It's infuriating, especially if she's right.

When I don't answer, Emma starts picking berries again. "So, what's your big rescue plan?"

I take a breath. At least she is willing to hear me out. I tell her how the prisoners bring their dead up to the top deck at dawn, wrapped in a blanket and weighed down by a cannonball. "The guards heave them overboard, letting them sink."

Emma is losing patience with me. "Can you never come to the point? What's your big plan?"

"One morning, before dawn, Tom's friends will wrap him in his blanket and pretend he's among the dead. The guards will heave him in the water with all the other dead souls."

Emma looks horrified. "What's to keep him from drowning?"

"He won't be wrapped with a cannonball. He'll free himself from the blanket and float to the surface."

"Even if he manages this impossible feat, then what? He'll be out in the choppy water and drown for sure."

"No, he won't. We'll plan it for a morning when we row out to the ship with Lieutenant Pritchard to sell our goods. As the bodies go overboard, we'll leave the ship and pick up Tom as we row ashore."

Emma speaks slowly as if she's explaining something complicated to a three-year-old. "Have you forgotten something? Dan won't row us out to the *Defiance*."

"That's where I'll need your help," I say. "We'll need to convince him the plan will work." Even as I lay it out, the whole idea sounds crazy.

"Dan would never do it. It's too risky. A million things could go wrong. So don't expect me to take part."

"I know it's risky, Emma. But what if we could free Tom? Wouldn't it be worth it?"

"They'll hang the lot of us."

She could well be right, but I press on, pulling out my strongest ammunition. "I've seen men starving so, that they gnaw on shoe leather to survive. Men so desperately hungry that they pore through the slop from the pigs on board."

"Stop!"

I hug her so tightly that the berries in our aprons squish. "Now we must convince Lieutenant Pritchard."

"Sarah, I haven't agreed to this."

"Will you see him this week?"

"He always comes to dinner at the Pendletons' on Monday."

"You could slip him a note."

"I'll do that much, but don't try to trick me into doing more. You have a way of doing that."

# Chapter Twenty-Three

Emma is true to her word. The lieutenant arrived for dinner, and as she took his coat, she pressed my note into his hand, just as we planned.

"I was shaking so badly I feared Mrs. Pendleton would think I'd contracted the palsy," she tells me at breakfast the next morning.

In the note, I took pains not to say anything that would get him into trouble. I simply asked him to meet us tonight at the Common under the grove of maple trees. It's always busy so no one would think it odd for the three of us to meet up for an evening stroll.

All day I can think of nothing else. Mercifully, Jonah is busy courting a new supplier of paper, and the effort involves much rum, the city's finest turtle soup, and beef pies, followed by fruit tarts and more rum.

I think Emma likes all the intrigue, though she'll never admit it. Or it could be she's just smitten. For tonight's rendezvous, she slipped on her lowest-cut gown, fixed her hair with new ribbons, and wore her heart-shaped locket. Even without all the extra effort, she is still far prettier than me. You might think it bothers me, but it doesn't. I barely notice.

Emma and I hurry through our supper of bread and cheese, barely listening to Mother's monologue about the shortage of good British tea. After cleaning up, we tell her we're taking a walk to cool off from the summer heat.

We dash down the front steps as a wagon loaded with barrels creaks by. "Do you think he'll be there?" Emma asks. "What's to stop him from thinking we're just a couple of silly girls out for a lark?"

"He knows better, and I've already shown him I can be trusted."

Her cheeks and lips are reddened with beet juice; Emma looks like she's off to a ball. I wish I'd at least tamed my curls into a manageable mound. Tom likes me the way I am, but I'm sure Pritchard prefers someone nicely put together, like Emma.

We approach the Common and see canvas tents scattered here and there, families still homeless after the big fire last year. People mill about, children play, and cows graze wherever they can, which is to say, anywhere they want.

At the maple grove, there's no sign of Pritchard.

"I knew he'd think it insane to meet us," Emma says.

"Not so fast. We're early. I haven't heard the 7 o'clock bell." I, too, worry that something has gone wrong. But the way he looked at Emma on our last crossing tells me there is more than a flicker of something there. He's never looked at me that way.

We stroll around the grove trying to appear unconcerned, even when we pass a group of drunk, raucous redcoats. They ignore us, likely focused instead on the next tavern they'll tear apart.

Finally, Emma says, "We might as well go home. He's not coming. I dressed up for nothing."

Just then, he appears from behind a rock outcropping. "Good evening, ladies," he says, removing his hat. "I'm sorry to have kept you, but I wanted to be certain I wasn't followed."

"Evening Lieutenant Pritchard," Emma says, grinning like a simpleton.

"Call me Dan, please."

Emma lets out a deep sigh. "We thought you weren't coming." He smiles at her as if I'm not even here. His eyes are warm and caring, and his uniform is neat and clean.

I get right to the point. "We have a plan to rescue Emma's brother Tom from the *Defiance*, but we need your help."

His smile disappears immediately. "A plan?"

I tell him the details, and he takes it all in without a word.

"Will you help us?" I finally ask.

"Please," Emma pleads, "for my brother's sake."

"No." His answer is immediate and firm.

My heart stops. "Why?"

He wipes the sweat from his brow with a white handkerchief. "I can't put the two of you at risk, nor myself. You know what happened last time you went out there. This war is a nasty business. It's no place for young women."

"We know the risk," I say. "We're not children."

"You realize that if there is any little misstep, we'll all be taken prisoner," he says. "They'll slip the noose around our necks with pleasure."

Emma winces.

"I'm sorry," he says to her, his voice softening. "But it's true."

"We better forget about this," she says. "I don't know what we were thinking."

"No, I still want to try," I say, ignoring her.

"You are a most determined young lady," he says.

I don't think it was a compliment, but I barge ahead. "I've thought it all out. I'm sure it will work."

"You've overlooked something," he says. "How will you let Thomas know of your plan?"

I smile. "I haven't overlooked a thing. I'll get a message to him with invisible ink."

They both look dumbfounded. I tell them about Father's formula, and that I've already written to Thomas about it and supplied him with a candle to read the secret message between the lines.

Pritchard is stunned. "The rebels could use you on their side."

"I am on their side," I say, uttering aloud for the first time my most private thoughts on the matter.

"Good."

"Will you help us, Dan? If you don't, I'll figure out a way to do it without you." I have no idea what I'm talking about.

"I can't let that happen," he says, letting out a deep breath. "I'll help you, though I must be insane to let a crazed young woman talk me into this."

"She has a way of doing that," Emma can't help but note.

I let it pass. I'm too thrilled.

Suddenly a man of action, the lieutenant takes command. "We can do it next Sunday. It's best we don't wait too long."

"We'll have to get a message to Tom before then," I say.

"I'll be at Captain Pendleton's home for dinner again on Friday," he says. "Emma could pass it to me discreetly. Are you with us, Emma? If you'd rather not, no one is forcing you."

She nods yes, but I can see she's terrified.

"Are you certain," he says. "We could all die, including Tom."

"Tom may die if we do nothing," I say, fearing Emma will change her mind any second.

"I'm in," she finally says. I can see she's so lovestruck she'd swim to Brooklyn if he asked.

"Good. If your plan works for Thomas, maybe it will work for the others," Pritchard says. "That's why I'm willing to give it a chance. Perhaps it's safer to rescue them one at a time than try to spring them all at once. We've tried that and it hasn't worked."

As we part ways, I wonder just what I've taken on. Deep inside I'm scared to death.

On the way home, Emma gushes about Dan. How handsome he is, how tall, and serious, yet warm and caring. When she'll see him again. What she'll wear. It's nauseating.

"You sound lovesick, and you barely know him," I tell her.

"I think you can love someone at first sight," she says.

"When you first met him, you thought he was a British soldier, a lousy redcoat," I remind her.

"I always suspected he was a spy, a rebel at heart."

"Emma, you did not! You had no clue."

When we arrive home, I decide to write the secret letter—an

invisible letter-within-a-letter, if you can believe it—to Tom. I have a deliciously devious plan for getting it into Tom's hands without arousing suspicion.

> *My dearest son,*
> *I have the most unfortunate news. Your brother Ichabod has died. He ran off and joined the rebels and died in battle last month. Death came quickly. He did not suffer, thank the lord.*
> *Your mother and I urge you to renounce this destructive rebellion and pledge your allegiance to the British. It's the sensible thing to do and will ensure that your life is not lost too. The rebels can't possibly win against the mighty British. Perhaps you can convince other prisoners to do the same. The sooner they do, the sooner this war will end. We desperately need you back at the farm.*
> *God bless,*
> *Father*

Tom will know immediately the letter is from me. His father would sooner die than renounce the rebels' cause and Tom doesn't have a brother named "Ichabod." I take out the vinegar formula, clean off the quill pen, and start the real message to Thomas, writing in the big spaces I left between the lines.

> *We have a plan to rescue you Sunday at dawn. You'll need the help of a trusted friend, and you'll have to play dead …*

I tell him he'll only be in the water a few minutes before our boat comes to his aid.

> *God willing, you have the strength to do this. I'll be waiting for you. Sarah*

I let the vinegar dry and examine the letter. No trace of the hidden lines. I pray he hasn't used up the candle I slipped him. By holding the paper over the flame he'll see the most important words I've ever written. That is, if I haven't blundered somehow.

143

Emma is sound asleep when I finally undress and slip into bed. I don't go to sleep right away. I keep thinking about Tom and our time together in Essex. I had no idea he cared about me then. Except he gave me a fine box of writing paper when his wounded leg finally healed. Perhaps I was too obsessed with Samuel to notice his gift was more than just kindness.

# Chapter Twenty-Four

I can barely concentrate at work, and I keep making stupid errors. When I misspell "apathy" for the second time Jonah explodes.

"Girl, what's wrong with you today!" he yells. "Your head is somewhere else. It's certainly not here."

I apologize, a task not easy for me. I can't stop worrying about Tom. Did he read the secret message, or has his candle burned to a useless nub? Is he strong enough to survive rough waters? Will his friends turn on him and tell the guards? I think of a thousand awful things that could happen. Of course, I tell Emma none of this. Her loyalty is a fragile flower.

I force myself to concentrate on the task at hand: writing an item about the new clockmaker opening shop on Cortlandt Street. Of course, the clockmaker just happens to be a strong supporter of the Crown.

With a war raging, I can't imagine the people of New York spending money on such luxuries, but Jonah assures me the wealthy British can well afford it.

I wonder what Father would think if he knew I'm now a rebel. I feel certain he'd switch sides if he'd seen what I've seen. How can Jonah turn a blind eye?

"Jonah, do you know how many men have died on those filthy ships? I hear it's up to 10 prisoners a day and that's only on the *Defiance*."

"The prison ships again? Girl, can't you just find a suitor?" he grumbles, as he shelves the latest batch of new books from London.

"Doesn't it bother you? The British throw rotten food at them as if they're pigs in a sty. I've seen it."

"Don't tell me you're still rowing out there?"

"Yes. It helps Mother scrape together a little money."

I expect Jonah will tell me to shut up and get back to work. But he doesn't. He seems puzzled.

"How many prison ships are out there?" he asks.

"It's grown to a half-dozen in Wallabout Bay and nearby."

"And how many rebel swine live on the ships?"

"Hundreds on each. Maybe a thousand on some and it can barely be called living. People need to know."

Jonah's mood changes in a flash. "I don't need advice from a know-it-all child about what to put in my newspaper. Now get back to work."

The man would be a tyrant if he weren't so inept. I finish the item about the clockmaker and set about to clean the press. Not that I enjoy it, but at least I'll be out of earshot of Jonah's demands and insults.

I didn't hear the door to the shop creak open. Before I know it, Samuel is standing over me while I'm on my hands and knees, sweaty, covered in ink, and horse piss.

"I see you're still mucking around in filth," he says, startling me.

"Why are you here? Certainly not to see me." I make no attempt to stand up and pull myself together.

"No, I've come to see Jonah. About the prison ships."

I freeze. "What about them?"

"If you must know, the Crown is offering a reward for information about the ringleader behind the bungled escape from the *Defiance*. That should flush out the culprit, whether it's some traitor in the British ranks or one of those scummy prisoners you care about so much."

My hands are trembling now. "Let me guess, you want Jonah to publish an advertisement about the reward."

"Yes. And I assume as a good loyalist, he'll do it without charge."

"Don't count on it." Just the sound of his voice grates on me.

"I suppose you're still rowing out there to peddle your wares. You and your mother." The self-righteous prig is bursting with contempt.

"And now Emma too," I add proudly. "She's here in New York. And we have no intention of stopping."

His upper lip rises in a sneer. "Is that why you're so passionate about these prisoners? Is it her brother, that bastard Tom? Your father would be ashamed of you."

"How dare you!" I grab the pail I'm using to clean the press and dump the foul, inky, mess on his shoes, spattering his precious velvet breeches and white stockings.

"Oh dear, how clumsy of me. Now get out!"

He stomps his feet in disgust. "Not before I have a word with your boss. And don't think I won't tell him about this … this latest insult!" As he leaves, he calls me a whore and says he's not finished with me, not by a long shot.

"What does that mean?"

"I think you know." Then he stomps away leaving wet, filthy footprints on the floor.

My breath comes in short bursts like I'm about to cry. I've never been so angry…and scared.

●  ●  ●

I walk home totally exhausted, my hands cracked and sore from scrubbing the press. I pass groups of British soldiers laughing and talking as if they're on holiday. If there are still families here that support the rebels, they're scarce and they keep their opinions to themselves. Like Emma, and now me.

I don't know how much more I can take. Will Samuel tip off the rebels that I was the one who set fire to their ammunition in New Hampshire? Not even Tom knows that, and he was there that night. He was guarding the arsenal.

I'd stashed that monstrous fear in the back of my mind, and now it's looming over me. What I did that night seems worlds away. But

I was a crack shot with a bow and arrow, thanks to my brother. Even so, I was astonished when I let fly the flaming arrow and it ignited the thatched roof of the century-old barn. In seconds, the place exploded, sending a huge fireball into the night sky. That was the night Mother and I fled Essex with Benjamin.

Emma helped me, even risking a whipping from her father to do so. All I wanted was to keep the rebels from ever using their blasted weapons on the British troops. I thought I'd save lives on both sides.

As I trudge home, I think about Tom. What will he say when he finds out it was me who dashed the hopes of the rebel forces that night? Will he hate me? Will he believe me when I say I've become a rebel?

My worries don't end there. I have Mother to contend with. She'll have a fit if she finds out about our plan to rescue Tom. And if she discovers that Pritchard is a spy, she almost certainly would run to Pendleton. There are so many ways for my world to explode. If I could run somewhere, I would.

# Chapter Twenty-Five

In the kitchen, a kettle of chicken soup is simmering on the hearth. Emma and I each take a bowlful while Mother puts Benjamin to bed.

"I saw Lieutenant Pritchard today," Emma says.

"Did you give him my letter?" I'm suddenly alert, not as dog-tired as I was earlier.

"He winked when he saw me."

"Emma! I can't wait all night while you blubber about the man. Did you give him the letter?"

"I was just getting to that part."

"It's about time."

"As soon as he came up the walk, I ran out to greet him," Emma says. "I gave him the letter and he read it quickly before we went inside."

"That's all?"

"No. He said, 'This might just work. Sarah is clever beyond her years.' Then Mrs. Pendleton greeted him with a sly smile and said, 'Daniel, I see you've met our Miss Emma'."

"Then what? Emma, quickly."

"I helped serve them dinner. They had roasted—"

"I don't care what they ate."

"During dinner, Dan said to the captain, 'This curious letter arrived today for one of the prisoners.' Then he read it aloud."

Emma acts out the rest of the conversation as if on stage:

"'Oh, the poor soul's brother died,' Mrs. Pendleton says, passing the platter of roast duck."

"'Poor soul? He's a damn prisoner and this is war, dear woman,' the captain says."

"'Certainly, you'll inform him about his brother,' she says."

"'Certainly, and I'll bring him his tea and crumpets,' he says in a sing-song voice."

"Then the children laugh at their father's hilarious impersonation, but Dan says, 'Maybe we have something to gain here.'"

"And then they go back and forth about this and that, and the ridiculous ban on letters to the prisoners now."

I can't stand it anymore. "Emma! What else did they say?"

"Well, Dan says that the father makes some good points in his letter and that maybe it would sway Tom and even the others to join up with the British."

"And?"

"Oh, and then Mrs. Pendleton says, 'Of course! How very clever of you, lieutenant'. Then the captain grew bored."

"'Fine, fine,' he says, stuffing his mouth with mashed potato. 'Pass it on to the prisoner. Now let's open this bottle of port and toast our men'."

Emma's face is flushed at the retelling of the story. I've never seen her so excited. Then she gushes on about her Dan's quick thinking when it was my idea in the first place.

"Enough about him," I say. I certainly never felt that way about Samuel. I don't even know if I feel that way about Tom, though I might.

"Sarah, have you thought about that?"

"What?"

"Pay attention. I just asked you whether Tom will need dry clothes when we rescue him. And what about shoes?"

My heart skips a beat. I forgot about the clothing. "Yes, of course. I've got a plan." Luckily, she doesn't ask just what it is.

150

I go to sleep puzzling over it, and when I awake, I know what I must do. And there's no use telling Emma. She'll never approve.

Instead of going straight to the *Loyal Gazette* after breakfast, I stroll down to Samuel's rooming house. I know he goes to work early so it should be easy to slip into his quarters.

I march up the steps, knock on the door, and pull my bonnet down low.

"Yes, what is it?" It's the old landlady, and I pray she doesn't remember me.

"I'm Samuel's sister. I've come to collect his washing."

"He's never mentioned a sister. I do his washing. On Mondays."

I didn't expect this. But I put on my friendliest face and look her in the eye.

"Oh, yes, I know. He's told me about your kindness. But yesterday he had a mishap with a pail of garbage thrown out a doorway. His clothing was spattered with putrefied fish, and he couldn't bear to trouble you with cleaning the mess. So, he asked me. I'm Rebecca."

"How kind of you. Come in. Samuel has been gone for hours." She starts down the hallway toward Samuel's door.

"Oh, I know where it is," I say. "I'll collect his things and be out of your way."

"Very well, then." She turns and is gone.

I lift the latch on the door and open it slowly, half expecting Samuel's mistress, the wretched Mrs. Stoneham, to leap out from behind a curtain. But the room is empty, save the neatly made bed, chest with brass handles, and a desk with piles of papers scattered here and there. I resist the urge to look at them. There isn't time.

Hanging on a peg next to the fireplace, I find the shirt and breeches he wore yesterday at the shop. They're still damp and stink so badly that I'm surprised the old woman didn't notice. On the floor are the stained shoes. I scoop them all up in a bundle and head for the door.

I feel not the least bit guilty about stealing his clothing. Samuel has more than he needs, no doubt, to impress Mrs. Stoneham. The prisoners wear rags. I'm just evening the score.

151

• • •

In Emma's room that night I proudly unroll the bundle to show her.

"What is that stink?"

"Don't ask. And don't ask me where they came from."

"I don't want to know."

"We'll soak them in vinegar, then wash them before Mother comes home. Even the shoes. We can hang them to dry in your room. Mother never goes in here."

"They'd better not smell," Emma says, picking up her knitting needles to work on socks for Tom.

"I'm sure Tom will be grateful to have them, whether they smell or not." She's strangely quiet for a moment. "What's wrong?" I ask.

Emma sighs deeply. "I'll just say it plain. I don't want to go with you Sunday to the ship."

"What? Why?"

Her face is contorted in pain. "I'm afraid. And I'm afraid for Tom."

"But you promised …" My carefully thought-out plan is falling apart.

"I never promised anything. You just assumed."

"But I thought you wanted to rescue Tom. What about all our planning? Do you just want to throw it all away?" How could she do this to me now?

"All *your* planning. And, of course, I want to free Tom. What kind of question is that?"

"Then what's the problem?"

"The problem is this. When you get an idea in your head, you're like a charging bull," she says, her eyes angry. "There's no reasoning with you or stopping you. You never ask me what I think. And I'm telling you right now, it's too risky. Tom could drown … you don't even know if he can swim."

"Of course, he can swim. Don't you remember the water fights he and Seth used to have in the pond in Essex?"

"It's not the same as swimming in rough, swirling seawater," she says.

"No one is going to die," I say, shrugging off a very real possibility. "And I don't think I'm anything like a charging bull. Is this about Dan Pritchard?"

"No!" Emma starts working the knitting needles at a breakneck pace. Her head is bent over so I can't see her eyes.

"I think it is. Now that you have him wrapped around your little finger, you don't want to do anything that might threaten your little love affair." I probably went too far but it's too late to take it back.

Emma slams down her knitting. "That's not it at all. See, you're doing it again!"

"What? Being a bull? Don't you see? Dan wants to free all the men, not just Tom."

"You've lost sight of what you're doing. It's not about Tom anymore. It's about you having to be the center of attention and controlling everyone and everything as if it's some big game. It's safer for him and us if we wait. This war surely will end soon."

"We can't back out now."

"Yes, we can. No one would be the wiser."

"No! We can't. God willing, Tom already knows we're coming for him Sunday." I want to shake Emma, bring her to her senses.

"What makes you think he'll even read the invisible part," she says. "You're assuming a lot… you and your invisible ink."

"It will work," I insist, knowing full well it might not.

"I thought you cared about my brother." Emma's voice drips with disdain. "I even imagined you and Tom might one day wed."

"Wed?" My voice cracks.

"It's obvious you have feelings for him. If it's real love, you wouldn't put his life in such danger."

I feel my world collapsing. "Of course, I care. That's why I want to rescue him before he dies of starvation or who knows what."

"Now you're being melodramatic."

My patience runs out. "Emma, if you're so afraid, then stay home Sunday. It's better without you, anyway. You'll just get in the way."

"Fine! Do it yourself."

# Chapter Twenty-Six

I fume all night, barely sleeping at all. I'm mad at myself for losing my temper with Emma, and for saying hurtful things I don't even mean. How can we rescue Tom without her? She's the one the guards and prisoners look forward to seeing. Curvy, flirty Emma. They don't look at me the same way.

She doesn't speak to me the next day, nor do I to her. At least she washes Samuel's foul clothing and lays it out to dry in her room.

Saturday night we gather the fruit and vegetables from the garden, Mother's biscuits and raspberry jam, honey, bits of pork leftover from dinner, and as much tea as Mother will part with. I add a newspaper or two that Jonah won't miss. Emma is still giving me the silent act while chattering away with Mother about the price of flour and the scarcity of sugar and every other stupid thing.

Finally, it starts to turn dark, and we climb the stairs and go to our separate rooms without a word. I should apologize but I can't. Sleep won't come, and by 3 a.m. I'm still awake so I get up and quietly dress. In the kitchen, I put a log on the glowing ashes in the fireplace and fill the kettle for tea. Spilling water, I realize my hands are shaking.

At dawn, I gather up the baskets, slip out the front door, and head for the wharves. After a few minutes, I hear a commotion and freeze. British soldiers patrolling at this hour?

"Wait, Sarah!" It's Emma, holding up her skirts awkwardly and sprinting after me. "You forgot something," she gasps.

"What?"

"The clothes for Thomas."

"Well, where are they?"

Emma smiles slyly. "Under my skirt, tied to my petticoat."

"Does this mean you've changed your mind about coming?"

"Yes. Against my better judgment."

"Good." I'm so happy I want to grab her and dance. "I'm sorry, Emma. I said things I didn't mean."

"So did I, though I meant some of them."

"The part about me being like a bull?"

She nods.

"I rather liked that part," I say.

When we reach the dock, Pritchard is already there. "Good morning, ladies. Ready for the rigors of the day?"

Emma puts on a lovely smile. "Yes, of course."

Once we shove off, he guides the boat through calm water, and the docks slip from view. In the middle of the river, he stops rowing. "Let's go over our plan," he says in a low voice. We must get this absolutely right."

He reaches over and squeezes Emma's hand. I'll admit it: I'm jealous.

"You ladies will sell your wares as usual, until the guards order the prisoners to haul up the dead. It takes several minutes, especially if there are 10 or 12 bodies all wrapped in blankets and weighted down with cannonballs. Except, of course, Tom."

Emma doesn't look the least bit relieved.

"When the order is given to throw the corpses overboard, we'll depart," he says, picking up the oars.

My mind is racing. "Won't they see us haul Tom out of the water?"

"I have a diversion all figured out. Now quiet! We're almost there."

"Act normal, Emma," I whisper as we tread up the gangway. As soon as I say it, I realize it's like telling a dog to act like a seal.

"How can I act normal, when I have a man's breeches and shirt and shoes tied to my undergarments," she hisses.

The usual crowd presses in as we unload our baskets. They're thrilled just to be in the presence of women.

We're selling the last of the biscuits when a man's rough voice calls out: "Prisoners! Haul up your dead!"

My eyes dart over to the stairwell, and the lieutenant gives me a stern look. I try to concentrate on the fat, foul guard fondling the biscuits.

"My mother baked them fresh this morning, sir," I say as pleasantly as I can.

"Did she now?" he says, looking me over from head to toe in a way that makes me want to throttle him.

Out of the corner of my eye, I see two emaciated prisoners struggle to haul the first blanket-wrapped body on the deck. Then four more arrive, dropped on the wood planks like slabs of beef. I scan each one for any sign of movement and see nothing. Emma stands utterly still.

Then two guards lift the first body and clumsily heave it over the side. I hear the loud splash.

"Good riddance, traitor!" one of them shouts.

"Ladies, let's take our leave," Lt. Pritchard says.

We head down to the boat. I hear a loud splash as each body goes overboard on the other side of the ship.

"Quickly!" the lieutenant whispers, shoving us into the bobbing boat. "Quickly!"

As we pull away from the *Defiance*, a rowboat filled with loud, heavily rouged women in their low-cut Saturday night best comes near.

Then a lusty, low-pitched voice belts out the ditty: *"What do you do with a drunken sailor."* The other three join in, waving jugs of whiskey. I wonder what kind of fresh hell we've slipped into now, but I have to say, I'm taken with their rowdy enthusiasm. I recognize Lucinda among them as they play the tease and raise their skirts well above their knees. The whooping guards rush over to the side for a look at the strangest sight I've ever seen.

The women wave and blow kisses as they launch into another song, this one even more off-key.

The men cheer as they take in the spectacle. "Ladies, raise 'em higher!" one yells. "Come aboard and bring the jugs."

As the women continue the racket, Pritchard eases our boat around the *Defiance*, to the side where the bodies were so unceremoniously tossed. I realize he's the one who devised this brilliant diversion.

"They're from the Holy Ground," I tell Emma.

"Prostitutes?" She's stunned, but the lieutenant tries to make their involvement sound like an everyday event.

"My dear, these ladies sometimes pass on valuable information to us," he says. "I can assure you they'll be paid handsomely."

As they launch into some bawdy ditty, Emma and I scan the water frantically looking for Tom. It's calm, with no sign of a ripple. Have all the bodies sunk? I'm sick with fear. Have I just taken Tom's life with my foolish idea of rescuing him?

Seconds later a head shoots through the surface of the water, gasping for air, choking on water.

"Thomas!" Emma screams, too loud.

"Quiet!" I caution. "They'll hear us."

"Hurry Dan, before he goes under again," she whispers hoarsely.

The lieutenant rows frantically. When we pull alongside, an arm grabs the side of the boat.

I'm so excited. Soon we'll have Tom hidden in the boat under a tarp and on our way to shore.

But something is wrong when I finally glimpse his face.

"You're not Tom!"

# Chapter Twenty-Seven

It's a full minute of gurgling and gasping before he catches his breath. Then it takes all three of us to haul him into the boat.

Once I have a good look, I recognize him. "Why, you're Nathaniel, Tom's friend." He sprawls onto a seat. Suddenly, Lt. Pritchard dives from his place at the oars and shoves him into the bottom of the boat.

"Be still!" he orders. "Stay down, hide under this tarp, and don't make a sound."

Poor Nathaniel is more boy than man. He huddles at our feet shivering, the soaked rags clinging to every crevice. The welts on his bony back are red and raised, fresh from a beating.

By this time, Emma has come to her senses. "Where's Thomas? Where's my brother? What have you done with him?"

"He's still on the ship," Nathaniel says.

"Is he ..."

"Yes, he's alive, barely. Like the rest of us."

My patience for this unwelcome guest is at its limit. "Why are you here on your way to freedom, and Tom is still trapped on that ship from hell?" I whisper an inch from his face. "Did you beat him?"

Nathaniel's sunken eyes pool with tears. "He insisted I go first."

"Why would he do that?" Emma demands.

"He said the strongest should go first. A weaker man likely would drown in the trying."

"And you? You're the strongest?" I say, in disbelief.

"Stronger than the poor devils gnawing on splinters for sustenance, ma'am."

As much as I wish it isn't Nathaniel shivering in the bottom of the boat, I can't bring myself to begrudge this poor soul a chance at life. I take off my shawl and, beneath the tarp, wrap it around his scrawny shoulders. I berate myself for giving away the last biscuits to those fool guards.

The city waterfront comes into view, and Pritchard stops rowing for a moment. "He can't get off the boat and walk down the street in those rags."

"I have breeches, a shirt, and shoes," Emma says.

"Where?"

In a move we'd all just seen from the raucous ladies of the night, Emma raises her skirt just high enough to reveal the stash she has tied to her petticoat.

The usually tight-as-a-drum Pritchard laughs out loud. "Well done!"

Nathaniel opens his eyes to what surely must seem a vision: Emma pulling warm, dry clothing from beneath her skirts. It takes all his energy to twist himself into the clothes that hang loose on his fragile frame.

"We'll get you to our house, where you'll be warm, well-fed, and safe," I tell him. How we'll do that without drawing suspicion, I haven't a clue.

"How can I thank you?" Nathaniel asks.

"You can get well and help us bring out other men," Pritchard says as we approach the dock.

Waiting near the landing is a wagon loaded with fish. The driver waves at us, and I fear we've been found out.

"That's Matthew Kittridge," the lieutenant says. "He's one of ours."

I recognize him as the man I met earlier in the shadows. But now he's dressed as a fishmonger.

"He catches and sells cod for a living," Pritchard says. "He picks up a lot of useful information at the docks."

"Why is he here?" I ask. "He might draw attention to us."

"Quite the opposite. He'll hide Nathaniel under his catch and give you all a ride home."

"I'm sure you'll be quite comfortable," Pritchard tells Emma, helping her onto the bench seat next to Kittridge. He doesn't offer to help me, but he lifts the tarp-wrapped Nathaniel like a matchstick and gently lowers him into the wagon's depths. Mr. Kittridge covers him with what seems like two tons of cod. "You'll get accustomed to the smell, son."

"I reckon I smell worse than they do," Nathaniel says from beneath the odorous pile.

"I reckon you do. You'll need a good scrubbing when we get home."

"Emma! Leave the poor man be," I say. "He's been through enough."

We lumber through the back streets. Emma is slumped over and silent.

"Next time we'll bring Tom out," I tell her.

"God willing there be a next time."

With each creak of the wagon, I worry about finally arriving home. Mother has no idea what we're doing. I figured she'd accept Tom; even though he's a rebel, he's from Essex and he's Emma's brother. But dragging home a stranger, one who fought against the British, is another thing entirely. She'd sooner let a thief into the house.

"What will we tell your mother?" Emma says as if she'd read my thoughts.

"I don't know. Maybe nothing."

"I hope you don't think you can hide him in the attic, or something crazy like that," she says.

Suddenly, that seems like the only thing to do, at least for a day or two until we come up with a plan.

"Good idea, Emma."

"You're a lunatic," she says. "We'll all die for sure.

"Why do you always think the worst?" Maybe, I figure, because she's a lot more logical than I am.

Mr. Kittridge steers his rig into the narrow back alley behind the house. Mother is gone, and she's taken Benjamin with her. He scoops a mountain of fish off Nathaniel and helps the poor, dripping boy up to the landing by the back steps.

"He needs water and food," I say.

"He needs a bath before anything else," Emma says. She fetches a stool and a bucket of cold water, and he scrubs himself to her satisfaction, while I head to the kitchen and make some tea. No sooner do I set down his teacup than he gulps it down with bread and jam, barely pausing for a breath.

"Go easy! Or it'll make you sicker," I warn. He sips the tea and within minutes he's asking for more.

"Only if you take it slowly," I say.

After a half hour, he seems stronger. "Rest," I tell him. But he wants to talk, and his story comes out in a rush.

He was 16 and a blacksmith's apprentice from Connecticut when he signed on with Washington. He met Tom at the Battle of Brooklyn when both were taken captive.

"We had barely enough food as soldiers, and we'd raid the farmlands for watermelon and corn," he recalls. "But that was a feast compared to the ship."

Then he tells us about the raw, putrid meat and all the other horrors below decks in the *Defiance*: the suffocating heat, the snow piling up on the men as it whips through the gaps of the boarded-up portholes. And there were the visions: the angels and devils, the long-dead loved ones, the hallucinations from being trapped like rats in a cage.

I'm fascinated, knowing I'll write it all down in my diary. What I don't understand is how any human being can do these things to another.

We hear Mother return, and I caution Nathaniel not to make a sound. Then Emma and I lope down the stairs to make it appear as if nothing is awry.

"How was your trip out to the *Defiance*?" Mother asks.

I empty the pouch and a dozen coins fill her hands. "We took a respectable amount off their hands," I tell her.

"Not as much as last week," she says. "Perhaps next Sunday will be better." Will she ever be satisfied with anything I do?

At dinner, Mother fills a platter with cornbread and chicken, payment for her latest birthing. When she isn't looking, I fill my napkin with as much food as I can shovel off my plate.

"My goodness you're hungry today, Sarah," she says.

"It's especially good, Mother."

"Thank you my dear and thank the Lord for his blessings."

"I certainly will."

Later, Mother dozes off in her rocking chair, and her Bible falls on the floor. She doesn't stir, so I take my food-soaked napkin up to the attic for Nathaniel.

He eagerly takes it. Already he looks better, but I wonder how long we can hide him.

I get my answer a few hours later when we awake to the awful sounds of retching and moaning. It's Nathaniel, and I rush upstairs in my nightgown. Mother is on my heels, armed with a fireplace poker.

"Who's there?" she yells.

Nathaniel is on his knees before a wash basin, choking up the last of the chicken and cornbread.

"Who are you?" she demands as he wipes his face with his arm.

"Mother, it's all right," I say as calmly as I can.

"He doesn't look all right. Tell me this instant what this is about."

"We found him this morning when we were walking home," I say. Then I recite the story that Emma and I rehearsed. How we found him shivering, half dead, in the bushes near the waterfront.

"He managed to escape from one of the prison ships," I say. "I don't know how."

"A rebel in my house?" Mother shrieks. "Is there a reward?"

Then I tell her everything Nathaniel told us about the ships. I leave out nothing. By this time Emma has joined us.

"You won't turn him in, will you?" Emma pleads.

"He's just skin and bones," Mother finally says. "Just a boy."

Nathaniel has crawled back onto the bed, but he's shivering again.

Mother feels his forehead. "He's feverish. Sarah, bring me a basin of cool water and a cloth."

Relieved, I head down the stairs. Mother won't do anything rash, at least not now. She doesn't have it in her bones to turn her back on the sick. No matter who it is. I feel a surge of love for her as I return with the basin. She's talking to him softly, gently examining him.

"He's had dysentery so long he can't even keep water down," she says. "And the welts on his back are infected."

Emma gasps. "Poor soul."

"He's a sick boy," Mother says, standing up beside the bed. "I'll fetch my bag and see which herbs will best help him."

"I think I've been visited by angels," he moans. Then he goes back to sleep.

# Chapter Twenty-Eight

Mother barely leaves Nathaniel's bedside over the next week. Gradually his fever lifts, and he's able to keep soup down, but she insists he stays in bed. I admit I'm a bit jealous of how she fusses over him.

Emma sees her dear Dan at the Pendletons' house the following week. To hear her tell it, the most exciting moment was when he kissed her neck in the pantry. She's so smitten she nearly forgot to tell me the best part.

"Oh, he said to tell you that the rescue worked so well that he wants to do it again this Sunday and the Sunday after that."

"Best news ever!" I say. "But I just want Tom to be the next one."

"The ladies from the Holy Ground are eager to provide their services again," Emma says. The last trip proved more lucrative than an entire week's earnings. I'm curious how well the lieutenant is acquainted with the patriotic prostitutes, but I'm not about to broach it with Emma.

"Dan said he would somehow get a message to Tom," she says.

"Hopefully, this time he'll have the sense to save himself," I say, laughing at my own stupid joke.

• • •

At the *Loyal Gazette*, Jonah spends the morning lecturing me on the futility of the rebels' fight while he unpacks the newest books from London.

"They can't hang on much longer, and when it's all over, they'll pay a steep price," he says. "You'll see."

I fear he's right, but I do a silent "Hallelujah!" every time they gain a small victory.

For the second time in as many days, a gentleman drops in to ask if Jonah might have a copy of John Milton's long, century-old poem, "Paradise Lost." Each time he has a copy sitting on his desk, ready to go.

"Why the sudden popularity of 'Paradise Lost'?" I ask him. It was a tedious, boring, incomprehensible read, even for me.

"It's a favorite of the King," he says. "I'm surprised you didn't know that, a refined lady of your intellect."

It's pointless to try to get anything else out of the old coot. I settle into my work, setting type for an ad drawing people to Flynn's Market for fresh cod and lamb.

All I can think about is the stranger hiding in the attic and the upcoming trip to rescue Tom. Does Pritchard expect us to house a parade of near-dead prisoners pulled from the harbor waters? A terrifying, yet exciting, thought.

My diary is crammed with details from Nathaniel's account. Now I'm sure the prisoners' treatment on the other ships is just as gruesome. Why doesn't someone put a stop to it? Jonah won't touch it. Maybe the *New York Bugler* would, as the owners are rebel sympathizers. I'm about to sneak out and pay them a visit when I come to my senses. They'll never trust a girl, especially a girl who works for Jonah Livingston, defender of the King.

Jonah leaves for the coffeehouse, and I'm glad to be rid of him. I set the type for an article about the King's latest speech to Parliament. It's pure hogwash. He's a tyrant who would tax everything from stamps to playing cards and dice, and we have every right to rebel against him. I wonder what Father would say about my change of heart. And I wonder why his opinion is still so important to me.

165

Jonah returns sputtering. "What are you fussing about?" I ask.

"Someone in our ranks has cozied up to the rebels."

"You mean a turncoat? How do you know this?"

"A most reliable source: Captain Pendleton."

Instantly, I grip the edge of the desk for balance. "How does Pendleton know this?" I pretend to look disinterested and fiddle with my hair.

"They somehow got their hands on the signal code."

"What?" I have no idea what he's talking about.

"The signal code!" he bellows. "The signals the British use aboard their ships."

I'm still confused.

"It's how the ships talk to each other. If you weren't so dimwitted, you'd know how crucial it is during battle."

I'm so relieved it has nothing to do with Nathaniel's rescue that I let pass his boorish comment.

"Pendleton is blind with rage," Jonah says. "He's turning his ships inside out to find the turncoat. I'd hate to be that sorry bastard."

Suddenly, I'm desperate to know if Dan Pritchard's days are numbered. If he's caught, would he be tortured and tell everything? I watch the clock until I can leave.

• • •

Racing up the front steps, I fling the door open and scream, "Emma! Emma!"

"Lower your voice," Mother orders. "You'll wake Nathaniel."

"Where's Emma?"

"She's not home yet, and I'm starting to worry. Perhaps you should walk toward the Pendletons' in case she had a mishap on the way home."

Mishap? Mother makes it sound as if she's skinned her knee. I have visions of Emma and the lieutenant behind bars.

"I'll have a look," I say. As I hurry toward the Pendletons' stately brick home, I glance down the side streets for a glimpse of her. Nothing but a few chickens. Tom will never forgive me if something happens to Emma.

I'm out of breath when I spot her with Pritchard, huddled in deep conversation behind the Presbyterian Meeting House.

"Emma!"

"Hush!" Emma beckons me into the doorway. "Pendleton is on a rampage."

"I know. Does he suspect you?" I ask the lieutenant.

"I don't think so. He still hopes I'll help him ferret out the traitor. He's either confiding in me or playing me for a fool."

He wraps his arm around Emma's shoulder and draws her near. I can see she's been crying.

"What now?" I ask him. I know that he can make his way back to Washington's lines, and we'd likely never see him again or Tom.

"I'm of more use if I stay right here, passing on information about the British as long as I'm able," he says calmly. I'm in awe of this man of few words, and I'm relieved.

"You mean you'll help us rescue Tom?" I ask.

"Sarah, you can't ask him to—"

"Yes. I'll get that message to him."

We walk home, all three of us. He and Emma are so moony over each other that I truly want to be sick.

# Chapter Twenty-Nine

Mother is on the front steps, waiting for us.

"Why Lieutenant Pritchard, how nice of you to walk Emma home. Won't you come in for a cup of tea?"

I know instantly what Mother is up to. Poor Dan looks hopelessly trapped.

"How nice of you," he says, and we all traipse inside.

Over steaming tea, we stumble through the most awkward conversation ever held. Mother harps about the rebels and their senseless war, and Dan tries his best to agree with her on every point. Meanwhile, Nathaniel sleeps upstairs.

I keep my mouth shut, hoping the torture ends soon. Emma is just happy to be with Dan, all decked out in his splendid red uniform. She even pats his hand at one point.

Mother can't stop gushing. "I was so pleased when Mrs. Pendleton told me you'd become acquainted with Emma."

Pritchard's face turns the same shade as his uniform. I see beads of sweat on his forehead.

"Oh, now I've made you blush. Have some more," Mother says, grabbing the teapot.

"No thank you. You're too kind, but I must return. The captain will need me."

"Yes, Mrs. Pendleton told me the captain won't rest until he catches the turncoat spilling secrets to the rebels. If that weren't enough, he's hunting down another escaped prisoner. I don't suppose you know anything about that, do you?"

I can't believe Mother's audacity. What will she say next?

"I can assure you, Mrs. Barrett, that British forces will bring both to justice in no time," he says. "That prisoner will have even more welts on his back from the beating I'll personally give him."

He starts to get up. "Now I must be going, ladies."

Before he's out of his chair, we hear a wracking, wall-cracking cough. Nathaniel has awakened.

Mother gives me a desperate look. Dan ignores the noise. "I enjoyed our tea. Thank you for your kindness." Another series of explosive coughs followed by a thunderous sneeze.

Dan is halfway to the door. "Emma, I'll see you soon."

"Just a moment, lieutenant," Mother calls after him.

He stops and turns to face her.

"Aren't you the least bit curious about that noise?" she asks. "With an escaped prisoner on the loose."

Sweat is dripping off Dan's cheeks and onto his collar. "Well, of course, I—"

"And how would you know about the welts on the prisoner's back?" Mother is out of her chair, inches from his face. "It's you, isn't it? The turncoat!"

At that moment, Nathaniel ventures down the stairs with his empty teacup, shambling into the kitchen wrapped in one of Mother's old quilts. How can this disaster get any worse?"

He sees a British officer and shakily turns on his heels.

"Hello Nathaniel," Pritchard says.

Nathaniel is confused. "You're here to arrest me?"

"I see the two of you are acquainted," Mother asserts as if she's just inserted the final piece of the puzzle.

"I'm not going to lie to you, Mrs. Barrett," Dan says. "I helped

Sarah and Emma rescue Nathaniel from the *Defiance*."

"Is that true?" Mother asks, glaring at me.

I nod, and the whole sorry story comes out.

"I'm surrounded by liars and lies," Mother says, clearly disgusted with all of us. "I don't know who to believe. Sarah, I don't know that I can ever trust you again."

I can't think of a single thing to say in my defense.

"And as for you, Lieutenant Pritchard, turncoat, spy, or whatever you call yourself," Mother hisses, "I need utter just one word to Mrs. Pendleton, and you too can call yourself a prisoner. That's what any right-minded person loyal to the Crown would do."

"No Mother! You can't," I cry.

"And why not?" she says.

"Tom. He expects to be rescued Sunday. If we're not there at the *Defiance*, he'll be stranded in the water and drown for sure. We need Lieutenant Pritchard to row us out there."

"Please Mrs. Barrett," Emma pleads. "He'll die on that ship."

"I'll die for all my sins," Mother says. "I'm hiding a rebel, consorting with a spy, and now you want me to hide yet another rebel? I'm glad your father isn't here to see his daughter conspiring with the enemy."

"This will be the end of it," I say. "Just this one time, for Tom." If she knew of Dan's hopes for freeing a stream of prisoners, it would kill her.

She grabs her ever-present Bible and presses it to her chest. "Oh Lord in Heaven, why hast thou forsaken me?"

"Mrs. Barrett," Pritchard says calmly. "I understand your dismay. Turn me in to the authorities if you feel so compelled. But I'll not stop working for General Washington. And I'll not stop helping the prisoners on those ships. Just imagine if one of them was your son."

I gulp. Dan has said the worst thing imaginable. But it's too late.

"Don't ever, ever bring up my son in defense of your rotten cause!" Mother shrieks. "He would be here today if the rebels in New Hampshire hadn't shot him dead."

"Mother, it was an accident," I say.

She looks at me as if I'm the devil herself. "How could you defend his murder! Do you not have eyes? Did you not see those miserable scum come to our home and turn your brother's heart against us?"

"Mother, Seth believed in the cause," I try to reason. "Father objected. Then things got out of hand, and a rebel, a boy, shot him."

"Enough!" Mother yells. "You, in your British finery, get out of my house right now."

Dan is thoroughly beaten. He puts on his hat and walks out without even a glance at Emma.

I'm stunned too. "Mother, what are you going to do now?" Will she go straight to Pendleton and turn him in? Maybe even turn in all of us?

"I don't know," she says wearily.

• • •

An hour later I hear Emma sobbing in her room. I knock softly.

"Go away!"

"Please, Emma. I know you feel awful, and I want to help."

"How can you possibly help? I'll never see him again."

"You don't know that." My upbeat chirping fails to convince even me.

"I never should have come to New York and let you talk me into this mess."

I have no answer to that. It's true. I've tangled her up in something dangerous. Not only that, but I've led her to the man she loves, and now he's gone.

I start to walk away, then I hear her door creak open. "Come in if you must," she sniffles.

Emma's eyes are so puffy they look like little slits. Her nose is running. She's never looked so miserable, huddled under her yellow quilt, and now she asks something else I can't begin to answer.

"Why does bad luck always find me?"

It's true. She'd likely be married to my brother Seth by now if he hadn't been killed. At the time, I was so upset about losing him that I paid scant attention to her pain.

"Your mother will probably turn in Dan."

"She won't!" I say with certainty. Having brought so many souls into the world, she wouldn't deliberately snuff one out. Of course, she never got over Seth's death and the cruelty directed at Father. The so-called patriots burned down his newspaper office and melted his type for bullets. They threw him in jail when he wouldn't sign their stupid loyalty oath.

For a moment, I don't know which side is worse. But Tom's fate is looming over us.

"Emma, we can't abandon Tom."

"As if we have a choice! We can't possibly rescue him without Dan."

"What makes you think we've seen the last of Dan?" I'm willing to throw out any scrap of hope if it makes her feel better.

She looks skeptical. I push the straight-back chair close to the bed and sit down.

"As long as Mother doesn't turn him in, he's safe. Captain Pendleton will never suspect trustworthy Dan. And remember: Dan said we should all proceed as if nothing is amiss. So another trip out to the *Defiance* won't appear out of place."

Emma has stopped sniffling. "How can we be sure your mother won't go to Pendleton?"

"Leave it to me," I say without a hint of a plan.

# Chapter Thirty

Nathaniel Fox gradually grows stronger, but he isn't safe anywhere except in the attic. Harboring an escaped rebel, even a sickly one, is the very definition of treason. Mother reminds us of this constantly, but still, she sits by his bed, checking for fever, preparing herbal remedies, and tending the welts on his back.

Back in Connecticut, Nathaniel apprenticed for a blacksmith who organized the local militia when the first shots rang out in 1775. Only 16, he went off to fight, against his mother's wishes. His father and his two brothers also signed on, leaving his mother and sister to manage the farm.

Mother takes quite a liking to him, even knitting him a pair of stockings. He knows his Bible, and the two of them playfully try to top each other with verses from scripture.

Nathaniel often thanks her for her hospitality with a warning from Proverbs: "Withdraw thy foot from thy neighbor's house: lest he be weary of thee, and so hate thee."

But Mother bats him away with a quotation from Matthew: "For I was hungry, and ye gave me meat: I was thirsty, and ye gave me drink: I was a stranger, and ye took me in …"

They laugh while Emma and I roll our eyes.

He tells her about a girl he fancies back in Connecticut. He blushes easily, his sandy hair falling over his brow. Slight of build, he's not much taller than me. Mother treats him with such tenderness, especially when he talks about the brutality on the ships, all done in the name of her precious Crown. Of course, I don't point that out to her. No use getting her worked up. So far, she hasn't spilled the beans.

But I know she's tormented. She prays even more than usual and pores over her Bible seeking guidance. She and Nathaniel study the Book of Job and discuss it for days. She's walking in Job's footsteps, her faith in God tested by one tragedy after another, or so she thinks. I don't understand why she's so conflicted. It's clear to me she should do whatever it takes to get suffering men off the ships, but she doesn't want my opinion.

We all know that as soon as Nathaniel is well enough, he'll make his way back to Connecticut. It'll be a dangerous journey. British soldiers stop everyone traveling through New York.

Luckily, I've come up with the perfect strategy. Emma will sew him a black linen shirt, white collar, and black cloak for the journey. And he'll carry an eloquent letter from the Church of England certifying that Anglican minister Luther Williams is entitled to unhindered passage. The letter, my contribution, will even display an official-looking stamp.

* * *

If matters aren't complicated enough, Emma arrives home a few nights later with a startling message. Captain and Mrs. Pendleton have invited Mother, Emma, and me to dinner. Even Benjamin is included.

"We value our loyal friends and want to share our bounty around the table. We have also invited Lt. Pritchard to join us," the elegantly written note says, hardly having to point out his tender connection to Emma.

"We can't possibly go," Emma says, as she lays out the dishes for supper. "It's too dangerous, especially if your mother takes the opportunity to denounce Dan."

I know it's dangerous, even foolhardy. But there's something intriguing about working behind enemy lines.

Emma gives me a horrified look. "You aren't seriously thinking of going, are you?"

"Well, it might be helpful."

"Or insane," she says, ladling cabbage soup into bowls. "Your mother won't be in the same house with Dan, much less sit at the same table. She'd shriek traitor till the walls fell in."

"Maybe not," I say, snatching a hunk of cornbread and stuffing it in my mouth. "I'll talk to her."

"And say what? It was all a misunderstanding?"

"No. Too late for that now. Maybe I can appeal to her softer side."

"Sarah, there was nothing soft about the way she ordered Dan out of the house. I think you're crazy."

"Maybe so, but I have to try."

I have my chance after Mother emerges from the attic with a supper tray for Nathaniel.

"He ate every bit of it," I say. "Soon he'll be well enough to be on his way."

"Not just yet," she says. "He needs to get his strength back." It's clear she can't bear to have him leave. Suddenly I see a way into her heart.

I tell her about the dinner invitation, and she reacts predictably. "I will not dine with him, not for a minute! I owe the Pendletons the truth. They've been very kind to us."

"But Mother, if you do that, we'll all be found out. Emma, Nathaniel, me, even you. Nathaniel will be hauled back to the ship and beaten to death. Tom will have no chance of escaping. And you'll be tried as a traitor for harboring an escapee."

"Me? A traitor?" She looks at me with angry eyes. The last time I talked to her that way, she slapped me. It's different this time.

"He's just a boy," she says, her voice softening. "A sick boy." I hear her resistance giving way.

• • •

We arrive at the Pendletons' in our Sunday best. Even Benjamin

175

is scrubbed and looks more like a little boy now that he is wearing breeches. Of course, Emma has spent an hour arranging her hair.

Amanda, the Pendletons' servant, answers the door and leads us into the parlor where a mahogany grandfather clock towers over us and the gold wallpaper gleams. Barely my age, Amanda says little, but she's happy to see Emma, a familiar face. She arrived from Vienna several months ago as an indentured servant. Emma told me the whole story.

The children immediately corner Emma and demand a story.

"No, she's our guest tonight," Mrs. Pendleton says, shooing them away. "Come in everyone, the lieutenant is already here." She gives Emma a sly look. "He's in the study with the captain."

The door to the study is closed, and I hear loud voices from within. My stomach jumps, and I see the pinched look on Mother's face. The men emerge a moment later, and from the angry look on the captain's face, it seems they've had a row.

Mother springs into action. "How good of you to have us for dinner. I've brought you the last of the apples from our trees." Not quite the last ones, I think to myself. Emma and I set aside nearly a bushel of them for our next trip out to the *Defiance*.

Mrs. Pendleton hands the apples to Amanda. "These will make a fine applesauce," she says. "Thank you, my dear. Now, everyone gather around the table before the food gets cold."

In the dining room, she seats Emma next to Lt. Pritchard, of course. Emma gives him a dazzling smile that I think is excessive. I can't take my eyes off the fine china and silverware, and the embroidered damask tablecloth.

Then the captain struts in and refills his glass with rum. He sits down at the head of the table with only a quick word of greeting. His wig is freshly powdered, and his red uniform is spotless. He is much taller than Dan and gives off a commanding presence that scares even me.

I wonder if Mother feels the same way. Will she keep our secret or feel compelled to tell him everything? I can't tell by her face, but I see the contempt in her eyes when Dan sits across from her.

"Let us bow our heads in prayer," the captain says. "Thank you,

Lord, for the bounty we're about to eat. And may you see your way to turn this battle in favor of our beloved King." I don't bow my head, and neither does Dan or Emma. We all exchange a look, hoping we'll survive the night. The captain drains his glass and demands another. Mrs. Pendleton ever so slightly scowls.

She recovers quickly with a big smile directed at Mother. "I'd like to commend Mrs. Barrett for her kindness and charity toward all the women of our city. This dinner is meager thanks for her hard work. Without her expert care, they would surely suffer greatly."

"You must be talking about the whores at the Holy Ground," the captain says, in a mocking manner. "Goodness no, we can't let these soiled lambs suffer even a moment for their sins."

"We'll discuss this later," says an embarrassed and angry Mrs. Pendleton. An awkward silence ends mercifully when Amanda, her blond hair wrapped in a braid around her head, brings out bowls of oyster stew made with thick cream and butter, and a hint of nutmeg. It's not at all like Mother's watery soup. I try to eat slowly and delicately, like Emma, but it's too good, and I slurp until Mother gives me one of her icy looks.

"I trust your men are faring well, Captain Pendleton," Mother asks.

"Not well at all." His tone is loud and gruff. "We lost in Saratoga." He's slurring his words, and Mrs. Pendleton is uncomfortable. That doesn't stop him from opening a bottle of French wine and pouring himself a full glass.

"And we have a spy in our midst, right here in New York. When I find him, I'd like to tear his heart out and stuff it down his throat."

I nearly choke on my soup. I don't dare look at Emma or Dan, but I hear gasps from all corners of the table and the captain realizes he went too far.

"Sorry, ladies. I do have strong feelings about the matter."

Then, to my horror, Mother speaks up calmly: "Not at all, captain. But how do you know there's a spy?"

She seems on the verge of thrusting a finger toward Dan. I hold my breath and wait for the awful truth to spill out.

But the captain heedlessly continues. "The rebels know about our plans before our soldiers do. Someone is leaking information, and I'll find him if it's the last thing I do."

"No doubt you will, sir," the lieutenant says. "But the trap you're proposing would be terrible for the men's morale."

I pray that's the end of it, but Mother has more to say. "If this traitor has any honor, he'll confess before he's found out." She looks straight at Dan. I realize my knuckles are going white because I'm holding my soup spoon so tight.

Dan looks straight back at Mother and advances his theory of honor. "Our man has lost faith in the Crown."

"Perhaps, but he's still a traitor," the captain booms.

Thankfully, Amanda bursts in to clear away the soup dishes. I'm relieved the meal is over so we can all go home soon. But she emerges from the kitchen with a platter of venison, followed by mashed potatoes, sweet potatoes, biscuits, and peas and baby onions in a creamy sauce. And more rum and French wine, which I've never tasted before.

I haven't seen that much food since Seth died and neighbors piled our table high with casseroles, breads, and pies. But now, no one has money for anything beyond the barest necessities, like Mother's abominable cabbage soup. Everything worth eating goes to the soldiers.

I can't take my eyes off the mounds of steaming food. I'm nearly drooling. In a feat of unimaginable strength, I regain my hold on reality. The spread laid out before us is a travesty. The more I look at it, the more incensed I grow. I can't let it alone.

"What a huge and magnificent dinner you've provided tonight," I say, smiling at Mrs. Pendleton, then the captain.

I think Mother will burst with pride as she beams at me. "There is more to come, so save room," Mrs. Pendleton says. "Amanda has made a custard pie, and chocolate pudding."

Chocolate! Mother must think she's dreaming. As much as I want to taste the chocolate pudding sliding down my throat, I'm overcome with self-righteousness. "How is it you have such luxuries when others are so needy?" I know immediately I've ruined the evening.

Mother's smile crumbles. Emma and Dan both look at me as if I've accused our generous hosts of theft and hypocrisy, which I suppose I have.

But the captain just laughs. A big hearty laugh that perplexes me.

"My dear, you have much to learn about war and Great Britain," he says. "The Crown always takes very good care of its commanding officers. That instills loyalty and respect among those in command and among those who are honored to be under their command."

Mother relaxes as if a disaster has just been averted. But I can't let go of it.

"The soldiers are wanting, and the men are starving on the prison ships," I say as the ruddy captain takes another huge gulp.

Then he gives me a condescending smile. "Well, my dear, that's why I'm happy to have you and your mother peddle your wares, your food, or whatever you have to the guards and those rebel prisoners. It helps the Crown, and it certainly brings your mother a little cash."

"But we can't possibly feed—"

"Enough talk about the bloody prisoners," he bellows. "Let us raise our glasses in a final toast."

We all raise our glasses, even me, though with some reluctance.

"To the King," he says. "May he continue to provide us with what we need to finish this war once and for all."

"To the King," Dan echoes with enthusiasm. I think Mother's eyes will pop out of her head.

We finish the meal mostly in silence. Mother glares at me. We say our goodbyes, and Mother leads us out with an exceptionally firm grip on my arm. Thank God she also kept a grip on her very own mouth.

# Chapter Thirty-One

It's cold and rainy at daybreak Sunday when I awake to thunder. For a moment I've forgotten that I slept in my clothes to save time. Sliding out of bed, I slip on my shoes and tiptoe down the stairs.

Our basket of food is by the door. Beside it is the folded red uniform Pritchard snatched from a guard, and shoes I bought from the cobbler. I traded one of Jonah's new books for them.

A year ago, I would have thought long and hard before stealing so much as a sheet of paper. But these days I'm desperate to free Tom, whatever the cost. Jonah won't miss his book, though the soldier will miss his uniform. Neither troubles my conscience at all.

Emma finally emerges from her room, wearing her yellow gown, with her blond hair combed and piled neatly under a yellow bonnet adorned with yellow and blue ribbons.

"We're not going to a ball, Emma," I say, wondering what lengths she'd go to if that were the case.

"I know. I like to look nice. You could at least wash your face."

Of course, she's dressing for Dan. I grab the basket and thrust the uniform and shoes at Emma. "Hide these in the other basket under a blanket. We'll put the apples on top."

The rain has slowed to a drizzle as we hurry along the quiet, wet streets. Other than the men working at the shipyard, we pass hardly anyone and that's a relief. The last thing we need is an inquisitive redcoat.

"This will never work," Emma says. "We'll be found out. Tom will be tortured, and Dan will be bludgeoned to death personally by that deranged Pendleton."

Emma dumping cold water on my plan does nothing to bolster my shaky confidence.

"Stop it! It worked before, and it'll work again." She knows, of course, that we'll be headed for the gallows if we're found out. I decide not to remind her of that sorry fact: No need for hysterics, is there?

"Captain Pendleton won't rest until he finds his so-called spy," Emma says. "Maybe he already knows and he's waiting to catch us in his trap."

"That's enough! And hurry up. We're already late, and you wouldn't want to keep Dan waiting, would you?"

After a few sighs and a nasty look in my direction, Emma pulls herself together. We hurry along the waterfront until we spot the lieutenant's docked boat. But as we get closer, there's no sign of him. We wait on the wharf, but there's nothing. Emma is close to despair.

"I knew it," she cries. "It's over."

Her face is white and her lower lip trembles. "We never should have come. Let's get out of here."

"No! What about Tom? What if he's heaved overboard like some actual corpse, and we're not there to pull him from the water?"

Emma stares straight through me. "Do you care for him so much that you'd risk all our lives? I don't think so. I think you love the notoriety of being the heroine in this little novel you've created. Or maybe you look at this adventure as fodder for your diary; the real-life story of the first woman to become an honest-to-God American patriot."

I can't deny that seeing my name in print would be the most thrilling thing I can imagine. But I'm also feeling things the likes of which I've never felt before, feelings with a far deeper imprint than words on a page.

"Emma, I do care about Tom, a lot. Is that so hard to believe?"

"Yes, it is. Just look at yourself. You slept in your dress. Your hair is a tangled mess, and your head wouldn't know a proper bonnet."

It's all true. How could Tom or anyone find me appealing? Samuel doesn't count. He considered me a challenge, someone to clean up and turn into a lady.

"Let's go home," Emma says, picking up a basket. "Without Dan, we have no way to get out to the ship. Tom will have to wait. God willing, he can keep himself alive."

I can't give up that easily. "No, Emma. We can do this."

"We can do what?"

"Row ourselves out to the ship. We'll do just what we planned. Tom is expecting us. We have to try. We might not have another chance."

I step into the boat and take my seat between the oars. "Are you coming?"

"You're going to row us out there? We needn't worry about being hanged. We'll drown first."

"If you don't get in right now, I'll leave without you."

"I can't let you drown alone," she says. "I must be as crazy as you." Emma lifts her voluminous skirts and lumbers into the boat. "Do you even know how to work the oars?"

"Of course! I rowed Seth's boat on the pond in Essex."

"You might have noticed that this isn't the town pond, Sarah," she said.

"I know, I know, but I've seen Dan untie the ropes and row us out to the ship so many times. How difficult can it be?" I grab the oars, push off and soon find out. We bob in a full, vicious circle before I gain control.

The water is choppy, and the drizzle persists. I'm cold at first but after rowing a few minutes I'm sweating, my shoulders ache, and I doubt I can make it all the way to the ship, much less return. Emma must have read my mind.

"It's not too late to turn around."

"No!" I keep rowing, though I feel blisters forming on my hands.

The waves come crashing over the sides the farther we go, and at times it seems we're going backwards.

"Do you want my help?" Emma asks. "I could take a turn with the oars."

"No!" Despite the exhaustion, I have to do it myself.

Emma looks disgusted. "You're the most stubborn person I know."

Finally, when I think my arms will fall off, the *Defiance* comes into view. As best I can, I sidle up to her, arriving with a loud crunch. The men on the top deck break into laughter and cheers.

"Ladies, you are a grand sight," one of them yells.

I tie up the boat with the thick, heavy rope in the bow, trying my best to emulate the knot Pritchard usually makes. We struggle up the gangway with our baskets. Emma's gown is drenched. I'm a mess too, sweat-soaked and streaked with grime from the oars. It's no matter to the men crowding around us.

There's no sign of Dan and, even more worrisome, no sign of any blanket-wrapped dead prisoners about to be thrown overboard like so much trash. The men wrestle over the apples, and everything is gone in minutes. My apron clinks with coins. We can't stay on board any longer. We'll have to row back without our scheme to pick up the "dead" Tom even getting a chance.

Suddenly, the men stand at attention, and I hear heavy footsteps behind me.

"Good morning, ladies," a deep voice booms.

I whirl around and there's Pendleton, towering over me. I feel my legs wobble.

"I suppose you're wondering what has happened to your Lieutenant Pritchard," he says.

I have no chance to answer.

"Well, I've taken care of him. He'll rue the day he decided to turn against King and country."

"Where is he?" Emma demands.

"He's a prisoner now, just like the other fools in the belly of this ship, licking his wounds from the flogging my men gave him."

Emma lets out an anguished cry. She is about to lose control and say God knows what. I say the first idiotic thing that occurs to me.

"Thank the Lord, you uncovered him for what he is, Captain Pendleton," I say, with totally believable phony indignation. "A spy right under our noses. It just makes my blood boil."

Emma looks at me with disbelief, dabs at her eyes, and regains her composure. "I hope he rots in hell."

I want to applaud her acting skills, but Pendleton isn't so easily taken in.

"Ladies, let's be honest."

My heart stops. Emma's jaw drops. He's on to us.

"Emma, I know that he blinded you with his professed love. But we've all been fooled by Cupid at some time, my dear. You might not believe me, but you'll get over it."

"Yes," Emma says without missing a beat. "Thank you for understanding, sir."

"I was taken in too," he says. "But fortunately, we have spies of our own who alerted us to this beastly turncoat. And by the time I finish with him, he'll give up the names of others—every one of the others—who've turned against the Crown."

Now I stifle a gasp. Who would turn in Dan? And would he name names—our names—under threat of torture?

"Well Captain, you're to be congratulated for your shrewd work. The King will raise a glass and toast your name," I say, feeding his enormous ego.

"I think I'll go below and do exactly that." He turns to his motley crew and urges them to join him in the galley. "Men, come and indulge in a dram of rum to celebrate my ... that is, our ... success."

"We'll take our leave now," I tell the pompous fool. "May this war end soon, and may the Crown be the victor."

"Thank you, ladies, for your service."

Just then another booming voice breaks the silence. "Prisoners! Bring up your dead!" The skeletal prisoners from down below, haul motionless bundles onto the deck. Each lands with a thud. I don't pray at all, but I pray Tom is among them.

By now the captain and his men are swigging their rum. Their inattention—and the dense fog blanketing Wallabout Bay—will be Tom's only chance.

Emma and I race for the gangway and practically leap into the boat.

"Don't say a word," I whisper. "They can still hear us." I take the oars with shaking hands and push off from the ship with a clatter, the oars squeaking with every stroke. I listen for the loud splash, signaling the first body flung overboard.

"Make yourself useful and tear the bottom off your petticoat," I tell Emma.

"Have you gone mad?"

"No! We can wrap the oarlocks, so they won't squeak."

She shrugs, then goes about pulling her petticoat apart. She hands me the bits of cloth without a word. Suddenly I realize her grief. "I'm so sorry Emma. Perhaps it isn't as bad as he made it sound."

"How can you find any hope in what he said?"

We're interrupted by a cry from the ship: "Heave ho, and may the sharks feast on rebel meat!" Then a splash, followed by another and another. Five altogether. The fog is thick as a good chowder. I scan the rough water for Tom. Nothing.

We wait, not daring to breathe, speak or move. Emma looks horrified. I refuse to think the worst.

"Maybe he wasn't among the dead this time," I whisper. "Maybe he's still on the ship." I can't tell her what I'm really thinking that he was unable to free himself from the blanket and has drowned, a victim of his own burial at sea. Maybe we asked too much of a man weakened by sickness and starvation. Guilt settles into my bones, where it feels all too familiar.

As we sit there in the gray nothingness, the only sound is a loon calling its mate with a quivering crazy laugh. Maybe he's mocking us for thinking we could do the impossible.

"Stupid bird," I mutter.

Then Emma's face lights up. "It's not a bird."

# Chapter Thirty-Two

"It's Tom! He's signaling us," she says. Frantically, we scan the water, but the fog is an impenetrable gray wall. Then we hear it again, that quivering warble. Maybe it's just a bird, I think.

"I know it's Tom," she insists. "He could imitate the loon call perfectly. It would drive Mother crazy."

Again, we hear it. It seems to be coming from the direction of the shore. I grab the oars and row as fast as I can. My achy arms come back to life.

"Over there, to the left," Emma whispers. "I see something. Can't you row any faster?"

I dig the oars deep in the water and pull with all my might.

"There he is!" Emma points at a small lump in the water. I row toward it, my arms and shoulders screaming.

"Yes, it must be him! Hurry!"

He's barely afloat, his face down. He could have been mistaken for a sodden log. When we finally reach him, I shove the oars aside and grab his hair, pulling his head out of the water. He takes in desperate, deep, choking breaths.

"Tom, you must be as quiet as you can," I whisper. "We're still close to the ship." He looks at me with faraway eyes, and I worry that it's too late, that he can't comprehend anything.

He moans softly as we each grab an arm and hoist his upper body into the boat. Then we grab his legs. It's easier than we think. His limbs are like willow branches, his body a bundle of bones that stick out everywhere from his taut skin.

And he's completely naked.

I try not to look but I can't help myself. I've never seen a naked man … only the baby boys I've helped Mother deliver.

Tom's breathing is ragged, but his eyes are alert now and darting about. They catch mine, then he looks away embarrassed.

"Emma, the blanket," I say.

I wrap him in it, but it doesn't calm his shaking. Even his teeth rattle. His face is so hollow, there's only a hint of the boy I once knew. I draw him close, hoping the warmth of my body will warm him. We sit like that for a few minutes, and gradually the shaking subsides.

"Is it really you, Sarah?" he whispers through chattering teeth.

"Yes. And Emma too."

"I've only dreamed of this moment."

"Freedom?" I ask.

"No, this moment with you."

Breathing, I fear, will ruin the moment.

"We must get ashore quickly," I say. "Stay hidden under the blanket."

"Tom, I have clothes for you," Emma says. "We'll get you into a warm bath as soon as possible. You may not be aware, but you stink worse than the foulest privy in all of New York.

"Thank you, dear sister," he says, his mocking voice weak with exhaustion.

I can just barely make out the outline of the docks on shore, but I row with what little strength I have left. My dirt-spattered dress is drenched from wrapping my body around Tom, and the wind feels raw on my skin. My cap has blown into the water, leaving my hair wild and free. I've never felt happier.

Before we reach the dock, Emma helps Tom put on the British

uniform we brought. It hangs so loose on his scrawny frame that he looks like a child playing soldier.

"I feel like a downright rat in this red abomination," he says, his voice hoarse.

"But you'll fit right in," I say. "We don't want to draw attention." Right, I silently figure. Who would possibly notice two young women with rain-soaked, clinging dresses shuffling down the street with a famine victim in uniform?

The shoes are too big, but they'll have to do. It doesn't matter to Tom.

"I haven't worn shoes for so long, I forgot how they feel."

"Hush. Save your strength," Emma says as we reach the dock and tie up.

Tom winces as we pull him out of the boat. How will we even make it to the house? He can barely walk ten steps without stopping to rest.

He leans on us as we meander down alleys to avoid the few people in the street. We're a few blocks in when two redcoats stride around the corner.

"Well, what have we here?" one of them says.

My mouth goes dry. Tom looks about wildly as if he's about to make a desperate run for it.

"What are you three doing out here on a stormy Sunday morning?"

I should have come up with excuses in advance, but I didn't. I can't help but rely on the obvious.

"I'm afraid he's had too much drink. We're taking him somewhere to sleep it off before he embarrasses himself more."

Tom collapses, whether from exhaustion or in the spirit of playing the drunk, I'm not sure. Emma and I hoist him back onto his feet.

The redcoats eye him with disgust. Do they see through our ridiculous charade, or are they more put off by a young soldier who can't hold his liquor?

The men draw closer, and I feel uneasy. "I see by your red ribbons you ladies are loyal supporters of the Crown," the larger of the two says, visually fondling Emma from stem to stern.

The shorter one looks me over not quite as enthusiastically, but not put off by my rumpled appearance. "What you ladies need is a little companionship. Why don't you dispatch this fool drunkard and let a couple of real men show you a good time?"

Emma is appalled. "How dare you—"

"What my friend means," I interrupt, "is we couldn't possibly consider such a kind offer on the Sabbath." I just want to get away.

"And my employer, Captain Pendleton, wouldn't look favorably on two of his men accosting ladies on the street," Emma says, much to my surprise.

The mention of Pendleton stops them short.

"Then we'll be on our way, ladies. 'Tis your loss," the larger one says with a wink.

"I'm sure it is," I say, stone-faced, as they round the corner.

"You scared them straight," I say to Emma.

Tom rallies for a moment. "I was sure I was a goner."

"Now let's hurry home," I say, "before we pique someone else's interest."

# Chapter Thirty-Three

Mother takes Tom under her wing, just as she did Nathaniel. I knew she would. She was there in Essex tending his mother when he was born. She watched him grow up alongside Seth. With tenderness, she bathes him and cuts his hair. The wound on his leg from Bunker Hill is filthy and oozing again. She cleans it as best she can and applies a poultice. Just as I thought, she pays no mind to his political views.

"He's a very sick boy," she tells us at supper, between bites of porridge and biscuits. "His escape may have been too much for him. He's feverish, and if I can't bring it down …."

Emma sighs. "I've lost Dan … I can't lose Tom too. He's been through so much." Tears fill her eyes.

"Tom won't die. Mother will see to that," I say with as much confidence as I can muster. "And we can't even pretend to know Dan's fate for sure."

"Sarah, I'm not stupid. We both know the penalty for being a spy."

She's right. But she doesn't need to know that death would be welcome after the British torture him to their satisfaction.

Mother already has her arm around Emma in a comforting embrace. "Have faith, my dear."

I look at the two of them and feel so inadequate, so selfish, so thoughtless. Emma is grieving, and Mother knows exactly what to do. Why can't I be more like her?

I reach out to take Emma's hand, but she yanks it back. "Tom would have been better off on that terrible ship. You couldn't leave well enough alone!"

"I only wanted what's best for Tom," I tell her.

"Don't you mean what's best for you?" With that, she rises from the table and walks slowly upstairs like a woman condemned.

Frustrated, I turn to Mother. "I was trying to help her. We rescued Tom, and I just about killed myself doing it. She should be thankful, not mad."

"Sarah, she's had a terrible shock." Mother looks exhausted. Her blond hair has come loose from its bun. "Do you have feelings for Tom? Is that what Emma meant?"

I start to deny it, but I can tell she doesn't believe me. "Well, yes, a little. But that's not why I wanted to rescue him. I wanted to help Emma." So, what if that isn't exactly the truth? I'm not the selfish princess Emma thinks.

"We'll do our best to keep Tom alive," Mother says. "And, God willing, no harm comes to us for harboring a rebel—now, two rebels—in our house."

"Thank you, Mother." I long for her to embrace me, just as she did Emma, but she gathers the supper dishes in a sudden burst of activity.

"I fear the worst for Emma's handsome lieutenant," she says. "I know he betrayed the Crown, but I can't abide hanging him."

"I want to know who betrayed him to Pendleton."

"You certainly don't think it was me?"

"Of course not, Mother. How could you even think such a thing?" Maybe I did for a half-second, but I don't mention it. Besides, I'm already certain it was Samuel. He'd do anything to torment me and to advance his so-called career.

"What if Lieutenant Pritchard tells them we're running some kind of hospital for escaped rebels? I've got Benjamin to think of. Pritchard only has his own dismal soul to keep him from turning on us."

"He won't. He's an honorable man, and he loves Emma too much to cause her trouble." I want to believe that. I can't bear to think otherwise.

"But they'll surely try to beat the truth out of him."

"Mother! Stop it!" I can't take more of her hysterics, so I tell her I'm going up to check on Tom. Mother has been so protective of him that she shooed Emma and me away from his bedside. She made Nathaniel move to the tiny alcove near the kitchen.

But now she seems to sense some benefit in my attentiveness. "Don't tire the poor boy," she tells me. "And take him some white willow tea to bring down his fever. Add some mint to soothe his stomach."

Mother grows herbs in her garden for just about any ailment that afflicts her patients. She hangs the sprigs to dry on strings next to the hearth. Then, she stores them in little canisters, each labeled according to the herb.

I brew the tea while we wash the dishes and carry it to the attic without spilling a drop. He's asleep and doesn't wake even when I put the cup down with a clatter. I study his face, a more innocent countenance, now that Mother has cut his straggly mess of shoulder-length dark hair. His nose is prominent, his chin strong, his eyebrows dark and thick above his sunken eyes, and his cheeks pale and gaunt now that his beard is gone. Despite the look of starvation, I think him handsome.

I know he needs to sleep, but I want so much to talk. I whisper his name. Slowly his eyes open to little slits.

"Sarah?" His voice is hoarse and weak.

"Yes, I'm here. How are you feeling?"

"So tired." He takes my hand and closes his eyes.

"You're safe now. I've brought you some tea."

His hand is icy cold, and he shivers under the heavy quilt. He looks as near to death as anyone I've seen. If he dies, is it my fault? Was Emma, right? Would he have fared better on the ship? I force myself to bury that thought, but I've never succeeded in trying not to think of something.

The next morning Emma avoids me. I know it's no use trying to talk to her. She allows a tiny smile when Mother announces that Tom's fever has broken … another of God's miracles. I'm so thrilled that I race up the stairs and find him sitting up, trying to put on a shirt.

He smiles broadly. "Good morning, Sarah." His voice is stronger, but I have to steel myself when I see his bony ribs and shoulder blades.

"Mother says you may begin eating, but only little bits until your stomach adjusts."

"Good. I could eat a horse or two." He tries to stand but collapses back on the bed.

"Not so fast. Your fever could return. It will take a while to get your strength back."

"I just want the strength to stand up and hold you."

I resist throwing myself into his arms, knowing it could squeeze the life out of him. "Let's get you healthy first," I say, tucking the quilt around him. "I'll bring you some gruel and bread with jam, then I must be off to work. But Mother will take care of your needs better than I could anyway."

He already looks sleepy again. "When you come back, you'll tell me all about your day." He squeezes my hand, and I think my heart will explode.

· · ·

I should have known Jonah would hear all about Lt. Pritchard before I hurry into the *Loyal Gazette*.

"I can't wait until they hang him," he says to me. "Just like that other incompetent spy, Nathan Hale. He wished he had but one life to give for his country; I wish he could have died a hundred times over! And as soon as they capture those two prisoners that Pritchard set free, they'll hang too."

I wince and don't even wait for him to tell me, yet again, that war is no place for women.

"If I don't share your enthusiasm for seeing a man die, then so be it!" I shout.

Jonah backs off. "Wasn't Pritchard the officer who rowed you and your mother out to the ship to peddle your wares?"

"Yes."

"And you had no idea he was a spy?"

"No. I was as shocked as everyone else." For a long few seconds, there's a cold silence. Then he's all business.

"Well, we have much to do. This hanging will be big news, and everyone in New York will want every detail. The crowds will be huge!"

He acts as if it's a royal visit, some grand entertainment. I'm horrified. "Won't there be a trial first? Maybe they'll spare his life in a prisoner exchange."

"Doubt it. They'll want to make an example of him. They have him locked up in the old sugar house on Crown Street with the other so-called patriots." With that, he saunters back to his desk.

Where does he get his information? It's always a mystery to me. Then I think of Samuel, Mr. Know-It-All. I want to confront him, but he would only laugh at me. He is truly repulsive.

I try my best to set the type for the next edition, but I can't concentrate. Who cares about an advertisement for a new hat shop, a play at the Theatre Royal, or the price of molasses? Not me, not with Dan in the shadow of the gallows and Tom fighting for his life. I keep thinking about his goodbye this morning. He wanted to hear about my day, about what I think, about how I feel. I can't remember anyone— not even Mother or Father—ever saying that to me. Can this be love?

Suddenly, Jonah is thrusting a handful of papers at me. "Make haste and set the type." Then he's out the door. Without his patronage, the city taverns and bakers of greasy meat pies would go bankrupt.

I read through the article about Dan. Predictably Jonah calls him "a nauseating rat" and "a treacherous enemy." Toward the end, I read a line that takes my breath away.

"Had it not been for the alertness of Captain Pendleton's servant, we might never have known about this treachery. Amanda Hoffman, a Viennese maiden under servitude for another three years in the Pendleton home, told her master about an incriminating slip of paper she'd found hidden in the lieutenant's boot."

My hands shake as I set the type. What else has Amanda told Pendleton?

# Chapter Thirty-four

"Emma! Mother!" I yell as I bound up the front steps and throw the door open with a bang.

"Come quick, I have news."

Emma rushes in, trailed by Benjamin. "Is it about Dan? Please let it be good news."

Mother calls from the kitchen. "What is it? Tell us."

"I know who turned in Dan. It was Amanda, the Pendletons' servant."

"I don't believe it!" Emma says. "I know her. She told me how much she liked Dan. He's boarded with the Pendletons ever since the big fire destroyed his quarters, and she would do his washing … gladly. She wouldn't turn him in … no, not ever."

"Well, she did," I say, "and it's going in the newspaper. She was polishing his boots when she found a note hidden under his false sole. It was in code, with strange letters and symbols. She gave it to Pendleton who managed to get it deciphered by some British code expert. Turns out Dan was working with Washington's men on a secret plan to take back New York."

"No, that can't be right!" Emma practically shrieks. I helped her with her English. She sometimes helped me with the children. She was paying for her passage from Europe through servitude to them. Once free, she hoped to be a seamstress."

"Maybe she was trying to buy her freedom by offering up that note," I say. "Or maybe she was tempted by the 50-pound reward the Crown offered."

Emma is visibly uncomfortable. "Did you tell Amanda anything?" I ask as gently as I can.

"She's a lovely, lonely person and she had no one else," she says, all but outright telling me what I suspect. "We confided in each other about a few things."

"What things? Remember, Emma!"

She breaks down in big choking sobs, and I fear the worst possible thing.

"Did you tell her about Dan being a spy? About Tom? Nathaniel? About us?"

She doesn't have to say a word. The look on her face says it all.

"Do you know what you've done?" I scream.

With a great, guilty exhalation, she lets loose a painful torrent. "I'm sorry! I thought I could trust her. I swore her to secrecy, and she said she understood in English. She was my friend."

Benjamin starts to cry, and Mother picks him up. "For God's sake, we're talking about surviving all this, not killing each other," she says in the low, serious tones she uses to get the attention of women in the throes of childbirth. "It does no good to blame anyone. Now we must figure out what's next."

"Tom and Nathaniel aren't safe here," I say. "And neither are we."

Nathaniel has heard the whole conversation. "No need to fuss about me," he says. "I'm well enough to be on my way." In fact, his tall, skinny frame has begun to fill out, and the color is back in his cheeks.

"Where will you go?" Mother asks.

"Home. Back to Connecticut. I'll pack a knapsack and be gone within the hour."

"But what if they stop you?"

"If they ask for papers, I'll show them the letter Sarah wrote and put on my best act as an Anglican preacher."

"You must take my husband's Bible with you," Mother says.

"I would be honored. Now, I must get ready."

"Sarah, it's clear to me, what we must do," Mother says. "We should have done it long ago."

I know what she's thinking, and I hate the idea. "I won't go back to England!"

"It's the only way," she says. "It's too dangerous here. I've tucked away enough money for passage."

"What about Tom? How can we leave him? And Emma?"

Emma has gathered herself. "I'll take Tom back home to New Hampshire. The sooner the better."

Everything is happening too fast. "No! He's not well enough for the trip. It'll kill him!" I say.

Emma, her eyes red and face blotchy, looks at me with a pained expression. "I know you care about him, but I'm his sister and I'll take him home. It's my responsibility, and I won't have it any other way."

* * *

Later that night, after we say goodbye to Nathaniel, I sit on Tom's bed and tell him what I've learned. "You're in great danger, and we haven't much time. Emma wants to take you back to New Hampshire. You can finish recuperating at your parents' house."

"Yes, Emma told me." He finishes his second bowl of chowder.

"Perhaps it's for the best," I say, hating every word. "The farther away you get, the safer you'll be."

"I see." He wipes the bowl clean with a hunk of corn bread. "Is that what you want?"

"I want what's best for you." I stare straight down because that's not exactly true.

"But do you want to be rid of me? This bag of bones you brought back to life?"

"No!" I blurt it out, and he looks surprised.

"Well, neither do I." He's smiling from here to New Hampshire. "I'm rather fond of you, Sarah Barrett, and I have been, ever since you tended my leg back home."

"But you never told me."

"You seemed so taken by your father's apprentice, you paid me no mind."

"Samuel! He proved himself a scoundrel of the lowest kind. I'm glad to be rid of him."

He smiles at me. "I'm a bit of a scoundrel too. Perhaps you're better off without me."

I take his hands, and he pulls himself up to a sitting position. Then he gently tips my face to his and kisses my cheek. A quiver of excitement spreads through my body like lightning. Then his chapped, rough lips find mine. He pulls me close, and a wave of joy washes over me.

We hear footsteps on the stairs and pull apart. Emma bursts in, and then looks embarrassed. Tom just grins at her.

"You might consider announcing your presence," he says.

"I didn't think it was necessary," she answers. "With you in such a very sickly state. Perhaps you're not as sickly as we thought."

"I'm not too sickly to enjoy Sarah's company. In fact, I think her presence is giving me a certain strength. Yes, an unmistakable strength."

I blush, but his words thrill me.

Emma then reveals a getaway plan for Tom and her. "Mr. Perkins next door has agreed to drive us in his wagon to the waterfront at dawn tomorrow. We'll get the first ship to Boston. From there we can find transport back to New Hampshire."

My heart sinks. Tom will be gone in mere hours.

"The whole family will be there," Emma says. "You can recover in peace and not worry about every knock on the door."

Tom lets out a deep sigh. "Seems you have it figured out. Do I have a say in all this?"

"Of course, you do. But—"

"Well, I choose to stay in New York. With Sarah." I can't believe what I'm hearing. "I'll take my chances. You go back to New Hampshire. Tell Father and Mother the whole story … how you plucked me from the water and rescued me from certain death. They must be worried sick about both of us."

"They are," Emma says. "They really want you home. I think it's for the best."

"Well, I don't," he says, his jaw set. "And I won't be changing my mind so it's no use arguing."

I'm so happy I throw my arms around him and crush him, extra gently, in a hug. I don't care that Emma is hurt and leaves in a huff.

• • •

Later I sit down on her bed while she packs her belongings in her trunk.

"I know you're mad at me. Can we at least talk about it?"

"Nothing to talk about," she snaps. "I've lost Dan, thanks to you, and now you're taking my brother. God have mercy on the two of you."

"That's unfair. Tom is a grown man, capable of his own decisions. And I don't see how you can blame me for Dan's capture. You're the one who blabbed to Amanda."

"Don't you think I know that?" Emma screams, nearly knocking me off the bed. "I'm ripping myself up over it." She stops folding a skirt and glares at me. "See, we have nothing to talk about. By tomorrow I'll be gone. None too soon. You spread chaos wherever you go, Sarah. If I never see you again, I'll be content."

Her words sting, and so do mine: "I think you're jealous of Tom and me."

"No, that is not it," she says, emphasizing every word, sounding very much like the schoolteacher she was and will again be back in Essex.

"Yes, it is. You've always been the pretty one, the one the boys flock around," I say. "I was the one nobody looked at twice, until now."

"No, you're the one people listen to. You're the one with the answers. You're the smart one. No one has ever asked my opinion. Not even Dan."

She closes the trunk lid. "I miss him so much. I dreamed we'd marry and have children. I never told him how I felt, and now, it's too late."

I wish I could take back my hurtful words and say something to comfort her. "He's a good man."

"You don't know the half of it." The rest comes out in fits and starts. Dan has been consumed with worry about his brother and the family shipping business. It seems the brother's gambling wiped out the family's fortune, and now they face debtors' prison.

"Dan is too good, too kind. He wants to help everyone," Emma says.

"Maybe the Crown will issue a last-minute reprieve. Stranger things have happened."

"Please Sarah. Don't patronize me. We know exactly what'll happen and so does he. He made his choices anyway. He told me he never regretted for a second taking up the rebels' cause."

"If he dies, he'll die a hero," I say.

"What good is that, if he's dead?"

Then her face softens. "I guess I am a little jealous of you and Tom. You have someone who cares deeply about you. I have no one."

I ache to make her feel better, though maybe it's my own guilt that needs easing. She touches my hand.

"I will miss you both so terribly," she says.

Then I can't help myself, and the tears flow.

"Don't cry," she says. "You never cry. You'd sooner eat nails than cry." Somehow that makes us laugh.

"Take good care of Tom," she tells me. It hardly needs saying, but I tell her I will.

# Chapter Thirty-Five

Emma climbs into Mr. Perkins' wagon just after sunrise. Tom hobbles down the stairs on his own to say goodbye. I thought he would weep, but he jokes as if she's merely going for a ride in the park.

"Tell Father not to expect me home to help tend the fields any time soon," he says. "And don't tell Mother I look like something risen from the boneyard."

"Stay out of trouble, Tom. If that's possible," she calls out as the wagon lumbers away.

I miss her immediately. The house seems so empty.

• • •

Jonah is gone when I walk into the *Loyal Gazette*. Only the two dimwitted apprentices are there, running the press and hanging up damp pages to dry.

"Where is he?"

"Just left for the hanging," one of them says.

"What hanging?" Of course, I know immediately but don't want to admit it. Jonah's imbecilic assistant professes cluelessness.

"How should I know?" he says.

"You must know. You can't be that daft."

"Went to Bowling Green, if you must know," the other one offers.

I dash out and run toward the patch of grass a few blocks away where men with means used to lawn-bowl the afternoon away. It's also where the statue of King George III stood until the rebels tore it down in a fit of celebration after the Declaration of Independence was signed in July.

Even before I arrive, I see a huge gathering of both soldiers and civilians. Out of nowhere, Amanda runs toward me, her face a portrait of pain.

"Sarah! They're going to hang Lieutenant Pritchard!"

It's all I can do not to explode. "What did you expect when you told your boss everything you knew? Did you think Dan would be commended for his cleverness?"

"I thought he'd be punished, but not hanged," she says in halting English. "I never meant this to happen. I only wanted my freedom. You couldn't possibly understand."

"And the reward? I understand that! What else did you tell Pendleton about me and Emma and our trips out to the ship? Everything?"

"Nothing. Emma swore me to secrecy."

"I don't believe you. Go peddle your lies elsewhere." I push my way forward through the crowd, toward the platform where the statue once stood.

Onlookers are chanting, "Hang him! Hang him!" Thousands have gathered, along with impressive ranks of redcoats.

I elbow my way to the front. Finally, I see Dan on the platform, his hands tied behind his back, flanked by a half-dozen stone-faced soldiers who have probably played guard at dozens of hangings. Gone is Dan's smart red uniform, replaced by bloodied rags. His face is battered, one eye completely shut. The noose lies limp around his neck, and he's supported by a guard on either side with a hand beneath his elbows.

This can't be happening. I'm dizzy, hot and nauseous. Suddenly, I feel my breakfast rising and there is nothing I can do. I'm a human volcano, and I'm mortally embarrassed.

"Don't have the stomach for it, my dear?" Of course, it's Samuel. "I told you women have no business meddling in war."

I wipe my mouth with my sleeve, wishing I had the strength to land a good blow on his face. He's having the time of his life as boys pelt Dan with garbage.

"You call this justice?" I ask, channeling every bit of my foul breath on Samuel. "He didn't even get a trial. Are you proud of yourself?"

Samuel recoils. "He doesn't need a trial. It's clear what he did. He deserves what he's about to get."

"It's you I'd rather see strung up," I tell him.

"You disgust me. Don't think Captain Pendleton doesn't know what you've done." He turns on his heel and fades into the crowd.

"Good riddance, Samuel!" But he doesn't hear me. The crowd's chants grow louder and faster.

Dan is standing just yards from me, but the noise is deafening.

"Emma loves you!" I yell, but I have no idea whether he hears me. The pained expression on his face doesn't change.

A redcoat shoves me back as Pendleton climbs the steps onto the platform. All the uniformed men salute.

"Daniel Pritchard, you are guilty of the high crime of treason," he reads from a document, citing a list of charges. "You are a disgrace to the British uniform and all these fine men who serve with loyalty and bravery."

Dan stares straight ahead, well over the heads of the churning mob. I see nothing in his face that betrays any emotion.

"You were in a position of trust," Pendleton continues. "I trusted you. The Crown trusted you. And for that gift of trust, you turned on us and sold the enemy vital information. For 800 pounds, you and the conspiracy you directed sold your very birthright. May God have mercy on your soul."

A pastor on the platform shouts, "Amen."

My mind is spinning … 800 pounds? That's news to me.

"Prisoner, have you any last words?" Pendleton says, more out of formality than interest.

"No." It's immediate and firm.

The mob goes wild with indignation, as if they expect at least an apology.

"Hang him! Hang him!"

The guards slip a white hood over Dan's head. The rope, dangling from a crossbeam, goes taut as the executioner releases a trap door and Dan drops with a thud. I can't take my eyes away. His body twitches for a few long moments, then goes still. It's over, thank God.

The crowd erupts in cheers, and I can't wait to get away. I spot Samuel chatting with Pendleton. Head down, I plow through the maze of people who laugh and gossip as if they've just seen a thrilling play. The captain's hateful words still ring in my ears. I'm scared for me, Tom, even Mother and little Benjamin.

I can't go back to the *Loyal Gazette*. Jonah will surely be there by now, gleefully writing his article about this grotesque event. Maybe he's already figured out what I've done. He'd happily turn me in if Samuel hasn't already done so.

There is only one place to go, home, and then, who knows? I lift my skirts and run as fast as I can over the cobblestone, hoping no one gives chase to a young woman, skirts flying, galloping through the streets.

Finally, I see the house and leap up the steps, panting and sweating.

What I see is chaos. Table and chairs overturned, papers scattered everywhere, dishes on the floor, the oak cabinet teetering on its side. "Mother!" She's kneeling on the floor gathering papers, trying to restore what she can of order. "What happened?"

"They just left. The redcoats came looking for Tom and Nathaniel. I said they weren't here, never had been. May the Lord forgive me for lying. Nathaniel was gone, of course. But Thomas ..."

No! It can't be! I run up the stairs to the attic. No sign of him. My old writing table is in splinters on the floor, the bed overturned.

Tom is gone. I check for my diary, my precious diary, and it too is gone; stolen from its hiding place behind a loose brick in the chimney.

I drop to my knees and close my eyes, letting it all sink in. I'm as good as dead. Even my account of the prison ships is dead, along with the one human being I cared about more than anyone else in the entire world.

Then I hear scratching. A rat; how fitting.

The scratching continues, and I scream, a futile effort to drive the rodent away.

"Sarah?" A soft, familiar voice. I look around and see no one. "Sarah, over here. It's me, Tom."

"What? Where are you?"

"The window. Look out the window."

I peer down to the ground. Nothing. No Tom.

"Up here, hurry."

I look up. There's Tom, clinging to the edge of the roof, feet dangling.

"I can't hold on much longer."

I reach as high up as I can and manage to get my arms around his upper legs. Giving it everything I have, I pull his body closer to the window and guide his feet in. Then my hands are around his waist, and he stammers, "I...have...to...let...go!"

"I've got you!" I yell, reaching up over his bony ribs as he lowers the rest of his emaciated frame through the window. Finally, we both collapse on the floor, panting hard.

"That's twice you've saved my neck." He grins at me. "Thank you, Sarah Barrett."

"Perhaps you can return the favor some time. I thought you were gone for sure, hauled off by the British."

He pulls me close for a full minute as relief floods my body.

"I was so close to dropping," he says, showing me the angry, bleeding cuts on his fingers that wouldn't let go. He lowers his head and presses his lips to mine. My head is swirling. "All I could think about out there, was you. They were up here poking around and yelling. I didn't dare breathe."

I tell him about Dan. "Poor Emma," he says. "First Seth, and now this. I can't say that I'm surprised he took the money. Desperate people do desperate things, especially for family. And I can't forget that he, and you, saved my life."

I don't know if I can be as understanding. What will I tell Emma about her perfect gentleman, or has she known all along?

Suddenly, I remember my diary. "Tom, it's gone. Everything I wrote about the prison ship, about you, Nathaniel, everyone."

"No, it's not." He smiles again.

"Where is it? Don't keep me guessing."

He reaches under his shirt and pulls out my battered soulmate. It's soaked in sweat, but all in one piece.

"How did you know where it was?"

"I saw you put it there; you thought I was asleep."

I kiss him roundly on the lips.

"I can get used to this," he says.

"I guess you're feeling much better."

Then I turn serious and, as ever, ruin the moment. "Tom, they'll be back for us. Maybe not right away, but soon."

# Chapter Thirty-Six

Tom is exhausted from the whole ordeal, but he refuses to go back to bed. Instead, he goes down to the kitchen and inhales a pint of cider and a pheasant pie that survived the raid. Then he gathers the splinters and shards of Mother's spinning wheel, figuring to fix what the redcoats nearly destroyed.

Mother is in quite a state. She's in the rocker, hugging herself with her arms folded tightly. Benjamin is howling, but she doesn't seem to notice. I pick him up, but it's not me he wants, and he howls even louder. Clearly, she's in no mood to hear about my worries.

"Mother, how can I help you?"

"Help me? You can help me by packing up and sailing back to London with me and your brother as soon as possible." There is no hesitation, no wavering in her voice.

I summon my calmest tones. "I've already told you. My ... our ... home is here." I leave Tom out of it.

"How can you call this home?" With disgust, she points to overturned jug of molasses and smashed dishes on the floor. "This wouldn't happen in London. I've been loyal to the King since this horrible ordeal started. Now, they barge in here and treat us like fugitive criminals."

I'm not callous enough to remind her that she already is a criminal just by giving aid to Nathaniel and Tom.

"If it weren't for your father's insistence, I never would have come here," Mother says, lingering for a moment over his memory. "Now there was a good loyalist, a good man."

"Father would have had a change of heart by now," I say. "He'd back the patriots, especially if he'd seen those ships."

"You're wrong and disloyal to your father's memory."

That rattles me. "Mother, I will not go with you."

"Yes, you will. I'm your mother and you'll do as I say."

"No! I'm a grown woman, old enough to make up my own mind."

"You're still an impertinent child!" Mother rages.

"Child?" I shout. "I can take care of myself. I have a skill, a job. You're still angry that I hate the idea of standing by your side to catch bloody, squalling babies."

Mother sticks out her chin. "I'm proud of what I do." She takes Benjamin from my arms, and he calms down instantly.

"Can't you be proud of me for what I do?" I yell.

"Spending all day in that dirty newspaper office, filth under your fingernails, ink all over your skirts?"

"Live with it, Mother! I'm a writer. One day I'll write something everyone will talk about."

I'm just getting started, but the pounding on the door stops me cold.

"Are they back?" Mother says. "What now?"

Tom, who's been silent during our bitter exchange, dashes up the stairs. I peek out the parlor window and see Jonah. That can only mean one thing. He's here to turn me in and win a handsome reward for his trouble.

"I know you're in there, girl," he yells. "I'm here to help you."

Help me? I don't trust him for a second. I open the door slowly, expecting to see a gang of redcoats, weapons aimed at my chest, charging around the corner. But it's only fat Jonah, puffing from the terrible exertion of knocking on the door.

It's over.

"Here I am," I say, wearily. "Mother had nothing to do with it."

"I don't care a whit about your mother," he says in his usual grumpy manner. "I'm here for you."

"Well, be done with it." I wonder if I'll be allowed to say goodbye to Mother and Benjamin.

"Crazy woman!" he mutters. "I'm not here to turn you in."

"Is this a trick?"

"For the love of God! I'm on your side."

"What do you mean?"

"I'm here to tell you Pendleton and his men will be here soon. Seems that boy Samuel gave him an earful. I told them you'd already left by wagon for New Hampshire, but they'll be onto that ruse by morning."

I'm still baffled, but a wave of urgency sweeps over me. "I've got to get out of here!"

"Finally, you're listening to me." He rolls his eyes.

But none of it makes sense. "Why are you doing this?" I'm desperate to understand. "I thought you were a loyalist through and through. I thought you despised the rebels. Why are you bothering to warn me?"

"I did despise them…at first. I thought your father was right, that it was wiser for the colonies to find some peace with the Crown."

"What happened?" I feel like I hardly know this man I've come to loathe.

For the very first time in the year that I've known this man, I don't see disdain in his eyes. "Taxes, for one thing. The Crown squeezes us for money. High fees on paper, ink, rum, molasses. Every time I turn around it's something new."

"So, it's all about money?" I'm still not sure I trust him. After all, taxes have been going on forever.

"No, it's not just the money. Their troops are drunken louts who would just as soon see us all burn. Just look at how they tore up your house, that can happen to any of us. And …"

"And what?"

He wipes his face, takes a deep breath, and continues. "I know what goes on aboard those prison ships. I knew all along that you were right, but I couldn't let on."

I can scarcely believe what's coming out of his mouth. Jonah, a sensible old codger after all. Just from his eyes and the set of his jaw, I feel he means every word. Still, it makes no sense.

"Then why does the *Loyal Gazette* continue to write about the glorious deeds of the British troops?" I say. "You've printed such hateful things about the rebels. Why do you keep it up if you don't believe in it?"

"Can I trust you?"

"Yes," I say warily. "If I can trust you."

"I've backed the Crown for so long that the commanding officers trust me. They tell me things at the bookstore, the coffeehouse, the tavern, even the theater. Things they probably shouldn't."

I'm beginning to understand, but it's still unbelievable. "Are you a spy, Jonah?"

"Don't ever use that word in front of me!" He lowers his voice to a whisper. "For the last six months, I've been passing information to people who get it to General Washington."

"But how?" Jonah is the last person on earth anyone would take for a spy, fussy, cranky old Jonah, newspaper publisher and book seller and postmaster. He's so public it's hard to picture him doing anything private.

"Usually with books. I hide a message in the bindings."

Suddenly, I remember. "Inside the copies of Milton's 'Paradise Lost!' I never understood why that book was suddenly so popular."

Jonah is surprised. "I hope you're the only one who noticed."

An idea is taking shape, and I approach it cautiously. "Jonah, do you believe a woman can publish an essay, or a pamphlet…a book?"

"No, of course not. That's the business of men."

I expected his answer, but it still galls me. "What if it was written so well it sounded as if a man—an accomplished literary man—had written it?"

His eyes narrow. "What have you done now, girl?"

"I've written all about the prison ships. I've kept an entire diary of details about the starvation, disease, and death. People need to know."

"Yes, so you kept telling me."

"I've not only been on the *Defiance* many times, but I've also helped two prisoners escape, and they've given me much to write about." I wonder if he believes me or thinks me a lunatic.

He looks skeptical. "Wait here," I say, dashing for the attic stairs.

"Tom, you won't believe what's happening," I whisper. I bound back down the stairs and hand my bedraggled diary to Jonah. He leafs through it and shakes his head.

"Sarah, I misjudged you," he says softly.

I'm beyond happy. "Then take it. Publish it if you dare. If the British come after me and find it, it'll be the end of me and my words. Please!"

"Of course, I will." He tucks it under his shirt and, in turn, withdraws a scrunched-up note. "If you need a place to hide, go to this address. They've helped others. "Good luck, my dear."

# Chapter Thirty-Seven

I race up to the attic two stairs at a time.

"Tom! We have to go! The soldiers will be back any minute. They know I helped you escape."

"How? Pritchard didn't tell them, did he?"

"I'm sure it was Samuel's doing. And God only knows what else he's told them about me."

"I knew he was a rat." Suddenly, Tom eyes me oddly. "What do you mean, 'what else he's told them'?"

"Nothing lewd, if that's what you're thinking."

"I wasn't thinking that at all," he says. "So, what is it?"

"Can't say just yet. You'll have to trust me." I can't bring myself to tell him the secret that I've been guarding for two years. Would he even believe it was me who nearly destroyed the whole town of Essex? Tom could have been killed in that huge blast, but mercifully no one died. Will he think so kindly of me if he hears the truth?

"Maybe someday I'll tell you. Right now, we have no time to waste."

"I don't like secrets," he says. "We'll return to this."

My eyes dart about the room. "We'll have to travel light. Bring only a change of clothes and a warm coat."

"As if I have an entire wardrobe. Sarah, why should I have to play guessing games with you? If you told Samuel something that could get you in trouble, it could also get me in trouble. So, let's have it!"

"Tom, this isn't the time. We're in danger and we have to go. Now."

He makes a grand, theatrical gesture toward the window. "And just where are you proposing we go in a city swarming with redcoats?"

"I don't know! Wherever we can be safe, at least for a little while."

I dread facing Mother and another go-around about fleeing to England. I find her in the kitchen slicing big hunks of bread and cheese. Does she think we'll have a casual supper at home, as if this is just another day?

She looks up at me with tears in her eyes. Is she trying to make me feel guilty about staying behind?

I couldn't be more wrong.

"I'm sorry, Sarah. You're not a child. You're a woman, and I must wrestle with that."

I stand there with my mouth open, unable to say anything.

"I heard every word Jonah Livingston said. You have no time to lose. I'm packing a sack of food for the two of you."

All my anger melts. I throw my arms around her and squeeze hard. "I'm sorry too, Mother."

She goes over to the flour bin, reaches deep inside, and pulls out a small leather pouch. Shaking off the flour, she hands it to me.

"What's this?"

"It's the money from everything we sold on the ship. I want you to have it. You'll need it, along with my prayers."

"I can't take that. You need it for your voyage back to London."

"I'm not going back there," she says calmly.

I'm dumbstruck. "That's all you've ever talked about. What will you do?"

"I'm going to Nova Scotia."

"Why so far north?" It's a virtual wilderness from what little I know about it. Hardly a place for someone eager to live in a more refined setting.

"It's kind of a sanctuary for people like me, Americans who still respect the Crown. They want no part of this miserable war. I can secure free passage on a ship leaving New York in a day or two."

"Free?"

"Yes. Seems they need midwives there. My services will be valued, not taken for granted."

The last part, I'm sure, is aimed at me. And I deserve it. "And they'll be lucky to have you."

Mother beams.

"Won't you miss London, though? What about all your family there and all the opportunities for Benjamin?" I'm still trying to understand this sudden change of heart.

"Yes." She takes a deep breath. "But Nova Scotia is closer to the colonies than London. It's not as far from you, wherever you go."

We're still embracing as Tom walks into the kitchen with his belongings in an old knapsack slung over his shoulder.

"What's this?" he laughs. "May I join you?"

"No. Ladies only." Finally, I tear myself away. "I'll gather my things quickly, then we must go."

In my bedroom, I pull a dusty old cloth bag from under the bed. It holds all the beautiful blue satin Samuel purchased for my gown; the one Mother never finished. I dump it out and throw in my good yellow dress, a nightgown, and my red wool cloak. I tuck in the comb Mother gave me and Father's favorite quill pen.

As I pack, a little seed of a plan starts to take shape. Tom is in no condition to travel yet, and there's no telling how far the redcoats will go to track us down. The only refuge I can think of is a place I don't even know, the address that Jonah handed to me: Henry Dawson, carpenter, William Street.

It's dark as we gather with Mother in the kitchen for the moment I've been dreading. Benjamin is fussing and squirmy, something that ordinarily would drive me crazy. But knowing I won't see him for God knows how long, he seems somewhat lovable.

Mother gathers us in for one last, long look. She strokes my cheek. "I must keep this memory alive until we meet again."

I don't know how long that will be, if ever. But I try to sound cheery. "Nova Scotia isn't so very far. I'll find you there someday, when all this is over."

"God willing." Mother wipes away a tear. "But right now, how will you make your way to this place on William Street? What if the soldiers stop you?"

I know Tom will hate this. At least I hope he will. "Tom will go disguised as a woman. No one would think it peculiar, two ladies out for an evening stroll."

"I think it's peculiar!" Tom bursts out.

A few minutes later, he's silent as I lace him into one of my old gowns. Mother produces a bonnet that hoods his face. Save for the stubble on his cheeks, no one would know.

As I survey my handiwork, I tell him about the letter I plan to send his sister. "Dear Emma, I'm happy to report that your brother looks absolutely ravishing in flowered gowns…"

Tom fires back with his own make-believe letter: "Oh, Emma dear. Sadly, your friend Sarah has lost her mind and is wandering the streets in a burlap sack. I'm sure you knew it would happen…"

Finally, we gather our few belongings and head for the door.

"Goodbye," Mother says in a quavering voice. "Don't forget your family, Sarah."

"How could I, Mother. Don't forget me…and Tom." I turn to leave quickly, so she won't see my tears.

Thankfully, it's dark as we walk toward William Street. The gown is too short for Tom, and with every step, his too-big shoes thrust themselves from beneath the skirts.

"Take dainty, little steps," I whisper. "Like a lady."

He gives me a withering look.

I change the subject. "We'll see our families again. I'm sure." Just hearing it makes me feel better, even if I don't really believe it.

"If we survive." I wish it were just battlefield humor, but I can tell he isn't joking.

It seemed like a grand adventure just hours ago. Now reality sinks in: One misstep and we could die at the hands of the British.

At first, I worry that Tom will collapse before we walk the half-mile to Dawson's. But I can barely keep up with him. As we draw closer, we see more people, men leaving the taverns, couples leaving the theater, but so far, no soldiers. We keep our heads low and hurry through.

I try not to think about Mother and Benjamin. Did I kiss the little devil goodbye? I wish I'd taken the caterpillar he offered in his little pink palm as we prepared to leave.

We pass shop after shop closed for the evening: the clockmaker I wrote about for the *Loyal Gazette*, the wig maker, the butcher, stonecutters, hat makers. In the stories over the darkened shops, I see figures in flickering candlelight, probably preparing for bed. It makes me wonder where I'll sleep tonight if I sleep at all.

When we arrive, I think for a second that Jonah has been true to form all along and played a cruel, stupid joke on us. The sign hanging outside the shop says, "Henry Dawson, Carpenter and Coffin Maker." The windows on the second and third floors are dark.

"Coffins?" I whisper. "I don't like this. What if it's a trick?"

"Do you trust Jonah?"

"Yes," I say hesitantly. "I trusted him with my diary. What choice do we have?"

"None."

I nervously rap the knocker. No answer. I rap again, a little more assertively. Finally, the door opens a crack.

"Yes? What is it?" It's a woman's voice.

"Jonah Livingston sent us," I say, barely making myself heard.

"Are you ladies friends of the Crown?" she says, opening the door another crack. I squint in and see an old woman, wrapped in a shawl, holding a candle.

"No." I worry that I've made a fatal mistake, but she motions us in.

Tom steps up beside me and, while clad like a lady, no longer makes a pretense. "Forgive the disguise. I'm Private Thomas Jordan of New Hampshire, and I'm in need of shelter for reasons you may accurately surmise. This is my... sister, Sarah."

"Oh my!" she exclaims. "Well, you two are a sight. We certainly have room for you, Private Jordan, that is, for you and your...sister. Come in, quickly."

We step into the parlor, and Tom throws off his bonnet. His outfit wasn't fooling anyone, and neither was his ridiculous pretense that I was his sister.

In the candlelight I see an ornately carved dresser with brass handles and a curved banister that goes up to the second floor. I sit on the fanciest velvet sofa I've ever seen. Twittering birds are carved into the wood frame.

"I'm Mrs. Dawson. My husband Henry is down in his shop working late. The need for coffins is most urgent."

I try to put her at ease. "Did Mr. Dawson build the sofa? I've never seen anything so beautiful. And the dresser—"

"Yes, he did it all. Now he has time only for the coffins the British demand of him. Yes, we prosper from loss, but I'd rather be less prosperous. This war will be the death of us all."

"It nearly was for me," Tom says, crossing his legs beneath the long dress. Then he tells her an abbreviated but no less harrowing tale of his time on the ship. "Had Sarah not rescued me from that hell, I'd be dead of starvation by now."

I hear footsteps and panic.

"Don't fret. That would be Mr. Dawson," she says. "I can tell his weary step. He's finally come up to bed."

The door creaks open and in steps a stooped old man with thinning gray hair and thick spectacles.

"Henry, come in here and meet our guests, Private Thomas Jordan, and his cousin Sarah. They've come for shelter from the British."

Tom clears his throat. "Begging your pardon, Ma'am. It's my sister not my cousin.

The old man steps into the candlelight. "Acquaintances of Jonah Livingston, I presume."

"Yes," I say, now curious about Jonah, the charmless curmudgeon I thought I knew.

"He's aided many others," the old man says.

"As have you, dear husband, at great peril to yourself and me."

Mr. Dawson scoffs, then turns to Tom and me. "You'll be safe here, for a spell. Where are you headed?"

"Thank you for your kindness," Tom says. "I hope to return to General Washington's troops in New Jersey. And Sarah, my sister, is headed to Nova Scotia where her, that is our, mother is."

I look at him with astonishment. What is he talking about? Go back to the fighting? That isn't the plan, at least not my plan. We never said what the future holds for us after this nightmare, but I believed we would be together. I certainly didn't intend to join "our" mother up north.

I gather my wits. "Tom, you're in no shape to go back into battle. At least not now. You can barely walk, much less fight."

I hope I sound sisterly. From the strange look on his face, I feel I've succeeded.

"I'll thank you not to judge my fighting abilities," he says.

"Listen to your sister," Mrs. Dawson says. "You're as scrawny as my chickens. But I'll fatten you up in no time. How about some custard pie before you retire for the night?"

After Tom has eaten half the pie, she takes us up the narrow stairs to the attic. It's full of odd scraps of wood, an old seamen's chest, a desk with a broken leg, a butter churn missing its innards, and a pile of ragged quilts. A half-filled bookcase against the wall catches my eye. Dust and dirt shroud everything. God knows how many mice took cover when they heard us.

Tom must see the disappointment in my eyes. "This will do us just fine, Mrs. Dawson."

"Yes, you and Mr. Dawson are very generous," I say with as much enthusiasm as I can muster.

"These are not your quarters." She goes over to the bookcase and leans against a corner of it. I can't imagine what she's doing, but the wall swings away, revealing a dark passage.

"In there," she gestures, handing me the candle. "You'll need this."

# Chapter Thirty-Eight

I can't even move. Who knows how many rodents await us in that inky hole, eager to nibble our toes and then leap for our throats. Suddenly, Mother's cramped, dusty attic seems like paradise.

"Don't make a sound in there," Mrs. Dawson says as she grabs a candle from a wall sconce and lights it off ours. "I'll bring up your breakfast in the morning. God willing, no one saw you come in. The British would love to get their hands on us and on you."

Tom leads the way into our pitch-black chamber. My hand is clamped on his upper arm. I expect a bat to fly into my face and spiders to crawl up my skirt.

My eyes slowly adjust. We're in a small room with barely enough space to stand. But there's a threadbare blue and red rug on the floor, similar to the one we had in Seth's room back in Essex. On the wall hangs an unframed painting of a ship tossed about on wild seas. A small table holds three tattered books. My eyes fall to the first, *Robinson Crusoe*, and my spirits lift. At least it's another bit of home.

Everything is scrubbed clean. A straw mattress on the floor is covered with a patched blanket. And a small window opens to the sky.

My eyes dart back to the bed. I wouldn't in a million years pretend that I haven't thought about this moment, alone with Tom. I've thought about it a lot. I imagined my arms around him, his arms around me. I've thought about him touching my breasts, caressing my thighs, and how that would feel. Every time I imagine it, a rush of excitement floods my body.

Tom looks at me with mischievous eyes. He must know what I'm thinking, and I feel flustered and embarrassed. He steps closer to me and pulls my chin up to kiss me. My knees feel wobbly. Then I remember what he said earlier, about going back to the fighting as soon as he's able. I pull away and look up at him.

"So, you can't wait to return to the fighting. You barely survived the last run-in with the British, and you want to risk it again?"

I know I ruined the moment, but I can't help myself. He looks at me, confused and a little agitated.

"Yes, Sarah, I do want to fight. More than anything."

I feel crushed, like the life has been squeezed out of me. "What about me? Do I mean nothing to you?"

He looks surprised. "Sarah, I'm so grateful that you saved me. I can never repay you for that. But I never told you I wouldn't go back to the fighting."

"Perhaps, you should have."

"I do care about you, Sarah. More than I ever have any other woman. I'm sorry if I misled you."

I break from his grasp, and he stumbles over the bed. His voice is hard and angry. "But you've misled me as well."

"What do you mean?"

"We're not supposed to have secrets from each other that you *might* tell me one day. I want to know today, right now. What have you kept from me?"

I knew I would eventually tell him, but I was hoping it would be underneath an apple tree by a country road, not here in this dark garret when he's already mad at me. Will he forgive me? Will he still want me?

"Well?" Then his voice softens. "Sarah, whatever it is can't be that awful. I know you. Just let it out, and you'll feel much better."

His words almost melt me, but not quite. "I'm not ready. I can't confide anything to you, not this way."

"Fine. But I told you I hate secrets. How can we trust each other if we can't say what's really on our minds?"

"Like you really told me what's on your mind about returning to the front lines?" I can't let go of my anger.

He sighs deeply, and I see exasperation on his face. "If it's about what you did with that damn obnoxious redcoat, Samuel. I can forgive—"

"No, it's not! And there's nothing to forgive."

"Then what am I supposed to do, guess? What am I supposed to think if you won't tell me?" His arms are folded across his chest, as if he's girding for some big blow.

I feel trapped. "All right, I'll tell you. Remember that night in Essex when someone blew up the rebels' ammunition? Well, it was me. I did it, and I wasn't sorry then and I'm not sorry now." There it is, out there in one big ugly burst of truth, something like the burst that lit the skies over Essex, but worse. I can't breathe.

I squint through the candlelight to search his face for any sign of horror or disgust. But he erupts in laughter. That rattles me. His words are soaked in condescension.

"You expect me to believe you? You'll have to do better than that."

"It's true." His smile is maddening and makes me feel like a little girl. I take a deep breath and fix my eyes on that stupid grin.

"I'll tell you exactly how it happened," I say. "I knew that British troops were planning to march into town and steal the huge cache of ammunition stored in the old barn. I also knew that the rebels had uncovered their plan and were about to beat them to the punch by mounting a counterattack."

"How did you know about that?" His face is somber now. "Only a few of us were in on that, and I trusted every one of those men with my life."

"Never mind. I just knew. I was sure it would be an awful bloodbath for both sides. I was worried Samuel and others would be caught up in it and die."

Tom grimaces at the mention of his name.

"I knew everything about it, you can't hide anything for very long in a town like Essex. I even knew the loyalist pastor who was tarred and feathered and had to flee, the one who abandoned the old barn where the rebels piled their boxes of guns and ammunition up to the rafters."

"But how could you possibly set that huge fire and trigger that massive explosion?" Suddenly my worst fears are realized. He's viewing me as the key suspect in a terrible crime, not as a heroine thwarting a gigantic bloodbath. "I was on guard duty at the barn that night. I would have seen you."

"I knew that."

"You did?"

If he doesn't believe me so far, he'll never believe the rest of my story. But I can't stop now.

"Do you remember my brother's hunting bow? How he'd practice for hours in the back when Father wasn't around to get him back to his chores?"

"Yes. His arrows were straight and true. Seth was a fine shot."

"So was I. Only better."

"What does that have to do with this fantastic tale?" The smirk is back on his face. I'm running out of patience.

"That night, I hid in the woods behind the barn with Seth's bow and his quiver. Emma carried a little bucket of hot ashes."

"Emma?" He gives me a dubious look, but I go on. "I attached a bit of cloth dipped in turpentine to the tip of the arrow, lit it, and fired it into the thatched roof of the barn."

"And just like that, it blew up?" he says. "Boom!"

"No, it took three tries before the dry straw in the roof really caught." After a few seconds, there was a tongue of fire bursting through the roof, and a crash that shook the hillside like an earthquake.

"I was right there," Tom says. "You knew that. Were you trying to kill me? If any of this is true, which I doubt, I don't know why I'm not dead."

"I can tell you why you're not dead. Do you remember that Emma brought your supper as usual that night?"

"Yes, she did," he says. "She was a stone's throw from the barn when she met up with that bear that had been terrorizing the town. I

222

remember hearing her screams. That's why I ran out, and when I got to her the bear was gone, but Emma was scratched up pretty bad."

"Tom, there was no bear. It was a ruse."

"But I saw the scratches, all that blood."

"I scratched Emma's arms with a thorny branch and bloodied her up with chicken guts beforehand," I say. "You can imagine how happy she was about that."

Tom is flabbergasted, speechless.

"So no one was inside when the barn exploded. No one was hurt."

"Well, thank you for sparing my life, I guess," he says with obvious sarcasm. "But it's not that simple. You do know that old Mrs. Twining across from the barn died of fright when her heart gave out that night. And the embers that flew onto the Farnhams' roof almost burned the place down. And George Kindley got pretty banged up when a falling beam hit his leg. You do remember all that, don't you?"

"I didn't know...all of it." Suddenly, my defense is looking a lot weaker than it did just a few minutes ago. "Mrs. Twining was already ailing and on her deathbed." My words feel hollow.

"Your little stunt didn't help."

"My stunt? There was no ambush, no bloody battle, no lives lost. To me it seemed worth it." I still feel no need to apologize, but my pride in aiming my arrow straight and true is somewhat tarnished now.

Tom just shakes his head. I wish he'd say something, anything, so I prod him.

"Are you glad you know my deepest, darkest secret now?"

"I don't know what I think. I can scarcely believe what I just heard. I do know that the entire Continental Army was furious over all those guns and ammunition being lost in a flash."

It's not quite what I expect. Here I am in this secluded hideout with a man I've dreamt about for so long, and it's turning out so badly.

"I'll have to think on it," he says. "You do know that your action set our regiment back severely? Gunpowder is like gold and just as hard to come by. And you must know too that a reward for your capture was approved by Washington himself."

"Here's your chance to be a hero," I say. "Turn me in. Get the reward, live like a king."

Tom scoffs. "I thought I knew you, Sarah." Without another word, he pitches himself down on the ragged mattress, well off to the side. In less than a minute, he's asleep, or pretending to be.

I lie there, as far as I can from Tom, fighting bitter tears as I second-guess myself for hours. Was I a criminal? Was I a fool to tell him?

• • •

Just after dawn I hear footsteps on the stairs.

"I've come with your breakfast," Mrs. Dawson announces. "It's safe to come out for a bit."

Tom and I avoid each other's eyes as we get up. Mrs. Dawson lets us out of our cave.

She sets a tray of oatmeal, cornbread, and tea, on a small, rickety table. The morning sun splashes over the setting as if pulled from some poem.

"It's all we can spare. There's so little food in the city. Fortunately, the soldiers haven't found my chickens yet."

"It's plenty," Tom says. "We're grateful for your kindness."

I nod and force a smile.

"Why didn't you and Mr. Dawson flee the city like so many others when the British took control?" I ask.

She sits down wearily on a dusty chair. "We're old, too old to pack up our things and move. My husband's trade is here. This is our home."

"You have no children?" I ask between bites.

"No. Not anymore." A great sadness sweeps over her face. "We had two sons, but they're both dead. Thanks to this terrible war."

"I'm so sorry." It's all I can think to say. I'm struck by what she's sacrificed.

"One died in the Battle of Long Island. A rebel pierced his heart with a bayonet. They tell me he died instantly; thanks be to God. The other was taken captive by the British. He was thrown in jail with hundreds of others, crammed in a space not fit for pigs. When he complained to the guards, they beat him to death."

I'm so moved, I take her hand. "Your sons were on opposite sides, and both died in the same battle? I am so, so very sorry, Mrs. Dawson."

She gives me something like a half-smile. "Thank you, my dear. But it's the same story in many families torn apart by war."

Tom has been listening carefully but his own horrific experience on the prison ship colors his words. "I'm sorry, Mrs. Dawson. But my duty is to fight the redcoats. We have to get rid of every last one."

His words show me just how much he wants to return to the fighting, and how little are my chances of making him see otherwise.

"You've given two sons to this war," he says to Mrs. Dawson. "And you're helping us now. May I ask you why you're being so kind, when it's clear that one of my comrades killed one of your sons?"

Mrs. Dawson piles our dishes onto the tray. "Joining up with the British was Jeremy's decision, and we've made our peace with that. We still believe in the rebels' cause. We've helped a dozen, or so, escape the British clutches. But we've opened our door to any frightened souls looking for a way out of a hellish situation, even a loyalist."

I'm stunned. They seem like such an ordinary couple. "Who were they all?"

"A young couple caught giving food to some hungry American soldiers. A newspaper man who dared write that the British are corrupt. A half dozen men who escaped the jails. Two young ladies driven half-mad by the demands of life in a brothel."

"Who did the painting of the ship hanging on our wall?" I ask.

"He was a rebel with us for quite a spell, until we could help him flee to Philadelphia."

"Aren't you afraid you'll be caught?"

"Of course. Every day I worry when I see a couple of redcoats in the neighborhood." Then a slight smile comes over her face. "But it gives me great pleasure—and not a little excitement—to know that I'm doing the right thing."

# Chapter Thirty-Nine

After breakfast, I start to read *Robinson Crusoe*. At least I pretend to read. It's impossible to concentrate with Tom inches away on the cave's miserable mattress, trying to ignore me.

Whatever we had between us is destroyed, beyond repair. Even if I apologized—and I don't intend to—he'll never get past what I did that night. In his mind, I'm back to being the enemy, a redcoat at heart. I was naive to think he'd ever choose me over his Continental Army sidekicks. Why didn't I see that? And if he thinks I would happily flee to the wilds of Nova Scotia and become Mother's helper birthing babies … well then … he's right, he doesn't know me at all.

We pass an hour without a word. He whittles a chunk of wood he found in the attic. Each pass of the knife against the pine causes me to lose my place in the book. I'm an absolute mess.

I read only 20 pages, none of which I remember even though I read the entire book two years ago. Tom finally puts down his little project and stands up as tall as he's able, still hunched over below the low ceiling.

"Sarah, how long do you plan to not speak to me?"

"As long as I please." I keep my eyes on the book.

"That seems silly, since we might be cooped up here for a while."

"Are you apologizing to me?"

"For what? That I didn't tell you I planned to go back to my regiment?"

"Yes."

"Well, if that's what it takes, then yes, I'm sorry. I can see why you'd want to know my plans, not that there's anything you could say to stop me."

"And you're not upset by what I did in Essex?" I ask.

"Yes, I'm upset. More than upset. I still find it unconscionable that you took it upon yourself to determine how, even whether, we would engage the enemy in a battle crucial to the colonies. That ammunition was paid for with the blood of brave men," he says, his voice rising. "What possessed you?" The tenderness is gone.

Not what I'd hoped for. Now the wall of ice, no, really a glacier, is back. I ignore him the rest of the afternoon as I force myself to focus on the book. He whittles two more chunks of wood into rough, ridiculous-looking spoons without saying a word.

Finally, he explodes. "Why did you do it? You couldn't leave well enough alone?"

"I told you. I wanted to prevent bloodshed. And I did. I don't regret that for a second. I'm sorry the Farnhams' house was damaged and Kindley was hurt, but there's always some price to pay in war. I still think my father would have been proud."

"Proud? Your father was a bloody loyalist just like your boss Jonah, and just like you, no matter how much you claim you've switched sides."

"That's not true! I'm on your side now. Would I have risked my neck to rescue you if I wasn't? Do you think I did that just for fun?"

"And I'll forever owe my life to you, oh Virtuous Lady of Good Deeds," he says with heavy sarcasm.

"A little gratitude would be nice!"

We both retreat to our icy silence for a few moments until I can't stand it any longer.

"At least let me try to explain," I say.

He nods.

"I was just a girl then," I say. "I thought Father was the smartest man in Essex, the smartest man in the world. His approval meant everything to me. He was a loyalist, and I wanted to be just like him. He wanted peace, so of course I did too."

"And now?"

"Do you have to ask?" I say, softening my voice when I realize how shrill it sounds. "I see things differently. The British have treated us—treated you and your comrades—like dogs. Conditions on the *Defiance* and all the other prison ships are a nightmare, a horror story that violates every rule of warfare. You might think I know nothing of war, but I read the words of those who do, Tom and I write."

Tom takes up his whittling again. I can't tell if I'm making sense, or if he thinks I'm unhinged, or maybe both.

"Don't you regret destroying the ammunition?" he says. "Are you just a little bit sorry you did it?"

"I'm not sorry that I saved lives that day." No way will I gush with apologies over saving lives.

"Sarah, grow up! Look beyond yourself and your little world. The rebels were desperate for those guns and ammunition. What if they'd used that stash in one big battle that left the British so badly trounced that it ended the war right then and there? That would have saved all the lives that have been lost since your little prank."

"Prank? I thought I was doing something noble at the time. And I did save lives. Since when is that a crime? Besides, who knows how your version of history would have turned out?"

We're nose to nose in this war of words. It's not at all how I imagined it would go. I offer a frail olive branch.

"Look, if I could magically bring the gunpowder back, I would. God knows we need it."

All I hear is an occasional "hmm" as he rubs his thumbs, again and again, up and down the spoons.

"Do I have to go into battle myself, armed with musket and bayonet, to make you see I'm on your side? No matter, I wouldn't anyway. My weapons are words, and I can be deadly accurate."

Tom starts whittling a new block, which is taking the shape of a freakish bird.

"It will take me some time to get over this. I thought I knew you."

"You do know me," I say, my voice trailing off.

I go back to my book, not sure how things stand between us. At least it's all out in the open, no more secrets. The drizzle outside turns into a downpour. I hear fat raindrops drumming on the roof, and soon I'm lulled to sleep. I dream about giant black birds descending over the city, devouring every last bit of food.

I wake in a sweat mumbling something, and Tom is gently shaking my shoulder. "You're having a nightmare," he says. "Wake up. What was it about?"

"Birds, scary birds," I mutter. But by then the dream has dissolved before I can summon it back. I'm conscious of Tom, still rubbing my shoulder.

"Did I say anything stupid?" I ask.

"Nothing too stupid," he says gently.

I'm relieved that he's in a better mood. Then I test the waters. "Must you go back to the fighting?"

"Yes," he says without hesitation.

"Will you ever be able to understand why I did what I did that night?" I ask, hopefully.

"I don't know. But that doesn't change how I feel about you."

"And how do you feel?"

"I love you, Sarah."

I'm not expecting that. "So, you're not going to turn me in?"

"No, of course not." He takes my hand, and I don't resist. "That's what I like about you. You're full of surprises."

My heart swells. "You don't care that I worked for Jonah, dirtying my hands with loyalist trash every day? You don't think me strange for wanting to be a writer?"

"Maybe a little strange." Then he chuckles. "I think there's better money in being a midwife."

"Now you're making fun of me."

"Enough talk." He pulls me closer and puts his arms around my shoulders. I wait for him to kiss me but finally take the leap myself. Our lips meet, and his tongue presses against my tongue. It feels odd at first, then pleasant, then, well, quite pleasant.

It's all new and different and a little scary. I don't know what to do with my hands, what to do with my tongue. Am I breathing too fast? I don't want to make a mistake and appear foolish. But Tom is calm, and sure, as if he's wrapped his arms around a hundred girls before me.

Perhaps he has. I think about the camp followers, the women who move with the troops, helping with the cooking and we all know what else. No wonder he knows exactly what to do.

He gently pulls me down on the mattress and I don't resist. He runs his fingers over my breasts, and I feel my nipples go hard.

"Sarah, Do you love me?"

"Yes!" He reaches under my gown, and I feel his hand on my thigh, and then higher. I shiver. I know I've crossed a line, and I don't care. I don't want him to stop, and he doesn't.

He unbuttons his breeches and I know what will come next. But, much as I'd thought about it, I'm unprepared. Will it hurt? I want to look, but I squeeze my eyes shut. Then I wait and wait. Finally, I open an eye and he's just looking at me.

"Sarah, I've never been with another woman."

I'm surprised, and somehow relieved.

"Do you know what I mean?"

"Of course, I know what you mean," I say, laughing and tousling his hair. "Nor have I been with a man."

"Not Samuel?"

"No. No one." Then I kiss him, hoping the moment hasn't been lost. His body settles against mine. It's over too soon, and he lies in a heap on top of me, exhausted and breathless. Finally, he kisses me again softly.

"Are you all right, Sarah?"

"Yes, I think so." I think I'm supposed to feel guilt or regret, but I don't. Mother told me it's a woman's duty to lie there and endure it without complaint. Is it wrong to feel pleasure? I don't think so…

Tom falls asleep. I put the blanket over him and quietly stand up, pulling myself together. I study my reflection in the small mirror. Do I look different now? Will Mrs. Dawson notice anything? I pull out the comb Mother gave me and let down my hair. I comb it until the red curls are smooth, and I fasten them just so under my cap. I take one last look in the mirror.

# Chapter Forty

"Tom, Sarah, I have news." It's Mrs. Dawson climbing the stairs to the attic. We scramble off the mattress and open the secret passageway.

She's carrying a tray of food: baked beans, half a loaf of bread, cheese and two apples. Tom's eyes nearly pop out when he views the bounty. He seems to be gaining weight every day, eating everything he can, including my share sometimes.

"I've brought the *Loyal Gazette*," Mrs. Dawson says. "And you'll be bowled over when you see it."

"What is it?" I grab the newspaper from her hand. "Is the war over?"

"Oh, mercy no," she says.

I look at the front page and know immediately. The headline covers the entire page: REBEL CAPTIVES DIE OF STARVATION AND ABUSE ON BRITISH SHIPS.

"Well, what is it, Sarah?" Tom asks.

"It's my article, my diary," I struggle to say. "It's everything I've been writing for months. Everything about the prison ships in the harbor."

Tom takes the newspaper from my shaking hands and begins to read aloud: "The old derelicts, under the command of Capt. Pendleton, are death traps for the thousands of rebel prisoners crammed aboard with no space even to lie down. The food—when there is any—is rotten or bug-infested. The men are so hungry they gnaw on wood, shoes, even their own fingers. Disease is everywhere, and so many men die every day there is no more space ashore to bury them. Their skeletal bodies pile up on the shore or are simply dumped into the sea."

Tom peers over the paper. "You are one courageous woman, Sarah. You're actually naming names."

"Jonah is the one with courage," I say. "He stands to lose his paper and his printing business and get thrown in prison. And God knows what this will do to his family."

Tom doesn't make his usual rush for Mrs. Dawson's hot, fragrant food. He's still reading the lengthy account, stopping occasionally to read a passage aloud. He raises his voice and inserts a telling emphasis when he comes to this nugget: "Word of the deplorable conditions has reached General Washington".

"He'll not take this kindly," Tom says. I've never seen him smile so broadly. I can only imagine him telling his comrades back in camp about his time on the *Defiance*, and the crazy girl, well, maybe his betrothed, who helped him escape. I suddenly know in my heart that, much as he might love me, I'm not in his immediate plans. Is following Mother up north the sensible thing to do?

"Young man, put the newspaper down and eat this food before it's cold," Mrs. Dawson demands. "You're still bony as a bird."

• • •

We're barely finished when I hear someone pound on the front door. Tom and I leap up and tumble into our little room with our dishes and pull the bookcase back in place.

I hear a man's voice.

"Can it be soldiers, come to get us?" I whisper to Tom. He grabs my hand and squeezes it. Have we left behind anything incriminating … a crust of bread, an apple core?

I hear footsteps on the stairs. Then Mrs. Dawson's voice. "Tom, Sarah, it's Jonah Livingston."

I'm so excited to see the old goat, I rush to hug him. But I stop dead. Jonah is a sight. His wig is gone, and long strands of straggly gray hair stick out from his bald head. His eye is swollen shut, and dried blood from his mouth and nose stain his shirtfront.

"What happened to—"

"Never mind! Sarah, you saw the newspaper. You saw what you and I managed to do?"

"Yes, I was—"

"Listen to me. You and that boy Tom are in grave danger. Pendleton came into the *Loyal Gazette* in a rage as soon as the paper was on the street. He demanded to know where you were. He wants to make an example of you, Tom, and no doubt, me."

"What did you do? What did you say?" I know only too well about the captain's temper.

"He threatened to shut me down if I didn't cooperate."

"Did you?" I ask.

"Hell, no! And I ordered him to leave." I can't imagine that. Pendleton, so tall and commanding, is no one to cross. "Then his men roughed me up a bit."

"They'll come back for you, Jonah."

"Let them. I'm tired of taking orders from those arrogant asses. If I must, I'll take my press to Boston or Philadelphia."

"Are we safe here, for now?" Tom asks.

"No! You should have left yesterday," Jonah says, using a stained handkerchief to wipe the sweat from his face. "One of my brilliant apprentices followed the captain out the door and didn't return for an hour. I don't know how much the jackass spilled but I fear the worst. He did return in an excellent temper and with a bottle of rum under his arm."

Before Tom or I can say anything, Jonah reaches inside his vest and yanks out a handful of coins.

"Sarah, this should pay for your passage to Nova Scotia."

I'm stunned by his generosity. "It's more than enough. Thank you."

"It's not a gift," he says. "It's payment for your writing. It's a fine piece of work, and it took the kind of courage I never expected from a girl, pardon me, I mean a woman."

I bask in the glow of delicious praise for as long as I dare. But I know each hour we stay is an hour too long. I have always prided myself on my ability to get out of trouble, but now I don't have the slightest idea how to escape the British web closing in all over the city.

"We need a plan," I say.

The room goes silent for a moment. Then Mrs. Dawson clears her throat. "We've helped more than a few flee New York."

"Pray tell!"

"Do you hear the sound of Mr. Dawson and his men sawing and hammering day and night? Oh, why am I even asking? Of course, you do. Well, we've had a number of our guests, still quite alive, depart in his coffins."

Tom and I look at each other, speechless.

"It's brilliant!" I burst out.

"But wait a moment," Tom, ever the strategic thinker, says. "The British are searching everyone going in and out of the city. What if they demand to open the coffins?"

That one takes a moment. Then I have it. "We'll be victims of the pox, that will scare them off. Just to be certain, we'll dab our faces with red spots."

"Good!" Mrs. Dawson says. "I'll ask Henry to get started quickly."

•  •  •

Mr. Dawson has two coffins ready in an hour. He and his workers load them onto his wagon in the back of his shop and scatter bits of straw all around to hide the tiny air holes along the bottom.

Meanwhile, Mrs. Dawson helps us turn our faces into scabby messes with drops of mud and red stain from berries. It's so convincing that I'm repulsed just at the sight of Tom, though he claims to find me alluring.

"Sarah, you've never looked more fetching."

"Neither of you will turn heads," Mrs. Dawson says.

It all seems like a grand adventure until I see the coffins, side by side, in the wagon. Then it hits me, this is no foolish lark. The coffins are real, made that morning from pine that I still smell. Lined with plain linen, they aren't fancy, no shiny silver hinges.

"I pray that you'll make it to safety," Mrs. Dawson says.

"Thank you for all you've done," I say to the kindest woman I've ever known.

"Hurry! We've no time to waste," Mr. Dawson says.

I dread this moment. I'm not scared of being in the coffin with the lid shut, in total blackness. It's the idea of being separated from Tom, maybe forever. I want to touch him one last time before we climb in but that's impossible. The way he looks at me I can tell he feels the same. What a sight we must be all moony-eyed with our pock-marked faces.

I step into the coffin and lie down. Mrs. Dawson covers me with a gray shroud, leaving only my face exposed.

"This will help with the chill," she says.

Then I hear Tom from his own pine box. "Godspeed, Sarah."

The lid comes down with a creak, and suddenly I'm alone in the dark, cramped space. The wood is two inches from my face. There's barely room for my arms at my side. I gasp for a breath of air, but everything is so close I think I'm suffocating. This isn't what I expected, but it's too late.

I feel a jolt as Mr. Dawson climbs into the wagon's seat. He flicks the reins, and the horse stomps his feet.

"Easy, Rascal, easy boy," he says, and the wagon rolls forward.

I feel every cobblestone as my back bounces against the hard wood. At least the sharp pains keep my mind off suffocation. Under the shroud I clutch a leather pouch containing Jonah's coins, Mother's comb, and Father's quill pen. Under my wool cloak I'm wearing my good yellow gown, an extra skirt, and stockings. Hidden under my gown is a sack of corn bread and cheese. If I appear great with child, so be it.

The wagon rumbles along at a painfully slow pace. Mr. Dawson says hello to a few shop owners as we pass. I hear the clop of an occasional horse passing. Droplets of sweat slide down my face. I tell myself it will be good to see Mother and Benjamin, even if it means being farther north and farther away from Tom. But Nova Scotia holds no bookstores, coffeehouses, theaters, all the pleasures I've grown accustomed to in New York. And no Tom.

I dread standing at Mother's side again, catching newborns. It's an especially tedious process after I've seen my words in the newspaper. *My words.* Tears come to my eyes as I replay Jonah's final words at the Dawsons: "Sarah, your confounded spirit drives me to drink, but I swear there's nothing you can't do."

I feel Mr. Dawson tug on the reins. "Hold up, Rascal." The wagon rolls to a stop, and I freeze.

Then Mr. Dawson's voice: "Good day, lieutenant. What's the trouble?"

"No trouble. We need to know who you are and where you're going."

"And why is that?" he asks.

"We're looking for enemies of the Crown."

"Yes, of course," Mr. Dawson says. "Damned rebels are everywhere."

"Indeed, sir."

"I'm Henry Dawson, carpenter, and coffin maker. The British depend on my services, especially now in these dark days. I'm delivering two souls stricken by the pox to the paupers' graveyard."

My heart is beating wildly as footsteps circle the wagon. Is Tom as scared as I am?

"We'll just have a look inside," the lieutenant says. "You can't be too careful these days. Could be muskets and ammunition for the rebels in there."

"I assure you, that isn't the case," Mr. Dawson says. "But suit yourself."

I close my eyes. The coffin lid creaks open, and I feel the warm sunshine. I hold my breath and will my body to be still.

A hand pulls the shroud back from my face, and a gust of cool air rushes over me. I can't hold my breath much longer.

"Good God, man!" the lieutenant shouts. "It's the pox!" The lid slams down and my body shudders.

"Move along, quickly," the redcoat orders.

I gulp what air I can and try to relax as the wagon bounces along the rutted road. We're close now. I hear the clatter of the rigging on the ships and the hubbub of workers on the docks.

Finally, the wagon rolls to a stop. "We're here," Mr. Dawson says in a low voice. He opens the lid and I sit up, gulping air and shielding my eyes from the light. We're in an alley a block from the water's edge. He helps me out of the coffin and for a moment I'm stiff and unsteady. Then he helps Tom.

"Close call back there," Tom says.

"Yes, your sister is quite an actress. She saved the day."

Mr. Dawson gives us rags to wash our pox off. I scrub until my face feels raw, and the evidence is finally gone.

"I must go now," he says. "Sarah, there's a ship heading north tomorrow. I'm sure you're able to spend the night aboard." I see the tips of the sails and feel a knot in my stomach.

"Young man, I don't know how you plan to catch up with your regiment, but God speed."

"I'll beg a ride across the Hudson into New Jersey, then I'll go the rest of the way on foot at night."

"Good luck to you both," he says, climbing aboard the wagon. "Let's go, Rascal." We watch the wagon disappear around the corner.

"Must you go, Tom?" I take his hand and squeeze it tight.

"Yes, we've discussed this. You'll be safer up north, with your mother." He puts his arms around me and pulls me tight. "I love you, Sarah. I'll find you in Nova Scotia when the fighting is over. I promise."

Every part of me recoils at the thought of Nova Scotia, never writing for a newspaper again or penning a novel. I know it's the sensible thing to do, but that's not who I am. Being part of the *Loyal Gazette*, going out to the dreadful *Defiance*, plotting Tom's escape, dumping Samuel, and seeing my name on a momentous story: All that has given me a new burst of courage and confidence. And, at that moment, I decide.

"I'm not going to Nova Scotia."

"What?"

"I said, I've decided not to follow Mother." It feels right. In fact, it feels joyous and liberating.

"What will you do?"

My path is uncharacteristically clear. "I'm going to Philadelphia." It's the most exciting place I can imagine, the heartbeat of the war. "I want to be a writer." I study his face for a reaction.

"But…I'm confused. What about your mother? How will you take care of yourself? How will you get there by yourself?"

"I'll take a stagecoach. There are newspapers there and printers and book sellers. I'll find work."

"No doubt you will. You're already published."

"I'll miss Mother and Benjamin terribly."

He gives me a shy look. "Will you care about me when you're rich and famous?"

I fling my arms around him. "Of course! I love you, Thomas Jordan." Then I tenderly kiss the tip of his nose.

The sweetest smile comes over his face. "Then I will find you in Philadelphia, Sarah Barrett. I promise."

# Author's Note

*Prisoner of Wallabout Bay* is rooted in a little-known slice of American history: Around 11,500 American captives died in deplorable conditions aboard British prison ships anchored off New York City during the American Revolution. The number is an estimate; no one knows exactly how many. It was far greater, however, than the number of Americans who died in combat.

Forced to live in squalor, they were crammed below deck where they succumbed to starvation, disease, and abuse. Fed scanty rations of spoiled, bug-infested food, they died at such an alarming rate that proper burial was impossible. For years, their bones washed ashore in Brooklyn.

From 1776 to 1783 the British firmly controlled New York City. They deployed the old rotting hulks when they ran out of prison space on land. As many as 16 were positioned in waters around the city, with most of them moored in Wallabout Bay off the shore of Brooklyn. The most notorious was the *Jersey*, a floating death trap that, at times, held 1,000 or more prisoners who wasted away in cramped, filthy conditions.

Today the Prison Ship Martyrs Monument in Fort Greene Park in

Brooklyn stands as a memorial to the men who died in the atrocity. Dedicated in 1908, it was designed by Stanford White, one of his era's most famous architects.

Over the centuries, the British named several of their ships the *Defiance*. None of the prison ships in New York waters was so named. However, the conditions I describe on the *Defiance* are a composite of what has been documented on the *Jersey* and others.

Sarah Barrett, the novel's protagonist, is my own creation. In the book, she gets to know the *Defiance* on trips to the ship with her mother, who sold produce and small items to British guards and those few prisoners with money. Historical evidence shows a number of enterprising merchants, like Sarah's mother, doing the same.

One of them was an old woman known only as "Dame Grant." Another was said to be Elizabeth Burgin, a widow with three children. While historians debate the scope and even the actual location of Burgin's efforts, her aid to British-held prisoners, whether in Manhattan or on the ships, ultimately prompted the British to offer a reward of 200 pounds for her capture. After fleeing to Philadelphia, she finally received a war pension through the intervention of General George Washington.

Jonah Livingston is also a fictional character, though there were pro-British newspaper publishers in New York at the time. The most famous was James Rivington, who, it turns out, may have been a spy for Washington.

Sarah's use of invisible ink to deliver secret messages to Tom Jordan is also based on historical fact. The armies of both sides used invisible ink to hide important messages often written between the lines of nondescript letters. They used other schemes to send secret messages, from elaborate codes to hiding tiny scraps of paper beneath the covering of a button, as Sarah did.

Jack Morton and his King's Tavern are my own creation. I was inspired by the real Samuel Fraunces, a rebel sympathizer and tavern owner. Fraunces Tavern continues to operate as a restaurant and museum at 54 Pearl St. in New York.

Captain Pendleton, the British officer in charge of New York prisons, and his aide Lieutenant Pritchard are also fictional characters, as well as embezzler Charles Laurence. There were, in fact, brutal British overseers who profited financially at the expense of the captives. The most notorious was Provost Marshal William Cunningham. There are reports that he gave a deathbed confession admitting to flogging and hanging hundreds of prisoners without trials.

Sarah's hometown of Essex, New Hampshire, is a product of my imagination but similar to my hometown of Keene, NH, as well as other towns in the region. No battles were fought in New Hampshire, but an incident in Portsmouth triggered my depiction of one in the fictitious Essex. On Dec. 13, 1774, a band of local residents stormed Fort William and Mary in Portsmouth and seized a cache of ammunition before British soldiers could arrive to secure it.

To research *Prisoner of Wallabout Bay*, I relied on numerous books. A big thank you to the historians and publishers behind these fine accounts. Here is a partial list:

- *The Ghost Ship of Brooklyn*, by Robert P. Watson, Da Capo Press, 2017
- *Hell on the East River*, by Larry Lowenthal, Purple Mountain Press, 2009
- *Recollections of Life on the Prison Ship Jersey*, by Thomas Dring, and edited by David Swain, 2010
- *Forgotten Patriots*, The Untold Story of American Prisoners During the Revolutionary War, by Edwin G. Burrows, Basic Books, a member of the Perseus Books Group, 2008
- *The Battle of Brooklyn*, 1776, by John J. Gallagher, Castle Books, 2002
- *The Battle for New York*, by Barnet Schecter, Penguin Books, 2003

Some of what we know about the brutality on the prison ships derives from accounts written by captives who escaped or were released. One of them, the poet Philip Freneau, gained renown for his sagas of the Revolution. Following his release in 1780, he wrote a blistering account of his imprisonment in the form of a lengthy poem, "The British Prison Ship."

# Prisoner of Wallabout Bay

*The various horrors of these hulks to tell,*
*These Prison Ships where pain and sorrow dwell;*
*Where death in tenfold vengeance holds his reign,*
*And injur'd ghosts, in reason's ear complain.*

# Acknowledgments

I want to start by thanking my husband, Steve Chawkins, for all his help from the beginning to the end. He suffered through early drafts, countless dinners where my mind was elsewhere, and numerous trips down the rabbit holes of 18th Century history. His editing expertise was invaluable and made the book a tighter read. His unflagging support and wit kept me going.

I so appreciate all the encouragement and feedback I received along the way from friends and fellow writers who took the time to read ever-changing versions of the book. You are the eyes and hearts of the readers.

Finally, I want to thank Mary Lou Monahan and Jacqueline Cook at Fireship Press for believing in Sarah's story and guiding me through the maze of book publishing.

# About the Author

*Photo courtesy of Lisa McKinnon*

Growing up in Keene, New Hampshire, Jane Hulse was surrounded by history. From her family's 1795 home, she could see the former tavern where 29 Minutemen rallied before fighting the British at Lexington. With her father, she explored caves that served as hiding places for loyalists who had been hounded out of town during the American Revolution.

After graduating from Syracuse University, Hulse worked for small newspapers in Colorado and then for the Rocky Mountain News in Denver, where she covered major criminal trials. She did freelance writing for the Los Angeles Times and was city editor at the Santa Barbara News-Press. For her leadership there, she was one of six staffers who received the University of Oregon's Arcil Payne Award for Ethics in Journalism, an annual honor for journalists who "report with integrity despite personal, political, or economic pressure." Most recently, she was editor of a Southern California agricultural magazine.

Hulse, who has a grown daughter, is married and lives in Ventura, California.

*If you enjoyed this book, please take a few moments to write a review of it. Thank you!*

# Other Fireship Press Titles

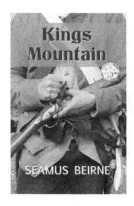

## Kings Mountain
by Seamus Beirne

*A New World Aflame with the Bonfires of a Budding Revolution*

In the year 1775, Michael Redferne and Isaac Malot break out of a penal colony in Barbados and go their separate ways. Redferne home to Ireland, Malot, a black man, to the Caribbean to captain a pirate sloop. Years later, a shipwreck and the search for a lost child land them, unknown to each other, in South Carolina, a colony in the grip of the American Revolution. From his sharpshooter's perch at the battle of Kings Mountain, Malot, a loyalist, adjusts the small telescope jury-rigged to his Ferguson rifle. Among the patriot enemy advancing into the killing zone, is none other than Michael Redferne. Malot faces a gut-wrenching decision, shoot his old comrade or risk forfeiting his newly won freedom.

## 1777: THE YEAR OF DESTINY
by Edward Cuddy

*The audacity of a handful of New World colonies challenging an eighteenth-century superpower.*

The victories of the continental army and patriot militia in Saratoga, New York, in September and October 1777, shattered the perception of the English Crown's military superiority. The capture of a British army persuaded France and Spain to ally with the Americans initiating a world war against the Empire. This is a story of those who fought.

1777: THE YEAR OF DESTINY parallels the heroic resistance of the Ukrainian people and may serve as a reminder to the reader of the price of freedom.

# For the Finest in Nautical and Historical Fiction and Non-Fiction
## www.FireshipPress.com

## Interesting • Informative • Authoritative

All Fireship Press books are available through
leading bookstores and wholesalers worldwide.

Printed in the USA
CPSIA information can be obtained
at www.ICGtesting.com
CBHW020810230624
10283CB00004B/12